A MESSAGE FROM CHICKEN HOUSE

This is a funny, fearsome, utterly Gothic story at the Frankenstein edges of early science – where the boundaries between living and dying become rather moveable . . .! It's also a charming *nearly* romance, in which burials – premature and otherwise – take us to strangely heart-warming places. Unique. You'll love it. Even the fly. Nicholas Bowling is a marvellous writer.

BARRY CUNNINGHAM
Publisher
Chicken House

The
Undying
of
Obedience
Wellrest

NICHOLAS BOWLING

Chicken House

2 Palmer Street, Frome, Somerset BA11 1DS
www.chickenhousebooks.com

First published in Great Britain in 2023
Chicken House
2 Palmer Street
Frome, Somerset BA11 1DS
United Kingdom
www.chickenhousebooks.com

Chicken House/Scholastic Ireland, 89E Lagan Road, Dublin Industrial Estate,
Glasnevin, Dublin D11 HP5F, Republic of Ireland

Cover and interior design by Micaela Alcaino
Typeset by Dorchester Typesetting Group Ltd
Printed in Great Britain by Clays, Elcograf S.p.A

FSC
www.fsc.org
MIX
Paper | Supporting
responsible forestry
FSC® C018072

1 3 5 7 9 10 8 6 4 2

British Library Cataloguing in Publication data available.

ISBN 978-1-912626-68-7
eISBN 978-1-915026-92-7

For Dave

SPRING 1832

I

NED

For my fifteenth birthday, my grandfather let me dig my own grave.

It was dawn when he woke me. He was standing over my bed with an oil lamp in one hand and a brand-new shovel in the other. I remember how bright its blade was in the darkness. I think he had been awake all night, going at it with his whetstone.

'Happy birthday,' he said. 'Shall we get started?'

He laid the shovel next to me on the bed, then opened the door of the cottage and went out into the morning.

I got up and dressed quickly. My shirt and trousers were still hanging above the washing tub, damp, because Pa – my grandfather, I mean – had insisted I make an effort to be clean for such an important day. I did not see the point of washing either my clothes or myself if I was just going to get covered in mud again, but I did as I was told. I put on my boots and second-best hat, since a crow had stolen my favourite some weeks earlier. I ate four of Pa's oatcakes and put another four in my pockets. Mosca was asleep in his jam jar, but I took him with me in my satchel because I knew he would be furious with me if he missed anything. Mosca is my pet fly. Back then he was probably my closest friend besides my grandfather. People say you can't tell one fly from another, but whoever says that knows as much about flies as they do about gravedigging.

There was a mist in the graveyard that morning, as I recall: wet and thick as cold soup. I could make out the church steeple and the great, dark boughs of the yew trees but the rest of the village had disappeared, and it felt like Pa and I were the only two living souls in the whole world. In a way that was true: we were the only two souls in *our* little world, unless you count Mosca and the birds and the animals in the churchyard.

I followed Pa's lamp along the path and through the cluttered headstones of the Old Quarter, hefting the shovel, enjoying its weight. I ran my finger over the blade. It was keen as a butcher's knife. Pa spoke over his shoulder.

'Now. You will remember that the soil in the New Quarter is a sandy loam.'

'Yes, Pa.'

'Not an ounce of clay in it.'

'Yes, Pa.'

'So you will need to be careful that the sides do not collapse.'

'I remember what you said.'

'And keep things neat. Most people think that gravedigging is just about—'

'Digging a hole. But it is not. I know, Pa.'

'Good. Remember, this plot is going to be somebody's home until Judgement Day. They will spend more time in their grave than any other place during their time on the earth, so make sure it is one that they will be happy in.'

Perhaps I should have been clearer from the start: when I say I was digging my own grave, the grave was not *for* me. It was for someone else. What I mean is that Pa let me dig it all by myself. Up until then, he was the one who always did the hard work, and I just had to watch, and listen, and take notes, and bring him his tea when he got thirsty. Now, in my fifteenth year, I had earned a shovel all of my own.

'Who is the new resident?' I asked.

'Lady from the village,' said Pa. 'Grammy Hickson. Nearly ninety years old, so the vicar said. A good run, by any reckoning.'

'Do you think she will be happy here?'

'I am sure she will, Ned. She won't be wanting for company, at least. Given her age, I dare say she knows most of the people buried here.'

The thought made me glad.

'I shall dig her quite the smartest grave that the village has ever seen!' I said. 'It will be the envy of the other residents!'

'That's the spirit,' said Pa. 'You will be in charge of the whole place when I am gone, so start as you mean to continue.'

To underscore this gloomy thought he coughed several times into his handkerchief, opened it to see what was inside, and then balled it up tightly as if it contained a secret. He had been coughing and wheezing for months, and by now I had stopped asking him if he was unwell, because the answer seemed to trouble him.

I watched him tuck the handkerchief into his top pocket and said nothing. My gladness was darkened somewhat. It's funny how even when you are surrounded by the dead you expect the people you love to be around for ever.

We left the Old Quarter and its great black yew trees and passed by the Nameless Grave, almost completely reclaimed by ivy, now. The church emerged from the mist and we took the passage around the side into the New Quarter.

'Here will do,' said Pa at the end of a row of headstones. He folded his arms and looked at me with his one good eye. It was almost silent in the graveyard. The only sound was Mosca buzzing in his jam jar.

'All right,' I said. 'Shall I just start digging then?'

'*Just start digging*, he says! I thought this was to be the smartest plot in the whole village?'

'It is!'

'Then you can't just start shovelling willy-nilly, can you?'

'No, I know. Sorry, Pa.'

'Then what are you going to do first?'

I looked in my satchel. First I took Mosca out so he could watch everything. He scuttled in quick little circles around the bottom of his jar and rubbed his back legs together. He seemed annoyed about something. I took out the two spindles of string we use for measuring the plots and began to stake out the area. When I was done, Pa inspected the dimensions and then perched himself on the edge of the next headstone along.

'Very good,' he said. 'Now then. Let's see how you handle that new shovel of yours.'

I set to work, Pa watching me the whole time with his good right eye while the other one rolled crazily in its socket. The sun came up and burnt away the mist and the New Quarter was as charming as I had ever seen it. Graveyards have a reputation for being gloomy places, but you should have seen ours in the springtime. Bluebells and marigolds and bright-pink campion. New ivy so green it seemed to shimmer with a light of its own.

I dug and I sang and I could not have been happier. The shovel was quite a marvellous piece of engineering. It was sharp and precise and very easy to wield. I cut and dispatched the soil with the efficiency of Pa working through a plate of liver. After half an hour the earth was up to my waist and after an hour I was in over my head. I called up to my grandfather, who by then had been quiet for a good while.

'What do you think, Pa?' I said. 'I have to say, I am rather proud of it! A stonemason couldn't get smoother edges than this.'

Pa did not reply. I worried I had done something wrong. Or perhaps I had spoken too vainly about my work.

'I know it's not perfect, by any means. But it must be nearly six feet by now. I can't see over the top. Could you pass me the string? Pa?'

There was silence again.

'Mosca?'

He buzzed distantly.

I hung on to the edge of the grave and hauled myself out. The sun was high and very hot by now and there was steam on the inside of Mosca's jar that seemed to be causing him some discomfort. I unscrewed the lid and he straight away flew up into one of my nostrils – his way of reprimanding me – and then off in the direction of the church.

'Well,' I said, 'there's no need to be like that.'

I tracked the erratic path of his flight and saw Pa on the far side of the graveyard. He was talking to the vicar. The vicar had a shining cassock and a rod-straight back and next to him Pa looked even more hunched and shabby than usual. His old coat and gloves were stained and full of holes. They were both looking at something on the ground. Pa was shaking his head.

I picked up Mosca's jar and went down the path towards the church with the shovel over one shoulder.

I knew something was wrong before I heard what they were talking about. The headstone in front of them was at a very strange angle, and the earth at its base was very uneven. I had not noticed when we first arrived because of all the mist, but in the clear spring light I could not conceal my horror. Someone or something had disturbed the plot.

The vicar, Reverend Biles, was speaking to Pa in a low monotone while my grandfather tugged anxiously at the ends of his sleeves. The vicar heard me coming and turned and looked at me without expression, his face another grey tombstone. He looked at Mosca's jar and frowned slightly.

Then he turned back to my grandfather without acknowledging me.

'I must admit,' said Reverend Biles, 'I am slightly at a loss as to how this escaped your notice after our last conversation.'

'Forgive me, Reverend, we – me and the boy—' He gestured in my direction but the vicar was done looking at me, it seemed. 'We have always taken every care to keep a watchful eye over the residents.'

The vicar pulled a grim expression.

'Residents?'

'I mean the parishioners. The deceased.'

A pause.

'I would be more inclined to believe you if it had not happened twice this year already.'

Twice? Pa had never mentioned anything of the sort to me.

'I'm sorry, Reverend. Really I am. Only it is the boy's birthday, and last night I was sharpening his shovel, and I suppose I was distracted.'

Reverend Biles looked at me again and I showed him the shovel with some pride.

'Many happy returns, I am sure,' he said. 'But that is really no excuse.'

'I know, Reverend,' said Pa.

The vicar sighed.

'Well, now you both have shovels, you can at least tidy it up twice as quickly.'

'Tidy it up?' said Pa.

'Yes,' said the vicar. 'Make it good as new. Before the mourners arrive for Mrs Hickson.'

'But the relatives—'

'The families would rather not know. I am certain of that. Fill this in and straighten the stone and we shall forget all about it.'

'But—'

'Much better for you, too, if the families do not know. Wouldn't you say?'

I looked at them both. Pa didn't reply.

'We all know what the villagers think of you, and we know what they would do if they were to discover any of this . . . unpleasantness.' His long, bony finger wavered between the two of us. 'You would do well to keep your mouths closed, or you'll both be on the gibbet before you've time to take your hats off.'

'Yes, Reverend.'

'Very well, then. Make it right. And be sure it does not happen again.'

Pa started coughing once more and took out his mangled and damp-looking handkerchief. The vicar wrinkled his nose. He looked at me and then turned and went billowing towards the dark archway of the church door.

With nobody standing in the way I finally got a good look at the disturbed grave. As a sexton it was really the last thing in the world you would hope to see. It was an awful mess, the headstone moments from falling flat and the soil piled in loose mounds as if a dog had been at it. Pa waited for the church door to close and nudged at the dirt with the toe of his huge boot.

'Barely been in the ground a fortnight,' he said.

'I remember. Young Robert Garrick, was it not?'

'And his wife. Damnable cholera.'

We looked at the grave in silence.

'Who do you think did it?'

'I don't know.'

'It was probably foxes,' I said. 'Or moles. You know what they're like.'

Pa straightened up and gave me a tired smile.

'Quite possibly,' he said.

'Why don't I ask our neighbours?'

'As you wish, Ned.'

Mosca had been flying in exploratory circles around the disturbed plot and finally came to rest in his customary spot on the tip of my ear. We went to the four corners of the graveyard and asked if anyone knew anything, in the yew trees, in the brambles, in the gutters of the church roof. The crow had seen nothing, and the family of foxes were asleep. The magpies just laughed and chattered nonsense, as per usual, and then got angry when I wouldn't let them eat Mosca.

I came back to Pa empty-handed. He was already patting and smoothing the earth on the top of the grave.

'No one seems to know anything,' I said.

Pa stood and leant on my shovel.

'No surprises there. It is no one's job to keep watch but ours. We shall have to keep our eyes open from now on. Both of us.'

'The vicar said it had happened before. You never told me that.'

'No, I didn't. I am sorry.'

I waited for him to explain but apparently this was all he had to say on the matter.

'He didn't mean the part about the villagers, did he?' I said.

'Which part?'

'About the gibbet. About hanging.'

He paused to examine the headstone and eventually said: 'No, Ned. Of course not. It would never come to that.'

I felt a tickle on the back of my neck that I thought was Mosca, but from the corner of my eye I saw him perusing the daffodils a few feet away. I watched Pa get on to his haunches to try and straighten the great stone slab. I will admit I am not the cleverest person in the village – I am not even the cleverest person in the churchyard – but I know when someone is not telling the truth.

II

NED

Mrs Hickson's funeral was a short and uneventful affair. Uneventful, at least, from her point of view. Pa and I kept a respectful distance and sat in the Old Quarter while the bell tolled and summoned the mourners and the pall-bearers, and after half an hour they emerged from the church and gathered at the graveside. There were perhaps a dozen men and women in attendance, most of them rugged sorts, farmers and labourers and the innkeeper from the village. I recognized all their faces, since they came to church every Sunday – all but one. A young and quite respectable lady who seemed nothing to do with the rest of the villagers, and whose face, even behind a black veil of mourning, stood out from the others like a pearl in the mud.

Reverend Biles droned through his eulogy. His voice sounded no different from the bell that had called them there. I watched them all very keenly, particularly the pretty young woman, because I wanted to know what they thought of the grave I had dug. I half fancied that someone might come over and shake my hand and tell me how pleased they were — what terrifically smart corners! how beautifully free of stones and worms! — but of course no one ever wanted to be seen talking to us, let alone shaking our hands.

When the funeral was done it began to rain. The relatives left the graveside and went back to whatever drudgery waited for them in the village. The vicar gave us the nod and hurried back to the church with his Bible covering his head.

I got up but the young lady was still there. She was slight and very pale. I might have taken her for a ghost, had I not known better. When you work in a graveyard and live in the company of the dead day and night, you quickly learn that such superstitions are mere silliness.

She drifted around Grammy Hickson's grave a few times and then started on the path towards us.

'Who is she?' I asked Pa.

He did not reply. He had barely said a word, in fact, since his talk with the vicar.

'Pa?' I said. 'She's coming this way.'

She moved like a phantom, too — floated, really, her feet all but invisible beneath the long black taffeta of her dress. She looked slowly from one side of the path to the other, studying the names on the gravestones. She passed the plot that Pa had recently tidied and seemed not to notice anything amiss, which was good. When she reached us, Pa finally looked up. The breeze gusted around her veil and I saw she was perhaps no older than I was. She inclined her head to both of us and touched the brim of her hat. Her hands were gloved, just like Pa's, although her gloves were made of silk or something even finer.

'Good afternoon,' she said.

'Miss,' said Pa, and returned the gesture.

The girl went on her way and floated around to the back of the church. And that was that.

I did not know what to say. I had never had anybody wish me a good afternoon, let alone a beautiful and well-to-do young woman such as this one. I breathed deeply and caught her floral scent even through the rain.

Pa heaved himself upright and every bone in his body seemed to click at once. He went hobbling over to the open grave. It was a moment before I caught up.

'Did you see that, Pa?'

'I did.'

'She nodded at us!'

'I know.'

'She nodded at *both* of us!'

'She was very courteous.'

'And she said good afternoon!'

'I heard her, Ned.'

Grammy Hickson's coffin had been scattered with a few handfuls of earth. Pa stuck the end of his shovel into the pile by the graveside and began filling in the hole. He seemed unconcerned with the apparition we had just encountered. I was more than a little preoccupied and lost concentration after only two or three spadefuls. I stopped and leant on the handle and tried to see what she was doing around the back of the church. The raindrops pattered into the open grave.

'Who do you think she is?' I said.

'She is from the manor,' said Pa, in between huffs and puffs. 'Mr Wellrest's daughter.'

'Really?'

'Really.'

I had seen the manor, but had never met a single member of the Wellrest family. Pa spoke of them sometimes but they did not come to church. They had their own chapel and their own family cemetery, and by all accounts they lived lives almost as private as our own.

'What is she doing down here? What's Grammy Hickson to her?'

'I wouldn't know.'

'Where has she gone now?'

'She is probably taking the air. That is what ladies do. So I am told.'

'Taking the air,' I repeated, trying the phrase for size. 'By herself?'

Pa shrugged and hefted another shovelful of dirt.

'She was very beautiful.'

'Are you going to help, or aren't you?'

I turned back to the work and began to shovel. It seemed the girl was, in fact, just taking the air because she reappeared quite soon afterwards and drifted up the path towards the gate. She was quite bedraggled by now, but seemed not to mind. When she passed us she stopped, took a few paces back, and peered into the plot, now perhaps three-quarters full.

I kept my head down. My heart thumped clumsily. I caught the smell of flowers again.

'Make sure you pack it all down properly,' she said. 'We wouldn't want the old hag climbing out of there tonight.'

We both straightened up. Pa and I looked at each other, then at her. She had pinned her veil up to reveal her whole face. She grinned.

'Excuse me, miss?' said Pa.

'I half expected to hear her rapping on the inside of the coffin when they lowered her down. Thought she might sit up in rigor mortis to tell me my hat wasn't straight, or that she was appalled by my posture.'

'You knew Mrs Hickson did you, miss?'

'I did. She was my governess.'

Pa frowned. 'Was she not a little old?'

'Quite right. But Father doesn't have two pennies to rub together. I believe she worked at the house many moons ago and he was calling in a favour.'

'Oh.' He paused. 'Were you very fond of her?'

She laughed out loud. It was not a sound I often heard in the graveyard. It rebounded off the headstones.

'Fond?' she said. 'No, sir. To own the truth, I wouldn't really call her my governess at all. That is the wrong word for it. Gaoler would be more accurate.'

'Gaoler?'

'That's why I'm here. To make sure she really is dead.' She nodded at the grave. 'And it looks like she is! So. Tremendous news all around. Seems I will have a break from needlework for a few days, at least.'

Pa and I stood in silence. Neither of us knew what to say. I had never heard anybody speak like she did, about the living or the dead. And Mrs Hickson right there, within earshot! I could not make up my mind whether I was impressed or appalled. Whether I liked or hated her. I think I liked her.

The wind changed direction and she must have smelt something on one or the other of us because her nose twitched and a crease appeared in her smooth brow. She turned suddenly and seemed to see me for the first time. I felt a small wave of terror break over me as she extended a hand towards my face. I thought she might touch my cheek but before my flush had finished blooming she flicked her fingers past my earlobe.

'You have a fly on you.'

Mosca buzzed with annoyance and circled my head and landed on my other ear.

'That is Mosca,' I said.

'Who?'

'Mosca. He's my fly.'

'Your fly?'

I nodded. She narrowed her eyes and smiled with only one half of her mouth, as if she could not decide if I was joking or not.

'I see,' she said.

There was more silence and more rain, but it seemed to cause her no discomfort at all. She laced her fingers behind her back and looked around the graveyard and seemed to be enjoying the day. Some moments passed. Pa cleared his throat.

'Is there anything we can help you with, miss? You're

getting awfully wet. You will catch a fever.'

'The grave back there,' she said. 'Behind the church. The lonely one with the cage around it.'

The Nameless Grave. My favourite spot in the whole churchyard, besides our cottage. I opened my mouth but Pa glanced at me and spoke before I could.

'A mortsafe, miss,' he said.

'What's that?'

'It's called a mortsafe. The cage.'

'How fascinating,' said the girl. 'To protect the grave's inhabitant, I presume?'

He just nodded and squinted, as if trying to fathom where the girl's curiosity might be heading. No doubt she was wondering the same thing that I had wondered for years.

'Who *is* the inhabitant?' she said. 'I saw no inscription on the headstone.'

Pa was about to answer but I could not contain my excitement and I said: 'We don't know. Nobody knows. It's always been blank. Hasn't it, Pa?'

He stiffened slightly.

'That's right,' he said.

'How strange,' said the girl. 'Well, it must belong to someone important, if the owner went to such lengths to stop people disturbing it. What do we think? Buried treasure?'

'Perhaps!' I said. 'I have always wondered this very thing!'

'No,' said Pa.

'No?' said the girl.

'This is a parish churchyard. Nobody in the village has any treasure to speak of, I can say that for certain.'

'Oh,' said the girl. 'Well, that is very dull.'

She hummed and surveyed the graveyard again. Pa drummed his fingers on the shaft of the spade as if suddenly impatient to get back to work.

'I suppose there's another explanation,' she said after a while. 'That the mortsafe – have I got that right? – isn't actually to stop someone from getting into the grave. It's to stop someone getting out.'

She widened her eyes in mock horror and then, when neither of us replied, she started laughing.

'Forgive me, sirs. Now I have no governess to look after me, my head is full of irrational, womanly fancies.' She gave a small, curious bow. 'Thank you for the conversation. It was lovely to meet both of you. Lovely to meet all three of you.'

Mosca's wings made a purring sound. She turned and started off down the path towards the gate, calling over her shoulder:

'Do let me know if she starts being a nuisance.'

It took me a moment to realize she meant Mrs Hickson. I wanted to reply but she was already out of earshot. The church gate groaned and the girl stepped lightly into the wet street, the scent of her still clinging to the headstones.

III

NED

Pa and I lived in a little cottage at the very back of the churchyard, hidden from view by yew trees and fir trees and an ancient clutch of ivy that was breaking the very stones of the building apart. Perhaps even 'cottage' is too grand a word. It was one room, really, with a stove against the back wall, hung around with old pots and pans and dried herbs from Pa's kitchen garden. Pa and I had our beds on opposite sides of the room. We each had a shelf, too; his laden with old leather-bound books and mine with interesting trinkets I had discovered in the churchyard — feathers, nails, pieces of glass, and once, inexplicably, a seashell. In the middle were two chairs and a small table and our tea set. I loved everything about the place, even though it was so small, and we had so few things we could call our own. I loved it for that exact reason, in fact.

When we had finished filling in Grammy Hickson's plot we came home and Pa revived the embers of the fire. It was spring but the bones of the house were not yet warm. I leant my new shovel against the wall at the foot of my bed and stood back and admired it.

'You're going to clean it, aren't you?' said Pa.

'Oh. Yes. Of course.'

'This time of year, all this mist and damp around, it'll rust up overnight if you're not careful. May as well clean mine while you're at it, if you wouldn't mind.'

He went back to blowing on the flames while I sat on the edge of my bed and polished the shovel's blade. He blew and blew and then inhaled too much smoke from the struggling fire and began coughing again – wheezy, gurgling coughs that brought up something dark and gelatinous from inside him. He spat on the floor. He noticed I was watching him and he glanced up at me. I went back to polishing and tried to fill the silence.

'I've never met anyone like her,' I said. I swirled the cloth around and around in the same spot and pictured the girl's face in the pale metal.

'Who?'

'The young lady.'

'Well, you've not met many people at all, have you?'

'I thought it was rather unkind what she was saying about Mrs Hickson, though.'

'Yes.'

'And yet, she did not *seem* unkind. She was very nice to us.'

'Nicer than most.'

'She called us "sirs", Pa! When was the last time anyone called you "sir"? And she said it was nice to meet Mosca.

Didn't she Mosca?'

My fly was back in his jar and feasting on some biscuit crumbs I had put in there. He seemed too focused on the task at hand to reply.

'I really don't know what to think of her,' I said.

'Whatever you're thinking,' said Pa, setting the kettle on top of the stove, 'you're thinking it an awful lot.'

I looked up from the spade, which was by now mirror-bright. He gave me a crooked smile and I flushed.

'I just thought she was interesting.'

'I know you're fifteen now, Ned,' he said, 'but it's a little early to be eyeing up a future wife, I think.'

'Pa!'

'Don't expect it to be a society marriage, though. She was right about her family not having a penny. The Wellrests are ruined. I suspect *we* could stump up a better dowry than her father.'

'But I thought they were the oldest family in the village? I thought that they lived in the manor? Not that it matters, at all,' I added quickly, 'since I do not wish to marry her.'

He smiled again.

'They *are* the oldest family in the village, and they *do* live in the manor, but you've seen the state of that house.'

'It could be smarter, yes. But it is so very big. I thought they would be sitting on a small fortune.'

'A long time ago that was true. But somebody in the family spent it all.'

His smile disappeared and he stared at the stove for a long time but did not elaborate.

The kettle began its ghostly whistling but he made no move to silence it. I got up from my bed and took it off the top of the stove and began to make the tea while he was lost in thought.

My grandfather had a very specific recipe for his tea. In fact I don't think it contained anything that you would actually call 'tea' at all – it was a mixture of herbs and roots that he grew himself. He said it was good for his rheumatism. Mallow root and hemlock and a few other things, I think. If it *was* helping his rheumatism, it did nothing for his lungs, because he seemed to be drinking more and more of it while his cough was getting worse and worse.

I poured the water into the teapot and sat opposite Pa while it brewed. It might have simply been the glum light from the fire but he looked particularly old that afternoon. I tried to cheer him again.

'At least she didn't notice the grave,' I said.

He looked up and scowled.

'The other grave, I mean. The one that the dogs dug up. That's a relief, isn't it?'

He regarded me sadly. His bad eye pointed towards the door. A few moments passed before he spoke.

'I don't think it was dogs, Ned.'

'Moles, then.'

'I don't think it was moles either.'

I racked my brains for other digging animals.

'Ferrets? Badgers? I would have heard about badgers, surely. The crow would have told me.'

'I think not,' said Pa.

'Then who?'

Perhaps it is hard to believe, but the real reason for the disturbance at Master Garrick's grave had not even crossed my mind. Pa always took pains to protect me from the unpleasantness of the world outside the graveyard. Looking back, I'm not sure if that was a good or bad thing.

'Withy Bottom is only a stone's throw from the university,' he said after a while, and then was quiet, as if this explained everything.

'I don't understand,' I said.

He checked on the tea and poured himself a cup and sipped it thoughtfully before continuing.

'Oxford is a centre of learning, Ned. There are many clever men there who are making great advances in understanding human beings. Our bodies. How they work. How they might be cured of ailments, and injuries, and so forth. But to do so, they need to . . .' He paused and searched for the word. '*Explore* our bodies. Thoroughly. Inside and out.'

I began to grasp what he meant but could not bring myself to speak it aloud.

'Certain opportunistic people have realized that the scholars' demand for raw materials is far greater than can be supplied. So these certain opportunistic people have taken it upon themselves to provide what cannot be procured through more, ah, *legal* means.'

I stood up and my chair fell backwards.

'They steal the bodies? The residents? No! Pa! That is too awful!'

'I agree. It is abominable. But where there is money to be made . . .'

'But you don't mean some devil snatched Master Garrick and his wife from their graves last night?'

He was quiet for a moment.

'It is very possible,' he said. 'Resurrection men, they are called. Or call themselves. To me it seems rather too grandiose. I think *bodysnatchers* a more fitting term.'

I paced back and forth a few times. I could not believe what I was hearing.

'But the gate was locked!'

'I don't think that is any particular obstacle. There are plenty of places to climb the church wall. Plenty of places where it's not even intact.'

'And the vicar? Why would he want to conceal such a terrible thing?'

'Reverend Biles is a proud man. He would like his church and his parish to be beyond reproach. And to his credit, he was trying to protect us. He was right about the villagers.'

'But you said—'

'They might not have us hanged, no. But you can bet the people of Withy Bottom would blame us the moment they discovered anything so disagreeable.'

'But we would never even think of such a thing! Quite the opposite! All we do is look after their relatives! Why would they be so ungrateful?'

'It is the way of things, Ned. Historically, gravediggers have not been afforded a great deal of gratitude.' He paused.

'Miss Wellrest was a pleasant exception to the rule.'

I marched about a little more. Miss Wellrest's pearly face drifted at the edge of my vision again, but my thoughts were now black with images of grave robbing and bodysnatching. I remembered, suddenly, that this had not even been the first disturbance. How many more had there been? Residents stolen from their very beds while they slept! And subjected to who knew what kinds of experimentation! The horror of it all!

I took up my shovel once more and let Mosca out of his jar and went to the front door.

'Where are you off to?' Pa said.

'To keep watch.'

'Can't we finish our tea first? It's not even dark yet. They're hardly going to come back in broad daylight.'

I opened the door and stood looking out at the evening. Everything was pale and silvered by the low sun and the remnants of the rain. It was an intolerable feeling, knowing that someone had been poking around the graves while we had been in the cottage, oblivious. They may as well have been rummaging in the cottage itself.

'I feel awful, Pa,' I said. 'Isn't there something we can do? Can't we get poor Master Garrick back?'

'If you were willing to take a carriage to the university and plead with the scholars, perhaps. And even then you would need to pay them an awful lot of money.'

I looked at my feet. I rarely left the churchyard, and had never been anywhere outside of Withy Bottom. The thought was unconscionable. Pa set down his tea, hobbled over to me and set a hand on my shoulder.

'You mustn't worry yourself, Ned. This is my responsibility. As soon as the day is done I will lock up the gate, and I will take our lantern. I will watch over our residents until the sun comes back.'

'I'll do it with you, then,' I said. 'And we could make use of Mosca. He sees everything.'

'You'll need to sleep at some point.'

'So will you. We can take it in turns.'

He smiled and looked somewhat distant.

'That will not be necessary, my boy,' he said. 'I haven't slept a wink since the day you were born.'

IV

NED

Regardless of what he said I kept my vigil with Pa that night, and the next, and the next. We walked laps of the New Quarter and when we needed a rest we sat together on the same tomb and talked of the world. We talked of St Bartholomew's and the churchyard in the times before I was born. We talked of the previous vicar, who had been a kinder and more charitable man than Reverend Biles, and had brought Pa not only food and drink but also the many books that were now on the shelf above his bed.

I tried to talk of my parents, too, buried side by side on the edge of the New Quarter, but it seemed painful for Pa and I changed the subject quickly. It had been fifteen years since they had been taken by cholera, so at least I could be sure the grave robbers would take no interest in them. At least, I hoped that this was the case.

The fourth night was a very cold one and Pa and I drank brandy and ate biscuits under a glassy, starlit sky. I drank too much and got tired quicker than usual and rested my head on his shoulder. I could see his breath in the lantern's yellow light. It was perhaps an exaggeration of his that he never slept, but it was true that he slept very little, and when he did it was with his eyes wide open, his good eye motionless and his bad eye rotating as slowly and regularly as the hand on a pocket watch.

A single loud clang woke me from the brink of a nap. I lifted my head from his shoulder and pretended I hadn't been dozing.

'One o'clock!' I said. 'Is it that late already?'

Pa didn't answer. He had turned to look back at the cottage and was sitting very stiffly.

'What?'

'That wasn't the church bell, Ned. I think someone's in our house.'

We crept back along the path with the lantern. Through a gap in the trunks of the yew trees I could see the door to the cottage was open. There was a dirty orange light inside but it was moving too much to be the fire. I heard whispers and heavy boots and the scrape of a bed on the stone floor.

'Who is it?' I whispered.

'I don't know.'

'Shall we go and talk to them?'

Pa shook his head.

There was a heavy clink of metal followed by the sound of someone colliding with a piece of furniture, the cracking of porcelain, and a great deal of cursing.

Two figures emerged from the cottage. The first was a large, lumbering man, remarkable for his long arms and enormous hands, like the great apes that Pa had described to me from his books. This man was also exceedingly bald, though only down the middle of his head, a strip of scalp gleaming between two thickets of tight black curls. After him came a woman who was perhaps half his height, very short indeed, with a very round head, and a quick tottering step that made her seem, to me at least, like an overgrown baby dressed in a housemaid's clothes.

She dropped something into the pocket of her apron. There was a clinking sound again.

'Oh, good God!' said Pa, taking no care to whisper any more.

They both stopped and squinted into the light of our lantern.

'Stop!' cried Pa. 'Those are not yours!'

They turned and fled. Pa set off after them but had only gone a few paces before he was coughing and wheezing. He doubled over, setting down the lamp and clutching his hat to his head with a gloved hand.

I watched the man and the woman disappear into the brambles and blackness behind the cottage, and knelt next to my grandfather.

'Are you all right, Pa? What shall I do?'

He couldn't get a word out in between breaths, but he flailed a hand in front of him and pointed in the direction of the two thieves. Mosca launched himself from the top of my ear and I went after him.

The wall to the north was in a bad way and, as Pa had said, no trouble to climb. Beyond it, things were more difficult. I had spent plenty of time exploring the woods behind the church, but usually it was in daylight and under far calmer circumstances. I hardly recognized the trees and I ran so fast I quickly lost my way. After the rain we'd had the earth was covered in a layer of thick mulch and I slid and fell twice, and when I picked myself up I was even more disorientated. If it hadn't been for Mosca I would have lost the thieves completely, and might have even lost myself in the process.

After a few minutes of zigzagging wildly through the tree trunks I saw their lantern and its wrinkled reflection on the surface of the river. I stopped a little way up the hill and doused my own lantern and watched the man climbing unsteadily into a boat drawn up to the riverbank. I hid behind an old oak and put my back to its wet and rugged bark and had no idea what I should do. I could easily catch them from here, perhaps even capsize their little boat, but then what? Then, as now, I was not much taller than the woman and skinny as a greyhound. I had never fought another person in my life. And I certainly could not swim, if they decided to hurl me into the river.

I waited and I listened. Mosca obviously thought me a coward because he flew so deep into my earhole I thought he'd reached my brain. I stuck a finger in there and tried to pluck him out. He buzzed indignantly.

'Stop it!' I said. 'I need to hear what they're saying!'

The overgrown baby was reprimanding the ape for his clumsiness.

'You're a bloody idiot! We're lucky enough to find the

place empty, and you have to go and knock over the tea set. We could have been in and out of there and they'd've been none the wiser!'

'Don't matter. We got what we was after.'

'Yes and they *know* we've got it.'

'So what? The old one's on death's door and the young 'un's no more'n a runt and they ain't got a brain cell between 'em.'

I took issue with this, especially the last part. Pa is the cleverest man I have ever met, and while I'll admit I'm no genius I definitely fancied myself wiser than this ape. I could feel my face getting hot.

'What if they tell someone else in the village?'

'And who in the village wants to listen to 'em? Can't get near 'em for the smell. Anyway, they don't know who we are, do they?'

'The boy might. The old man doesn't leave the graveyard but I've seen the young one lurking around the village of an evening.'

'Then we'll have to make sure he don't say anything. Drown him like a puppy. Not like he'll be missed, is it?'

The woman did not agree or disagree. There was a creak and a splash and then several rhythmic clunks of the oar-locks. I swallowed hard.

'Where are we headed then?' said the ape.

'Usual place,' said the woman.

'Thought you'd say that. I hate the usual place.'

'Well, just be glad he's not asked us for a bloody body this time.'

'Ay, that's true enough.'

They stopped talking after that and I listened to the splash of oars grow more and more distant. Even when the river and the woods were completely silent, and they were well out of sight, I still did not dare come out from my hiding place for another half hour.

I came back to the cottage to find Pa on his hands and knees picking up the fragments of the teapot. His breath still came in long and ragged gasps. Behind him the kettle lay on its side in a pool of water. I must have mistaken its clanging for the church bell.

I stood on the doorstep for a moment and I quivered in the draught. My body felt like a husk, hollowed out by cold and tiredness and not a small amount of terror. I did not want to be drowned. I'd seen the size of the man's hands.

Pa sat back and saw me and had some trouble getting to his feet.

'Ned! Ned, did you get them?'

I shook my head.

'I'm sorry, Pa. I saw them get in a boat but they just rowed away. They said some awful things about me. About both of us.'

'I mean the keys. Did you get the keys?'

I frowned.

'Is that all they took?'

'Oh, Ned.'

He briefly got himself upright and then slumped into the chair that had not been knocked over. He clasped his head in his hands and massaged his mottled temples but didn't say anything. His keys were on a great iron ring, large enough to wear around my neck, which hung above the stove along with everything else. They opened our cottage door (though it was rarely locked), the churchyard gate (though it was easy to climb the wall), and the back door to the church spire (which led only to the bells and the bats' roost). It seemed things could have been far worse.

'They didn't take the tea tin?'

Pa had an ancient, rusted tin containing a few coins, which he kept in the toe of a pair of boots he no longer wore. He shook his head.

'And they didn't take any bodies this time.'

'It seems not.'

'Then it's not so bad, is it? I mean, having your keys doesn't change very much. They got into the churchyard without them in the first place. And there's nothing to steal from the belfry, is there? Unless there's a key I don't know about?'

He just sat and shook his head and then went back to sweeping up the broken remains of our tea set.

V

ⱰEDE

The gossip among the servants – all three of them – was that the visitor was the most handsome gentleman they had ever laid eyes upon. It had been almost ten years since he'd last come to the house but they all remembered the spell he'd cast over the place, how the lamps had burnt a little brighter, how the clouds of worry had lifted from my mother's and father's brows for those few short days. Not just handsome but intelligent, they assured me, and well respected in social and academic circles. And, yes, of course, extraordinarily wealthy. No need for me to even ask.

He arrived shortly after four o'clock in the afternoon and we assembled our meagre household at the front door of the manor to greet him. I already resented the man for keeping me from my books, but Father was insistent that we put on a good show for such a distinguished guest. As if by dressing properly we might distract him from the crumbling façade of the house, the weeds in the drive, a pigeon infestation on the scale of a biblical plague. In the end I was glad to be there, not least to witness the servants' reactions when he emerged from his carriage. The sun was low and his face was golden in the dying light. I would have called him *striking* rather than handsome. For one reason in particular.

'Where's his nose?' I whispered to Father.

'It's between his eyes like everyone else's.'

'You know what I mean, Father. Where's his *original* nose?'

In the centre of what was, admittedly, a very well-proportioned face, the man had a nose-shaped metal prosthesis which was attached by a slim leather strap that tied around the back of his head. It sparkled in the sunlight.

'I have no idea,' said Father.

'Have you asked him?'

'No. And it is under no circumstances to be a topic of conversation while he is staying with us.'

'Is it real gold?'

'What did I just say?'

'Or brass?'

'*Bede.*'

My father glowered at me and went to greet the gentleman, who was instructing the coachman in unloading the luggage from the rear of the carriage. The servants cast glances at me as if to say: *No, this is not him! This is a different man altogether!*

'Phineas! My boy!' Father cried. I remember thinking how odd it was that he called him 'boy', since he must have been at least thirty years old. He turned and they shook hands very warmly. I did not remember his face at all, with or without his golden prosthesis, though Father claimed we had met. Phineas' father and mine had been childhood friends and cherished drinking partners. Our families had met often, apparently, until Phineas' father had drunk himself through most of the family's wealth, and subsequently into the waters of the Thames.

My father patted the younger man on the back and led him by the elbow to meet us. Phineas surveyed the driveway and the front of the manor house and shook his head and said: 'It is every bit as beautiful as I remember.'

Father gestured at me, like he was showing the man a particularly interesting coat of arms.

'You remember my daughter, Obedience?'

'Of course,' said Phineas. 'Little Bede!'

He took my hand and kissed it. Back then I always wore my gloves in company – rarely took them off at all, in fact – and was glad that Phineas' nose was false. I had not washed them for some time and the smell was fairly abominable.

'I am very glad to see you again,' I said, and made a curtsy.

'I should like to say that you are also as beautiful as I remember, but I fear I would be branded a liar.' I looked at Father and a frown passed briefly over his brow. Then Phineas added, with what he no doubt considered a rapier-point of wit: 'For you are many times *more* beautiful than you were when we last met.'

'You are too kind,' I said. 'I was not aware my beauty

made any impression on you when we last met. I believe I was six years old.'

Phineas' smile did not falter, though he wasn't sure how to respond. My father sensed the awkwardness and introduced the man to Mr Elmet, his footman, and Mr and Mrs Gilly, our two servants. They bowed and curtsied and tried to look absolutely anywhere that was not the gleaming centrepiece of Phineas' face.

There was a lot of grunting behind us as the coach driver continued to unload several large chests from the carriage.

'Perhaps Mr Gilly might help you with your luggage?' said Father, but Phineas waved a hand breezily.

'No, no, my man can manage. Can't you, Perkins?' Perkins appeared not to hear this. He also appeared to be not managing at all. The driver looked quite ancient and shuddered under the weight of what he was carrying. There was a lot of glassy clinking from inside. It sounded like Phineas had brought half of his wine cellar with him.

'I thought you were only with us for two nights, Mr Mordaunt?' I asked. 'Are you staying longer than expected?'

'Oh Bede, you do sound disappointed!'

I did not correct him but Phineas smiled anyway.

'Do not worry, my dear, I will not outstay my welcome. Your father has simply agreed that I might keep some of my equipment here while I am away from London.'

'Equipment?'

'Phineas has agreed to give us a demonstration tomorrow,' said Father. 'That's exciting, isn't it?'

'A demonstration?' I said. 'Of what?'

He leant in conspiratorially.

'That, my dear, is a secret,' he said, and he tapped the side of his metal nose as if daring me to make some mention of it.

'Mr Gilly,' said Father, 'perhaps you could show Mr Mordaunt to the Blue Room? You must be tired, Phineas.'

Phineas straightened up.

'Tired? No, not at all! I have been cooped up in that tiny carriage for hours. I simply must stretch my poor legs. Perhaps we could take a walk. And perhaps you would like to join us, Bede?'

Father agreed heartily.

For the next hour or two, while the light lasted, I trailed behind Phineas and my father as they toured the grounds and spoke of what I believe are called 'society matters'. They mentioned a lot of names of men I had never heard of: who was married and who was not; who was in debt and who was not; who had been invited to which balls and who had not.

We wandered to the orchard in the east and the folly in the west and back through the 'deer park', which was really just a large, overgrown meadow since all the deer had been sold long ago for venison. Before we reached the house we passed the hedge maze, also overgrown, to the point where it simply resembled one enormous square hedge with no paths running through it at all.

'Ah!' said Phineas. 'These are very amusing. Have you seen the one at Blenheim?'

'I have not,' said Father.

'I was there last summer. The gardens are beautiful but the maze is fiendish.' He laughed. 'Do you know the correct route through this one?'

'I do not,' said Father. 'I got lost in there as a boy and vowed never to go inside again. Bede – I mean, Obedience – she was always in there when she was younger. She knows the whole thing back to front, even now.'

'Does she?' Phineas looked over his shoulder. 'How clever!'

We went indoors and Father showed him the least embarrassing sections of the house. He had done his best to conceal the state of the manor but there was a limit to what dusting and cleaning and tactfully arranged curtains could achieve. I loved the house as it was. I thought it a noble ruin, far more characterful and charming for its dilapidation. In the drawing room I noticed a new and rather garish tapestry hung outside the dining room.

'Where has this come from?' I asked.

'It's always been there,' said Father quickly. 'Perhaps we should get ready for dinner?'

'No, it hasn't.'

'It has.'

I poked around behind it.

'Oh,' I said.

I moved the tapestry out of the way to reveal a spreading damp patch and an irremediably large crack in the plaster.

'Obedience!' Father snapped.

'Please don't worry, Gregory!' said Phineas and slapped

him hard on the back. 'It's an occupational hazard with these old houses. I have much the same problems with my properties in Russell Square.'

'Properties?' said my father. 'You have more than one, now?'

'Oh yes,' said Phineas. 'I have found it quite convenient to have one residence where I can work, and another where I can be at leisure. I would rather keep the two separate.'

'Two houses in Russell Square!' exclaimed Father. 'You are quite the man of means! And unmarried, too. It is beyond belief!'

He looked at me and raised his eyebrows, and I knew exactly what he meant by it. To me the remark sounded more than a little sarcastic – it seemed well within the realms of credulity that a man as wheedling as Phineas might struggle to be wed.

VI

ƆBEDE

It was strange having someone else at the dinner table that evening. The dining room at Wellrest Manor was a gloomy place, panelled with dark wood and overseen by austere oil paintings of past Wellrests, but when it was just Father and myself eating we seemed not to notice. Having a visitor only made us aware of quite how sad the house had become. Phineas' constant smiling did not so much light the room as throw it into sharper relief.

Father was looking at me as we took our seats.

'You haven't changed your dress, Obedience.'

'No, Father. I have not.'

'But we have a guest.'

'I know.'

'What were you doing in your room?'

'Reading.'

'Bede . . .'

'My dress is already dirty from the walk, and I shall probably spill food down myself anyway, so why give Mrs

Gilly two dresses to wash instead of one?'

Father frowned. Phineas laughed and unfolded his napkin.

'There is reason in that, Gregory!' he said, and Father shrank into his chair as if he had been ambushed.

Mr Gilly brought us dishes of Mrs Gilly's soup and laid them in front of us. We fell into silence and the room echoed with the clink of spoons on crockery and thinly disguised slurping. Underneath all of it I thought I could hear Father simmering.

'Tell me, Mr Mordaunt,' I asked, when the silence became intolerable, 'how do you plan on spending your time while you are with us? Besides preparing your mysterious demonstration.'

He dabbed at his mouth and considered this.

'I think I would like to simply enjoy the charms of the countryside while I am free of London's busyness. On the way here I saw that wonderful windmill that we visited last time I was here. Do you remember, Gregory? You were perhaps too young, Bede. We all went up to the windmill and took our luncheon out of doors, you, your father and . . .'

We looked into our soup bowls.

'Forgive me,' said Phineas.

'There is nothing to apologize for,' said Father. 'It was a very long time ago.'

'I was so sorry to hear of your wife's passing.'

Father tried to smile.

'It is the way of the world,' he said. 'Life must go on.'

Something hot fluttered in my chest. Indeed it must. But it is not the same life that it was before.

'We would not be able to visit the windmill now, anyway,' I said. 'It is a ruin, and the men from the village say it is too dangerous to go up there. It is my understanding that it could fall down at any minute.'

'A ruin?' said Phineas, glad for the change of subject. 'It seemed to be standing when I passed it – though, I only saw it from the road.'

'It was struck by lightning some years back. The stones are still standing but the whole structure is burnt out.'

'Lightning? How fascinating.'

'It is also haunted.'

Phineas glanced at my father over the top of his soup spoon, but Father was not looking. He was obviously still thinking about Mother. I felt sorry for him, then. Loved him, too, for all of his strictness. Perhaps I even loved him *because* of it, since it was only his strange, severe way of showing that he loved me.

'Haunted?' said Phineas after a few moments, a slight smile upon his lips.

'So they say.'

'I am a man of science, Bede. Generally, we do not entertain ideas of ghosts and spirits.'

'Perhaps you should.'

He waved a hand.

'Mere folktales.'

'Well, I would never think to go anywhere near it. There is not a bird or an animal within a mile of the place.'

'In my experience there is usually a reasonable explanation for such phenomena.'

I swallowed another spoonful of soup and said: 'They say it reeks of death up there.'

'Obedience, please!'

My father slammed his palm flat on to the table and the crockery jumped. I cast my eyes into my lap.

Another minute or so passed in silence. Mr Gilly came and took our bowls while Phineas desperately cast around for some way to lighten the atmosphere again. I could hear a strange wheezing noise from around the seams of his brass nose. Suddenly he stuck a finger in the air and grinned as if he had received some kind of revelation.

'You said you were reading before dinner.'

'Yes.'

'Was it a novel? I'll bet it was a novel. There is the problem, Gregory! That is why she is talking of ghosts and hauntings. These works of fiction unleash all sort of grotesqueries from the female imagination.'

I stared at him.

'No,' I said, 'it was not a novel.'

'You have no reason to be ashamed, I have no quarrel with them at all! I am assured that they are very enjoyable. Which was it? A lady I met just the other day was reading . . . now what was it . . .? *The Castle of Otranto*! She seemed to have quite lost her wits over it. Spoke of nothing else.'

'I do not read novels,' I said. I was gripping my knife and fork so tightly by now I was sure they would leave bruises on my palms.

'Then what?'

'I read journals.'

'Journals? What kind of journals?'

'Scientific journals.'

I may as well have told him that I was a wolf from the waist down, or that I could conjure the weather. He sat back in his chair and put down his napkin and looked at me with an expression of amused disbelief.

'Well,' he said, 'that is astonishing. Good for you.'

Nobody spoke for a while. He kept staring at me, then he looked at my father, as if we were both conspiring to make a fool of him. In the meantime, the main course arrived, one of Mrs Gilly's brown and inscrutable casseroles. Phineas didn't even seem to notice when the plate was put in front of him.

Father cleared his throat noisily.

'Obedience's governess, Mrs Hickson, passed away rather suddenly last week,' he said. 'She has rather too much free time on her hands now.'

'Oh, I am sorry to hear that,' said Phineas, though I didn't know if he meant Mrs Hickson's death, or the fact that I wasn't being kept busy with needlework and the wretched pianoforte.

'There is no need to be sorry,' I said. 'She was a harpy.'

'Please, Bede,' said Father.

Phineas leant forward on both elbows.

'Which scientific journal are you reading at the moment?'

'I do not think it is one that you will have heard of.'

'I think I might have.'

'The *Allgemeines Journal der Chemie*.'

He looked at me blankly for a moment. I do not think he spoke any German.

'Ah yes. I know it. Very . . . thorough. Did your father tell you that chemistry is my specific area of interest?'

'No, he did not.'

There was a flicker of disappointment on his face. He tried the casserole, licked his lips and put down his fork.

'Perhaps he did not want to spoil the surprise of tomorrow's demonstration,' he said.

'As far as I understand,' I said, 'the subject of chemistry covers a multitude of sins, depending on who one's teacher is. Tell me: do you consider yourself a chemist, or an alchemist?'

'Well, it is a *very* good question. Sometimes I think people draw unnecessary distinctions between the two. These days it would be unthinkable to call oneself an alchemist – I would be laughed out of the Royal Institution – and yet, I wonder if we still have much to learn from those serious men of antiquity! I myself would never disregard the findings of previous ages – I seek them out, in fact! – for, after all, is not the very *principle* of science to build upon the discoveries of one's forebears?'

He seemed very proud of this conclusion. I studied him a while and wondered if he knew – about the history of the family, about my own forebears. I thought it better to try and draw it out of him there and then.

'Presumably you know of the alchemist who lived here?'

'Bede,' said Father, 'that's enough.'

Phineas made a show of confusion that only confirmed my suspicions. He frowned and said: 'Here? In this house?'

'Old Uncle Herbert.'

'Goodness me!'

'He died perhaps two hundred years ago. He was killed by his experiments.'

'Killed?'

'Poisoned. Very slowly. After he had gone completely mad, of course.'

Father began waving his hands and shaking his head.

'No,' he said. 'No, no, no, no, *no*. The man was not even an alchemist. He was a mountebank! A cheap magician! To think of the fortune that he wasted on his silly little hobby. And now, look at us, two hundred years later and unable to afford a roof that keeps the rain out! All because of him!'

He suddenly realized how poor a picture this was painting for our guest, after we had taken such pains to conceal our destitution.

'Enough of him. I will not have Herbert Wellrest mentioned anywhere in this house, let alone at the dinner table, let alone in front of guests. I am *sorry*, Phineas . . .'

'Gregory, there is nothing to be sorry for!' he said, laughing. 'Now that you mention it, I believe I *have* heard the name Herbert Wellrest.'

Father looked mortified.

'You have?'

'As I say, I consider no text outside my purview, however old-fashioned. I believe I saw Herbert's name mentioned in a letter . . . Yes, that is it, he had caused some consternation among his fellow alchemists by stealing a manuscript of Paracelsus from a library in London.'

'Yes, thievery. It is said he was very prone to that too,' said Father.

'I never made the connection with your family. But of course he is one of your ancestors! You know, despite all you say, I would be very interested to know what it was he discovered, if anything.'

I let my spoon clatter into my bowl.

'I am afraid you will be disappointed,' I said.

'Will I?' said Phineas.

'He left behind none of his research.'

'None at all?'

'They say that he destroyed everything. His books, his apparatus.'

'His family,' Father added, grimly.

Again, Phineas looked from Father's face to mine like he suspected we were both lying. In fact, only one of us was.

'Well, that is a shame,' he said. 'Still, now you are a woman of science yourself, perhaps you can pick up where he left off!'

He forked a greyish lump of meat to his lips, chewed and forced it down. His smile was still there but, for the first time since he had arrived, it seemed that maintaining it was causing him some discomfort.

It was quite obvious, now. The only reason that Phineas had chosen to endure our hospitality was to find out more about Uncle Herbert. And it was equally obvious that I should do everything in my power to get him out of the house as quickly as possible.

'You're very kind to say so,' I said. 'But I know my limitations. I could never be a chemist of any real standing, or alchemist, for that matter. I am far too bookish.'

Phineas nodded in agreement, and, it seemed, relief.

'Quite so,' said Phineas. 'The theoretical aspects of science are fascinating, but the real discoveries will always be made in the laboratory, not the library.'

I watched the satisfaction bloom across his face.

'You have your own laboratory, do you?' I asked.

'I do. In Russell Square.'

'Oh! It makes me giddy just to think of it. All those strange contraptions and colourful potions.'

'I wouldn't call them potions . . .'

'Is it very dangerous, the research you do?'

'Yes, it can be.'

'Is that how you lost your nose?'

Even Mr Gilly, standing stone-like in the corner of the dining room, emitted a gasp. Father was too shocked to say anything at all.

Phineas blinked a couple of times. He raised a hand to touch the cold brass protrusion as if he had forgotten it was there.

'I beg your pardon?' he said.

His smile never left his lips, though it was more of a rictus grin by now and the rest of his face was trembling.

'Off to your room, Bede,' said Father. 'Now.'

'Why?'

'Go. We have had quite enough of your company.'

'I have not finished my supper.'

'Nor shall you.'

He stood up and gestured to the door. I did not protest and pushed my own chair back. Phineas began to say something apologetic, but I could not hear him for the blood singing in my ears. I caught sight of myself in the silverware as I left the room, and had not realized how much I had been grinning.

VII

BEDE

I returned to my room and spent an hour reading by candlelight before the inevitable knock on my door. I tucked all the books but one underneath my bed and went to open it. Father was outside, his face looking even more purple than it was in the darkness of the landing.

He came inside. I sat at my bureau. A few moments passed in which he tried to catch his breath, which he had lost either in anger or in climbing the stairs to the room. He had to stoop a little under the ceiling because we were up in the roof, among the servants' quarters. I had always insisted on having my room up there, since I was a little girl. I have always liked small spaces. It felt particularly tiny that night, struggling to contain me and my father and my father's rage.

'I have never been more ashamed in my life,' he said. He spoke quietly. That was how I knew he was truly inconsolable.

I looked at him for a moment before answering. I felt it

again, that familiar, violent commixture of defiance and pity that I could never get to settle. At last I said: 'It was a perfectly reasonable question.'

'I told you not to mention his . . . condition. It was my *one* request while he is staying with us!'

'I forgot.'

'You forgot?'

'I was staring at my reflection in it all the way through dinner! How could I *not* mention it?'

'Keep your voice down!'

'It's true, though!'

He met my eyes for a few seconds and then went to the small square window and looked out into the night.

'Your disobedience confounds me.'

I allowed myself a small laugh at that.

'Well. You gave me the name. It's not my fault if I took it as a challenge.'

'Don't try and be funny with me!'

I came over to him.

'Does it really matter, Father?' I said. 'Will anybody care if Phineas returns to London with tales of my bad behaviour? Are you worried our name will sink yet lower in fashionable circles? This family has no reputation to begin with. You can't just put up a new tapestry and pretend that we're respectable.'

'Our financial circumstances are not a reason for you to be uncouth, and unkind, and, frankly . . .'

'Frankly?'

'Feral.'

'Feral, am I?'

'I hardly know where you are half of the time!'

'Then I suppose you'll have to find me another governess, won't you? One who isn't five hundred years old and can actually keep up with me when I leave the house.'

Father's eyes were beginning to shine, and I regretted some of what I had said. But not all.

'You will apologize to Mr Mordaunt tomorrow.'

'Will I?'

'Yes. And you will do what is necessary to repair your friendship for the future.'

'Our friendship? We have no friendship. I know nothing about him, save that he is conceited, and excessively prideful, and he never, ever stops bloody smiling! As for the future—'

I stopped, realizing what Father was implying.

'Ah, I understand,' I said. 'I know what you're doing. I saw your look, earlier.'

'What look?'

'You want us to be married, don't you? That is why you wouldn't tell me *why* he was coming.'

He blinked a couple of times.

'His father and I were very close, Bede. He is a very wealthy and well-respected gentleman.'

'I am sixteen, Father! And you are already lining me up a husband!'

'It is really not so uncommon, for a young lady of your standing.'

'Our family has no standing! I am sorry to be the bearer

of bad news, Father, but we are quite unheard of.'

'Phineas has heard of us.'

'That is what worries me.'

'He is intelligent. And he *was* handsome, once upon a time. You may find him strange, but your children . . . Well, they would all have noses. Handsome noses.'

'It is not his nose, or lack of it, that I find disagreeable – it is his personality!'

'Bede, this could be very useful.'

'No.'

'Think about it.'

'The answer is no.'

'Your mother would—'

'Don't bring her into it!'

There was a pause in hostilities. We were both breathing hard.

'She would at least insist that you apologize,' Father said. 'She would ask that much.'

I turned back to the bureau, knowing he was right.

'And at least consider Mr Mordaunt. He has come here because he has heard much of your beauty and your wit.'

'From you?'

'Yes, from me. We have exchanged several letters in the last year.'

'So, it is all arranged, is it? Well, thank you for letting me know.'

'It is not arranged, no. He is here to get to know you.'

'He is here because of Uncle Herbert.'

'Nonsense!'

I raised my eyebrows, but he had nothing else to say on this matter.

'So,' I said. 'This demonstration tomorrow. That is part of his courtship, is it? To woo me?'

'Perhaps. You know, if you *were* to wed, he could perhaps teach you what he knows. You might even share his laboratory. You know I don't approve of any of this sort of thing –' he gestured at the book I had open '– but under his guidance your reading habits might be more seemly.'

'*Seemly?*'

'Consider it, Bede,' he said. 'You say we have no reputation to salvage, but that is not what I am thinking of. I am thinking of your happiness. That is all. I do not know what else I can say to make you believe that.'

He stood in the middle of the room a while longer, cocking his head at a more and more severe angle to try and draw a response from me. When it was clear to him that none was coming, he sighed and sagged and went out of the room and closed the door. I listened to his footsteps retreating down the landing.

My blood was too hot to let me sleep, so I did what I have always done in times of crisis and buried myself in my books. I studied for another few hours and pretended that the matter was settled. I would not be apologizing. I would not be getting married. I would continue with my work as per usual.

It was past midnight when I finally decided I should think about sleeping. My eyes were sore and the words and diagrams of the journal were beginning to blur into nonsense.

I undressed and slipped into a nightshirt and lay on top of the bedsheets, my brain whirring at such a velocity I fancied I could hear a high-pitched hum emanating from the top of my scalp. As if in counterpoint my belly was also rumbling, since I hadn't been allowed to finish my dinner. I thought a trip to the kitchens would do well to empty my head and fill my stomach.

I got up with the remaining stub of my candle and went down the servants' staircase at the far end of the hallway. The stairs were narrow and pitch-black but when I reached the door to the kitchen there was light coming from the cracks at the top and bottom, along with the sound of footsteps and a kind of frustrated muttering. Someone was already in there. At first I thought it was Mrs Gilly – in those days she was no stranger to continuing her tasks through the dead of night – but it became clearer that the voice was a man's and he clearly didn't know his way around the kitchen.

I listened a little longer. There was the sound of pans clanging, cupboards opening, and at long last a quiet 'ah!' of triumph. I heard the intruder come to the door at the foot of the stairs and I saved him the bother of opening it.

It was Perkins, Phineas' coachman and footman and all-round dogsbody. He was stooped and twisted and his face was seamed as driftwood. He looked more frightened than guilty. In one hand he held a candle of his own. In the other was a plucked, limp chicken. We looked at each other. Eventually he remembered to bow, and the chicken bobbed up and down in time with him.

'Good evening, miss,' he said.

'I think it's actually morning, now,' I said.

'Is it so late? I hadn't noticed.'

I nodded at the bird.

'Midnight snack, is it?'

He held it up and looked at it as though he was surprised to find it in his hand.

'Oh! This? Ah. Mr Mordaunt asked me to fetch it for him.'

'Was the dinner not to his satisfaction?'

'Quite satisfactory, miss. This here chicken is for his research.'

'And what research is that?'

'I wouldn't know, miss. I am, as you can see, not a man of letters.'

He lowered his eyes as if ashamed of himself.

'It does not take a man of letters,' I said, 'to know that it is wrong to steal from one's hosts.'

He looked up, aghast.

'He has permission, miss!'

'Has he?'

'Oh, yes, miss! Your father said Mr Mordaunt could have all that he wanted to make himself at home.'

'Did he?'

Poor, deluded Father. Neither of us moved. Eventually Perkins gestured with his candle.

'If I may, miss. He'll be waiting for me.'

'He's awake, too, is he?'

'Oh yes, he's quite the night owl, miss – like yourself!'

'Like myself,' I said. 'Well, tell him to send it back when he's done with it or there will be no lunch for him tomorrow.'

He frowned and then gave an uncertain laugh.

'Ah, yes. Very amusing, miss. I will pass that on.'

I stepped out into the kitchen and allowed him to come past. He bowed again and went up the stairs, muttering something that sounded very bitter, though if it was about me or his master or both of us I did not know.

I had a cup of water and some dry cheese and drier bread. I thought as I chewed. What on earth did a chemist need with a raw chicken? Phineas seemed an ambitious man, and I was quite sure the great scientific discoveries of the age were not being made in the field of poultry. And how dare he simply swipe it from the kitchen? As if he were already master of the house! No, I resolved again for the tenth time that night, I would not be marrying Phineas Mordaunt.

I went back up the stairs and listened on the landing outside the Blue Room but could not hear Perkins or his master. I returned to my room and sat on my bed. I still felt wide awake – rather than clearing my head, the trip to the kitchen had only filled it with more busyness. I sat there for some time and let the candle flame burn to nothing. I removed my gloves in the darkness and began the nightly battle to snatch a few hours of sleep.

VIII

ᴄBEDE

I missed breakfast but no one came to fetch me, so I assumed Phineas and my father were happy to eat by themselves. Perhaps Father was apologizing on my behalf. At any rate I was glad for the lie-in.

Around mid-morning another carriage pulled up outside the house delivering even more apparatus for Phineas' demonstration. Perkins staggered wearily back and forth to the ballroom with another half-dozen boxes. I suspected this would keep Phineas busy for an hour or so and took the chance to finish the *Allgemeines Journal der Chemie*, started on *The Proceedings of the Royal Society 1812*, and made some notes in my own journal. By ten I was getting thirsty and I risked a foray downstairs to refill my jug of water.

Father was waiting for me at the bottom of the stairs.

'Mr Mordaunt is staying for another week,' he said, as if I would be glad to hear it.

'I see,' I said. 'Well, perhaps you could tell Mr Gilly that I will be taking my meals in my room until he has gone.'

He closed his eyes and exhaled through his nose.

'I thought a good sleep would have helped you to see things a little more clearly.'

'I didn't have a good sleep. I never have a good sleep.'

Father looked me in the eye, caught somewhere between frustration and compassion.

'Why is he staying longer?'

'He is in correspondence with many of the scholars at the university, and he has invited several of them to visit us and view his demonstrations. It is much more convenient for him to be based here while he continues with his research.'

'You mean while he sniffs out Uncle Herbert's research.'

Father's mouth became a flat line.

'I told you not to mention him, Bede.'

'It's true, though.'

'It's not true. You're too suspicious by half. It is a matter of convenience. He is but an hour from Oxford and says our ballroom is three or four times the size of his laboratory in Russell Square.' He paused. 'He also says he would like some time to get to know you better.'

'Would he?'

'Yes. In fact, he would like to take a ride with you this morning. I was coming to tell you. He is waiting by the stables.'

'Then he will be waiting some time. I'm going to fetch some water and then return to my room.'

I went to pass him but he held my arm.

'Please, Bede. Just talk to the man. Get to know him.'

There was more than a little desperation in his voice. His eyes always seemed very dark and very wet. They had done since Mother had died.

'Very well,' I said. 'I will go for a ride with him. But nothing else.'

'There's a good girl.'

'Is that all it takes?'

I went and dressed, and then came back down and left by the kitchen door. It was a bright and flawless day. Phineas was in the stable yard talking to Mr Gilly about something, and as soon as I arrived Mr Gilly bowed clumsily and took his leave. I greeted him as he passed and he tipped his cap and hurried into the kitchen.

Phineas had not seen me, or at least pretended he had not, and began stroking one of the horse's noses. He was in clean and starched breeches, his face rosy, a single chestnut curl dangling over his forehead, looking not at all like he had been burning the midnight oil. He turned when he saw me coming and beamed, as if the altercation at dinner had been simply a horrid dream that only one of us remembered.

'Good morning, my dear!' he said, and bowed smartly.

'Good morning, Mr Mordaunt.'

He stood up but his eyes remained fixed on my legs.

'Very modern,' he said at last.

One of the few good things to come out of Grammy Hickson's guardianship, and her obsession with sewing and needlework, was the creation of a pair of pantaloons that fitted me very comfortably. Of course she was appalled, as was my father. But they were my garment of choice when riding or walking any great distance, since they were tough and easy to scrub clean and did not snag and tear like any of my gowns.

I ignored his remark, as I did everyone else who thought my attire worthy of comment.

'I see you have befriended Mr Gilly,' I said.

Phineas remembered himself and looked up.

'Hm? Oh, your manservant! Yes. Just passing the time. A helpful fellow, though, I must say, not a terribly good conversationalist.'

'I do not think conversation is what one looks for in a servant.'

'What does one look for?'

'Loyalty. Discretion.'

'Yes, both excellent qualities.'

I paused.

'Would you say that your man had them?'

'Who, Perkins? Why, of course!'

'I met him in the middle of the night, you know. In the kitchen.'

There was another pause. He seemed to be weighing up how much I knew.

'You did? What was he doing?'

He made no mention of his work, of the chicken theft. It seemed that Perkins had not mentioned our encounter to him, either. I pressed on with feigned ignorance, curious to see how far Phineas might go to conceal his night-time activities.

'I don't know,' I said. 'I suppose he was looking for something to eat.'

'That sounds about right,' he said, laughing, 'I've never known such an old fellow with such a voracious appetite!' He looked suddenly horror-stricken. 'He didn't wake you, did he?'

'No, I was already up.'

'Ah, that's a relief. Oh, poor Perkins. You must think I work him far too hard. I know *he* thinks that. Always grumbling. But very discreet, and very loyal – as you say, one cannot put a price on that.'

I smiled. Obviously Perkins was not so adept at keeping secrets as his master thought. Phineas went back to patting the horse's nose.

'You've met Victor, then,' I said.

'I have! A fine beast.'

Victor was older than I was and all skin and bones, but for once I agreed with Phineas.

'I've ridden him all my life,' I said. 'Clerval is the younger one. In the stall over there. I think he will be better suited to you.'

'Ah, I had not seen him!'

'He's a shy soul.'

'Hardly suited to me at all, then!'

I forced a smile.

'Where would you like to ride to?'

'On a day as beautiful as this – and in company as sparkling – I'm sure we can go anywhere at all.'

'Perhaps to the watermill and back, then. We have only

a couple of hours before luncheon.'

I wondered what grisly substitute for the chicken Mrs Gilly was plotting, and while I was lost in thought Phineas wandered to the end of the stables. He pointed and called over his shoulder.

'Tell me, what is that building over there? We passed it on our walk yesterday but I never enquired after it.'

I looked to the low rise at the very edge of the estate. There was an orderly row of cypress trees on the horizon and in the middle of them a small stone building with a vaulted roof.

'That is the Wellrest family cemetery,' I said, and again I thought I guessed at his motives.

'Ah, I see. Well, if we rode there we would have very pleasant views over the countryside, would we not?'

'I suppose we would.'

'Excellent!'

Mr Gilly had already saddled the horses and I led both Victor and Clerval out into the yard. Phineas fussed around Clerval for a few moments, checking the tack and getting the measure of him – perhaps he thought I had given him a deliberately skittish horse, and I would have done if I could, but Clerval was a pussycat. I had been in the saddle for a minute or two before he mounted up alongside me. He sat and stared at my pantaloons again.

'My dear, what are you doing?'

'I'm waiting for you, Mr Mordaunt.'

'But your legs . . .'

'I beg your pardon?'

'Forgive me, only, I have never seen a woman ride in this way. I mean . . . astride.'

I looked down. I rode like a man because I had never known any other way. I had seen ladies riding side-saddle and thought it the most absurd, impractical, downright dangerous practice.

'It is how my mother taught me,' I said. 'Does it embarrass you, sir?'

'No, no, not at all!' he said, but the bobbing lump in his neck suggested otherwise.

We trotted at a leisurely pace through the deer park and for the first few minutes I could almost forget he was there and enjoy the day. There were new buds on every tree and the grass was a lush, green ocean under the sun. It was good to fill my lungs and be free from my studies and my father, just for a few moments. I rode a little ahead of Phineas and did not look back. When we were halfway to the cemetery he came up alongside me and I saw the glint of his nose among his flying curls.

'There is no need to apologize for last night,' he said.

I had not been planning on it.

'Last night?' I said.

'Your questions.'

'Ah.'

'It is perfectly understandable.'

I said nothing and watched a pair of rabbits lolloping in the long grass. He wanted to pursue the conversation, though.

'To answer you plainly, I lost it in a duel.'

'A duel?'

'Yes. In London.' He paused. 'I was defending a lady's honour.'

'I would expect nothing less of you, Mr Mordaunt.'

'Miss Evenly. Of Hampstead. Do you know her?'

'I do not.'

'A young man accosted her very rudely in a coffee shop. I saw that no one was willing to intervene on her behalf and when I challenged the man he accused *me* of being envious because I fancied the young lady for myself.'

'And did you?'

'Absolute rot! I called him a liar and said that if we must duel for the sake of the truth, then so be it.'

'So really you were defending your own honour. Not the lady's.'

'You don't miss anything do you? Well. As it turned out I never got the chance to defend *anybody's* honour. Before I could set the terms of the duel the madman was upon me with a knife. I believe he would have taken my whole head off if I had not moved quickly enough.' He paused and looked distant. 'Still,' he added, 'I got my satisfaction.'

'I am sure you did,' I said, but did not ask him to elaborate.

'I am sorry if it perturbs you. My prosthesis, I mean. One day I hope medical science will have progressed enough to repair the injury, but for now I must make do.'

'It does not perturb me. Not in the slightest.'

He did not seem sure if I was mocking him or not, and we rode on in silence until we reached the top of the rise and the flaking iron railings of the cemetery. Within was the old charnel house, built of the same biscuit-coloured stone as the manor. Set around it were tombs and gravestones of Wellrests from hundreds of years back, some grey, some yellow, and most so furred with lichen that they looked dredged from the seabed. The hills rolled gently away on all sides and gave a good view of the village, the church steeple, and, far beyond, the black and crumbling hulk of the windmill.

Phineas took in the panorama and turned back to the cemetery.

'Well, this is a sombre little place, isn't it?' he said. 'Beautiful, but sombre.'

'Have you ever visited a cemetery that was festive?'

He laughed.

'No, I suppose I have not. May I have a little look?'

'If you would like.'

We both dismounted and he went through the gate and began wandering among the headstones, hands clasped behind his back, studying the names. He took his time. I stood with the horses and stroked their manes as I watched him.

'He knows exactly what he's doing,' I whispered to Victor. He flicked one ear. 'I will bet you one hundred guineas that he says something about Uncle Herbert's grave.'

Phineas came back with the wind tousling his hair. He wore both a smile and frown.

'I might be wrong,' he said, 'but isn't there one missing?'

I patted Victor's neck.

'How do you mean?'

'Your Uncle Herbert. When did you say he died?'

'I do not know exactly. Sixteen hundred and something, I believe. He was acquainted with Doctor John Dee. Or his son. I cannot remember which.'

'Gracious me, the good doctor himself! Well, as I say, there are far older headstones here. Is he buried elsewhere? Forgive my curiosity!'

I regarded him steadily.

'You are right,' I said. 'Herbert Wellrest is not here. He was quite the pariah by the end of his life and nobody wished him to be buried with the rest of the family.'

'But what on earth could he have done to be so hated?'

'As my father said, he ruined us. He spent all the family's money on his research. On absurd occult matters. Books of magic and such. I would hold him as a warning, Mr Mordaunt – obsession with such things will drain your coffers dry.'

'You think his work absurd?'

'Of course. There is nothing in it that has not been thoroughly disproven by modern science.'

'Once upon a time, there was little difference between what we call science and what we call magic. Do they not have the same ends? To lay bare the things that nature keeps hidden from us? To look beyond the veil, as it were?'

'Herbert's interests were nothing but fantasy.'

'Fantasy? And what about the things you mentioned last night – haunted windmills, ghosts, curses – are they, too, fantasies?'

I did not answer him. He smiled.

'So, if Herbert is not buried here, where is he?'

'I do not know. Nobody does. His body disappeared.'

'Just like his research.'

'Indeed. And good riddance to both.'

We looked at each other and then out over the village again. The wind gusted and sent ripples through the grass and down the slopes of the hill. There was a long period of silence.

'Very invigorating up here,' said Phineas.

Some broken tufts of clouds scudded across the sky and concealed the sun briefly. We stood there in the shadow, both preoccupied, I think, with the realization of what we were: a pair of liars, each as skilful as the other.

IX

NED

Pa seemed worse the day after the robbery. He spent most of the morning sprawled on the bed coughing and wheezing and in such discomfort I could not bring myself to ask him any more about the keys he had lost. He was more upset about them than seemed reasonable. It gnawed at me that he should be holding back the truth of their importance, but, as it turned out, this was only the smallest of a great many secrets.

While he was bed-bound I did my best to fill his shoes and act the part of sexton. I hardly convinced myself, let alone the residents. Mosca buzzed around me constantly, reminding me of the tasks I had forgotten and the ones I still needed to do. He refused to go back in his jar because he assumed – correctly – that if he did I would screw the lid tightly shut and not let him out until he was quiet.

In truth I felt as if I was getting ill myself. I had not slept at all. It was another beautiful spring day but the sunlight and birdsong seemed to reach me through several curtains of fog. The trees and bushes that had been so vibrantly green in the days before were now ashen and brittle, as if spring and summer had passed in the night and autumn was already well upon us. Every other thought was of the tiny woman and the giant man and at times I found myself gasping involuntarily because I had so vividly imagined my death: his great ape-palms forcing my head under the water.

It was midday and I was explaining these feelings to my parents when I heard a bell out in the road. A handbell, bright and cheerful and vigorously rung. The sound quite brought me back to myself. I ran to the cottage and flung open the door.

Pa sat up.

'Ned? What is it?'

He looked at me as if we had been robbed again.

'The Meat Maid!' I said.

'She's here?'

'I heard her!'

'She's two weeks early.'

'It's definitely her.'

'Then you'd better catch her up.'

He rolled over in his bed and fished the tea tin out of his old boots. He emptied a single tarnished gold coin on to his palm and stared at it a while.

'Last one?' I said.

He nodded and handed it over. Such a strange-looking thing, exotic somehow, as if it had been rescued from a shipwreck in tropical waters. He had once had hundreds of them, he said – his inheritance from his own grandfather, but there had only been a few dozen left in my lifetime.

'We can get some more, can't we?' I said.

'Not like that one, no. But the reverend might perhaps offer some as charity.'

I thought that optimistic.

'Well, I shall make the most of it,' I said. 'What should I buy?'

'Whatever she can give us, as long as it's fresh,' he said. 'Lawks, her timing could not be better. I feel completely dreadful.'

I pocketed the coin and took Pa's hessian sack from the nail it was hanging on and set off with Mosca down the path.

When it came to provisions Pa grew almost everything in our little garden, but it was difficult to find meat, and Pa liked meat. The village of Withy Bottom was too small to have its own butcher's shop, and we never, ever ventured into the city of Oxford. Instead, we had to make do with the Meat Maid. She came every month or so. She may have had another name, but I never found out what it was.

Since the keys to the gate had gone, I had to scale the church wall. Mosca buzzed impatiently around the bars of the gate. I dropped down on the other side and set off after the sound of the bell. I usually try to avoid the main road through the village, but I had no choice if I was to catch the Meat Maid's cart. I passed the villagers going about their days. It was the usual gauntlet of hard stares and lowered eyes. A woman sweeping her doorstep shooed me with her broom, then took a swipe at Mosca. A girl, much younger than me, made the sign of the cross and then walked quickly through ankle-deep mud with her father to the opposite side of the road. I did not think ill of them. I know I am strange, and I had grown used to such things.

I finally caught up with her at the far end of the village, between the inn and Wellrest Manor. Her cart was labouring very slowly through the rutted and sodden road. She sat up front in a shawl with her long, grey hair tossed like cobwebs in the wind. She was so thin it seemed she would be thrown into the mud every time her horse staggered or her wheels hit a puddle or a stone.

'Hold on!' I cried. 'I'm here!'

She brought the cart to a standstill and turned very slowly in her seat.

The Meat Maid's trade was actually not meat at all. It was hooves and hair, mostly. She went from village to village and farm to farm collecting the bodies of horses and other animals that could be used to make glue, plumes for helmets, strings for bows. It is no small task to bury a dead horse, and people are glad to have the bodies taken off their hands. She had two horses in the back of her cart now, and most of a sheep's carcass.

'There you are!' she said. 'I was beginning to lose hope.'

After the reactions of the other villagers it was a relief to see a smile, even if that smile was crooked and full of brown teeth.

'I was looking after Pa. He's not very well.'

'Well, there's a shame. Normally he's a vision of rude health.'

She laughed, but I did not find the joke particularly funny.

'I'm sorry, lad,' she said. 'I'm sure a good meal will restore his spirits. What's he after?'

'He said anything, as long as it's fresh.'

'*Fresh?* Ha!'

She dropped the reins and stood the bell on the seat of the wagon. She could not have been younger than sixty but she jumped down in quite a sprightly fashion and went around the back of her cart. She slapped one of the dead horses on the rump. Her fingers were stained dark red, her nails almost black. There was something of the witch about her, and the villagers greeted her with the same suspicion as they did Pa and me, which was perhaps why we got along so well.

'This mare broke its back yesterday and had to be shot,' she said. 'The other one was an old nag, just expired of her own accord, day before last. As for the sheep – found him on the road just now, God knows how long he'd been out there. Might get something for the wool, though.'

She shrugged. I looked at the sad heap of animals.

'We'll have something from the mare, I suppose,' I said.

'All right then,' she said. 'What'll it be?'

'Liver is Pa's favourite.'

She sucked her stained teeth.

'Now then. There might be a problem there.'

'Why?'

'Well, you see, someone has already staked their claim to that.'

'Their claim? What on earth do you mean? There's no one else who buys meat from you, is there?'

'Never used to be. But I've found myself a new customer. Someone who's after all sorts of bits and bobs. That's why I'm round these parts earlier than usual.'

Bits and bobs? What did she mean by that?

'Who is it?' I asked.

'I'm sworn to secrecy, I'm afraid.'

'Please, miss. Pa is in a bad way.'

She half closed her eyes.

'I suppose I might auction it off to the highest bidder. What's he paying?'

I took out the coin that Pa had given me. There was a worm curled around it. I shook it off and handed it to her. She examined it and shook her head.

'God knows where your grandfather gets these doubloons from. Like no coin I've ever seen.' She bit into the gold and seemed satisfied. 'Very well,' she said. 'But you'll not be getting any change from it.'

My heart sank.

'None at all?'

'It's like I say, more demand means higher prices. And this new customer's got a coin or two, I'll tell you that.'

'Well I don't want to go back empty-handed. So I suppose I don't have a choice.'

She looked up and down the road. A woman was herding geese out of the village, and two farm hands were leading a cow into it.

'Hop on,' she said. 'Let us do our business where things

are a little quieter.'

We rode up past the great rusting gates of Wellrest Manor and pulled to the side of the road when we got to the woods. She climbed into the back of the wagon and I watched as she took a knife from her belt and began to roughly open the horse's belly. The stench was quite overwhelming and while I had to pinch my nose, it threw Mosca into paroxysms of delight. The Meat Maid swatted him out of the way and delved in up to her elbows. She scooped out virtually everything, cut out the liver, then heaped everything back inside. The whole operation took a matter of minutes.

The liver itself was dark blue and dripping with something that was not blood. She slipped it with both arms into the sack and it looked to me like one of the enormous jellyfish I had seen in Pa's books on natural history. I tied the drawstring and hefted it over one shoulder. It was extraordinarily heavy.

'What's wrong with your old man, then?' she said, trying to clean her hands on the grass.

'I don't know,' I said. 'He seems very tired. He has a lot on his mind.'

'I can imagine,' she said, and got to her feet. 'Digging holes. Filling in holes. Must drive him mad having all that to think about.'

I made my mouth very small so she knew I was not impressed.

'I'm sorry,' she said again. 'You need a laugh in my line of work.'

There was a pause while I thought about what to tell her. Eventually I said: 'He seems very troubled. We've had people breaking into the churchyard. They stole our keys. And they stole . . . something else.'

I thought I had been vague enough about the matter but she leant on the edge of her wagon and nodded as if she understood perfectly.

'You've been paid a visit by the resurrection men, have you?'

'You know about them?'

'Oh yes, they're ten a penny these days! I dare say I would have been one of them if I hadn't already found my calling.'

'You don't mean that! You know what they do, don't you?'

'I do. It's not so different from my line of work, is it? No bad thing if you can still make yourself useful, after you've snuffed it. Ain't that right, Whiskey?' She slapped the dead horse again.

'These are *people*, though!' I said. 'You can't just take them to a laboratory and open them up without their permission.'

'Does it matter? People, horses, makes no difference. Dead is dead.'

I did not agree with that at all, and it bothered me that she could be so flippant about something so very serious.

I shifted the bag. My shoulder was already aching from the weight and I could feel my back getting wet.

'I should be getting home,' I said. 'Pa will be waiting.'

'Right you are,' she said. 'I should go and see my other customer.'

She winked and climbed up into the driver's seat.

'Give your grandfather my very best. If I meet any of these resurrection men I'll tell them to leave you well alone!'

I did not know whether this, too, was a joke.

I watched the wagon wobble away down the road and wondered who that next customer might be. I could not imagine anyone else quite so strange as Pa and myself, with the same strange requests. *Bits and bobs*, I thought. And then it struck me. It didn't seem beyond the realms of possibility that whoever had dug up the bodies was also getting materials from the Meat Maid.

X

NED

I lugged Pa's dinner the long way around the churchyard to where the wall was broken and climbed through the same gap the thieves had used. I rested here a while and looked at the ruin of mossy stones. Someone would have to build it back up, or there was hardly any reason in having a wall and a gate at all. Who that would be I did not know – neither I nor my grandfather was strong enough to do it, and without mortar it would only fall down again anyway.

Pa was engrossed in one of his books when I got back to the cottage. He had made himself tea, too. The teapot and one of our cups were still in pieces so he was drinking from an old communion goblet. He turned when he heard me come in and set aside the cup and book. He looked very ill.

'Any joy?' he said.

I came over and heaved the sopping bag on to the table next to his open book. The pages were open on a diagram of a plant, labelled in Latin. I understand only the King's English, but Pa is well versed in Latin and Greek. As I have said: he is quite the cleverest man I know.

He poked around in the bag and gasped.

'Oh, Ned!' he said. 'You've done marvellously well. Yes, this will do very nicely indeed.'

I thought of mentioning our rival bidder, but he seemed so pleased and I did not wish to spoil his mood.

He got up with a sudden lease of life and went over to the stove. He put the liver on a tea tray and took a knife from the wall and began to cut slices from it. Inside of its bluish exterior was a deep red. I could smell the iron in it.

Pa put a pan on the stove and fried two of the slices with onions from the garden and kept the rest back. He gave the fried slices to me on a plate, charred and delicious. The others he ate himself – raw, as usual, and swimming in dark blood. His diet of tea and vegetables must have been lacking in some very important kind of nourishment because he perked up almost immediately. The colour returned to his face and he sat a little straighter.

We enjoyed our luncheon in silence and while we ate the troubles of the last few days seemed to evaporate. It felt almost like old times – as if Pa were hale and hearty, the wall were intact, and no one had ever breached our little world. When he was done he licked his lips and slapped his belly and grinned at me through red teeth.

There was a knock at the door.

'Mr Graben? Are you there?'

It was Reverend Biles. Pa looked at the remains of the liver on the table. He scrubbed at his mouth but could not get it clean. He shooed me to the door.

'You speak to him!' he whispered. 'Tell him I'm ill! Don't let him see all this mess!'

I went and opened the door a fraction and found the vicar's grey, slabby face a few inches from mine.

'Is your grandfather here?' he said. 'I mean to say: I know he is here, because he is never *not* here.'

'He is sick, Reverend.'

'Too sick to talk?'

'Yes.'

'Then perhaps you can help.'

I slipped out and he craned his neck to see inside but I quickly closed the door behind me. He looked at me and was about to speak when something struck me.

'How did you get in?' I said. 'I thought the gate was locked.'

'That is precisely why I came to see you,' he said. 'Thankfully I have my own key, though I was forced to walk all the way back to the vicarage to find it. I am far too busy for all of this to-ing and fro-ing.'

The vicarage was next door to the church and could not have been more than half a minute's walk away but I did not mention this.

'May I ask why?'

'Why what, Reverend?'

'Why the gate was locked! You are to open it at dawn and close it at dusk. That is all you need remember. On top

– 83 –

of allowing every Tom, Dick and Harry to go rummaging in the graves, I would say you are hardly fulfilling your responsibilities.' He paused. 'Unless this is your attempt at keeping the churchyard safe? I'm afraid that will not suffice at all. You cannot simply lock everybody out of your little domain. As much as you might like to.'

I paused and looked at my feet.

'We could not open the gate. Pa is missing his keys.'

'Missing? He has lost them?'

'No, they were stolen. We had intruders again. Last night.'

'God in heaven! And the graves?'

'Nobody was disturbed, Reverend! At least, as far as I know. The only thing they took was Pa's set of keys.'

'And did you see the thieves?'

I nodded.

'There were two. A very big, very bald man. And a very small woman.'

'Did you pursue them?'

'I followed them through the woods to the river, but they got in a boat and escaped.'

He frowned.

'A big man and small woman. You can be no more specific?'

'The man looked like an ape.'

'An ape?'

'Yes. And he did not speak well.'

The reverend looked at me as if waiting for more information. Eventually he just sighed and said: 'This is most aggravating. No doubt these resurrection men – and resurrection women, God help us! – have taken the keys in the hope that they can come and go as they wish. I shall have to find an ironmonger to change the lock on the gate, though how long that will take, and how the church will pay for it, I do not know. In the meantime you will simply have to be even more vigilant than you already are. As for the key to your cottage and the key to the mortsafe – I do not know what can be done about that.'

'The mortsafe?'

'Must I teach you your own trade? The cage, boy. Behind the church. I believe your grandfather held the key to this, too.'

This was entirely new to me. I did not know there was a key to the Nameless Grave. Pa had never mentioned it. Yet another revelation that I had not expected.

'Do you think someone might try to open it?' I asked.

'I do not know,' he said. 'I think, perhaps not – they would hardly find any fresh cadavers in that plot.'

I lowered my voice a little.

'What *would* they find, if they did open it?'

'You mean you do not know?'

'Pa won't tell me.'

'Then perhaps he has his reasons.'

'Do you know?'

The tiniest hint of a smile tugged at the corner of his broad, thin mouth. He leant in.

'My predecessor told me that it contained a great evil,' he said.

'Evil?'

'Oh, yes. The owner was a cursed man. A magician, in fact. He sold his soul to the devil in return for forbidden knowledge. So Reverend Mooney said.'

All the warmth that had gathered in me during lunch drained away. Pa had always spoken very highly of the previous vicar. I did not know what was more disturbing – the story itself, or the fact that Pa had kept it from me.

The reverend straightened up and said brightly:

'Then again, Reverend Mooney was drunk as a wheel-barrow for eight hours of the day, so you can put as much trust in that story as you see fit! I hope I have not worried you.'

I did not reply. The reverend looked at the cottage door again, then back at the church.

'I have work to do. I shall inform the pair of you when the gate is to be replaced.'

'What about the wall?'

'The wall?'

'It's fallen down. Where it meets the woods. Anyone might simply step over the boundary however they please.'

This seemed to irritate him. He winced and swatted the news away as if Mosca were bothering him.

'Then put it back together. Must I do everything? I am quite sure you are capable of lugging a few rocks around.'

I was quite sure I was not.

'In the meantime, I urge you to double your vigilance. I am sympathetic to your grandfather' – he did not sound it – 'but I can only indulge you so many times before I must consider a new sexton altogether.'

And he set off up the path and disappeared into the darkness of the trees.

XI
NED

The Nameless Grave was isolated and overgrown, and very beautiful for it. It occupied a dim and lonely corner behind the church steeple and was no doubt overlooked by most visitors to the graveyard. The headstone itself was so weathered and misshapen it seemed more that it had grown from the earth, like a fungus, rather than been made by a craftsman's hands. In front of it, the iron grid of the mortsafe was so entwined with ivy it looked almost as if someone had prepared a soft bed of foliage for weary parishioners.

It certainly did not *seem* evil. How could it be? The churchyard was hallowed ground, and no kind of devilry was permitted to make a home inside of it. That was the point. *We* had made a home inside of it, and I had never felt anything remotely sinister lurking inside the wall.

Mosca and I took a tour of the grave. I squatted and poked around the ivy and examined the bars. They were badly rusted but still very robust. I found two hinges on one side, and then heard a wet buzzing from the opposite side that seemed to set the whole frame vibrating. I looked and found my fly creeping around a single dirt-clogged keyhole whose existence I had never noticed.

'I thought I might find you here.'

Pa's voice made me jump. I got up and dusted my knees and straightened my hat. He seemed much recovered after his meal.

'Oh! I was only checking. To see if it was secure. The Reverend Biles, you see, he said that—'

'I heard what the reverend said. You should know better than to listen to silly stories about curses and magic and whatnot.'

'Then there is no truth in it?'

'None at all.'

'But you *did* have the key to it?'

'Yes.'

'Why?'

'In case I need to open it.'

'Why would you need to open it?'

His bad eye ceased rolling in its socket.

'What have I always told you, Ned?' he said. 'Do not ask questions about this plot, or its owner. There is a reason it is nameless.'

'Which is?'

He looked at the grave and not at me.

'It belongs to someone who does not deserve to be remembered.'

From around the corner came the sound of raised voices

echoing against the wall of the church. Pa looked up and frowned.

He hobbled back to the path and I followed him to the front of the churchyard. Beside Mrs Hickson's grave two men were having an argument. They turned and confronted us before we could reach them. They both had the look of wolfhounds, I thought – tall and wiry and their hair silvered and slightly bedraggled.

'You!' said the shorter of the two men, and thrust a finger at Pa. 'What have you done with our mother?'

From a few feet away I recognized them from among the mourners at Grammy Hickson's funeral.

Pa and I looked at each other.

'We have laid her in the earth, sir,' said Pa, carefully. 'And made her comfortable.'

'Comfortable, is it?' the man said. 'Then why's there rumours in the village, saying you've been creeping around this graveyard with a lantern in the dead of night?'

I looked at Pa again. He tried to smile at the brothers. His lips were still slightly rouged from his luncheon.

'It is no rumour, sir,' he said.

The taller of the men, who had been silent and very still until then, seized Pa by the front of his old coat.

'Shameless dog!' he spat. 'You'd admit it, would you?'

Pa raised a gloved hand to defend himself. The man's nostrils twitched.

'We were not *lurking*,' Pa said. 'We were keeping watch, I assure you.'

'There's talk of grave robbing all over the county. I'll bet half of the time it's you two!'

He shook Pa and Pa struggled to keep his hat upon his head. I did not know what I could do. I looked around the graveyard for any kind of assistance and saw the reverend half concealed by the door to the church, but he seemed unwilling to be involved.

'There *is* talk of grave robbing, indeed, sir,' said Pa. 'That is why we keep our vigil.'

'Well, that's a very convenient excuse,' said the first man. 'And how do you explain the loose soil around our mother's grave? These footprints?'

'She was buried only a few days ago, sirs!' said Pa. 'You were here yourself. There has been no time for the grass to grow.'

'Are you trying to be clever with us? You think we'll be outwitted by dullards like you and your boy?'

I cleared my throat.

'If I may, sirs,' I said, but got no further than that.

'You can shut your mouth and all! Nothing but filth coming from both of you!'

At this Mosca began hectoring him, flying into his nose and ears while he flapped and cursed. The taller, quieter, angrier man was only infuriated further and let go of Pa to reprimand his brother. The other man yelled back, at his brother, at Mosca, at Pa and me. Pa protested his innocence and I tried to calm him. Mosca kept up his wild and bothersome assault.

And then, into the chaos, another stranger emerged. He strode down the path from the gate and seemed to bring things to order with just his smile.

'May I help at all?' he said.

The gentleman's voice was loud and commanding and the men stopped their scuffling almost at once. He was just as impressive to look at, being tall and well formed, wearing breeches and riding boots, a tailcoat and a very fine top hat. He looked radiant in every aspect of his appearance, but most radiant of all was his nose. Marvellous to relate: the thing was made of polished brass and attached to his head by an inconspicuous strap of pale leather. I had never seen anything of the sort and have not since.

Neither of the brothers Hickson replied to him. They were perhaps as transfixed by his nose as I was.

'Don't need your help,' said the smaller of the two eventually, with a good deal less self-assurance than he had shown so far. The taller one took a step back and regarded the newcomer suspiciously.

'Well, I suppose that depends on what it is you are attempting to do,' said the gentleman. 'What, may I ask, is the problem?'

Again, the smaller brother was the one who spoke.

'The problem is that these two have been digging up graves and selling on the bodies.'

'And what makes you think that?'

'There's people saying it all over.'

'Are there?'

'And we seen it. With our own eyes.'

'Ah! A fellow empiricist!'

The man tried very hard to repeat the word with his own

lips. It gave me a small glimmer of pride that I understood something that he did not.

'And what is it that you have observed?' said the gentleman. 'Where are these disturbed graves?'

'This one right here!' said Mr Hickson, pointing to his mother's plot.

'It seems quite all right to me.'

'Well,' said Mr Hickson, 'they've been covered up, haven't they? They're gravediggers, they know how to conceal what they're doing.'

'I see. Then you cannot point to any evidence of the crime?'

The brothers looked around frantically, as if another open grave might simply appear before them.

'The evidence is in their faces, sir,' the taller Mr Hickson said. 'You just need to look at them to know they're not to be trusted.'

'Their faces?'

The gentleman stepped forward and for a few baffling moments seemed to be measuring the taller man's head with the span of his thumb and forefinger.

'Phrenologically speaking,' said the gentleman, 'you have the skull of a primate. And not even a particularly intelligent one. So, if you are insisting on judging from appearances, I may have to discount your testimony.'

I tried very hard not to laugh.

'It seems to me that you are mistreating a hard-working, honest man – two hard-working, honest men – on the basis of nothing but prejudice. You accuse them without reference to the law, and certainly none to God. On holy ground, as well! I insist you leave them in peace and, furthermore, that you apologize and return to your homes.'

The taller brother stepped forward.

'And what, sir, is your authority?'

The gentleman beamed.

'Ah, how remiss of me! I should have introduced myself. I am Mr Wellrest's future son-in-law.'

I fancied I saw the colour drain from both of their faces.

'I will be taking up residence in Wellrest Manor very shortly, and it has been agreed that when I do, I will take on the running of the Wellrest estate. Including setting and collecting payments from the estate's tenants. Which, I hazard, includes you.'

A few moments passed in which I thought all five of us might yet come to blows. Then the shorter Mr Hickson made a curt bow to the gentleman and scurried away. His brother followed a little later, glaring at us both but giving not the slightest glance to the man who had saved us.

'The rest of the village will know of this,' he said as he retreated. 'Mark my words.'

They both made their way to the gate and went out into the road, heads together, conspiring.

'Thank you, sir,' Pa said to the gentleman. He bowed, too, his cap pulled so far down his face was barely visible. 'The villagers have never been well disposed to us.'

'It baffles me that they should be so beastly,' said the gentleman. 'You perform perhaps their most vital service.'

'It is kind of you to say so, sir,' said Pa.

'Tell me, if you do not mind my curiosity. Was there any truth in what those two were saying?'

Pa frowned and tugged at his sleeves in discomfort but did not reply.

'Your silence is telling,' said the gentleman, though he seemed unconcerned.

'It was not *this* grave,' I interjected, and immediately knew I should not have. Pa gave me a meaningful look.

'Ah,' said the gentleman. 'Then whose?'

I tried not to look in the direction of Master Garrick's plot.

'Do you know who is responsible?'

'It was not us, sir. Truthfully. There was a big man like an ape, and a little woman—'

'That's enough, Ned,' said Pa.

'A man and a woman? You mean a couple? Hardly the likely sort to be bodysnatching. How strange.'

The gentleman looked at us and when it was clear Pa was going to say nothing more, he took off his top hat and shook his head. His curls tumbled around his ears.

'A grisly business,' he said. 'No doubt they have ended up on the slabs at the university.' There was something about the word 'slab' that made me shudder. 'I could prevail upon the doctors there for information? I know many of them quite well. Perhaps they might know something of these resurrection men. Perhaps the bodies might yet be recovered.'

'You are too kind again, sir,' said Pa.

'I shall look into it.'

The gentleman nodded and looked around the graveyard as if searching for something polite to say. He gasped suddenly.

'Ah! Forgive me, I had forgotten the very reason I came. I have a question for you.'

'Yes, sir?'

'You must know every inch of this churchyard.'

'Of course.'

'Do you know the names of all the deceased?'

'Yes, sir, I believe we do.'

'Very good. Could you tell me, is there a Herbert Wellrest interred somewhere here?'

Pa did not reply at first. He frowned and sniffed and rubbed at one eye. A very long time seemed to pass.

'Pa?' I said.

Eventually he shook his head and said: 'No, sir. The Wellrests have their own cemetery on the grounds of their estate. They are all buried up there.'

'All but one, in fact,' said the gentleman. 'I was wondering where Herbert had got to. He would have died a couple of hundred years ago, I think. Maybe more. But surely that is not long enough for his grave to disappear entirely.'

Pa shrugged.

'As far as I am aware there are no Wellrests buried down here. None at all,' Pa said.

'I see. How odd. Perhaps I should look in the neighbouring villages?'

'Perhaps, sir.'

There was a little more silence between us.

'Well,' said the gentleman, 'since I am here, I think I will take a stroll around your delightful churchyard. So beautifully kept! Of course, you would never do anything to make the place look untidy. Those men were quite out of their minds.'

He put his hat back on and dipped the brim to us both and went strolling down the path. Pa watched him go and tugged at the patches of his beard.

'How about that, Pa,' I said. 'I cannot remember a time when everyone was so keen to speak to us!'

Pa turned and scowled at me.

'Everyone?'

'I mean Miss Wellrest. I wonder if they know each other? They both seemed very kind souls.'

'Knows her? Did you not hear what he said?'

'About what?'

'He said he is due to come into the estate. Which means he knows her very well. That man is Miss Wellrest's future husband.'

My heart seemed a deadweight behind my ribs. Of course, I had not made the connection between the two of them. The girl was to be married, and for reasons I did not yet understand, that news seemed more devastating than anything else that had happened that week.

XII

ᴮEDE

After our ride Phineas disappeared for an hour on some errand he would not discuss. When he finally returned we sat down together to a late and meagre lunch of soup and hard bread. Father was the only one who mentioned the absence of the roast chicken, explaining, for his own benefit as much as Phineas', that Mrs Gilly was probably saving it for dinner since their guest was staying on for more than one night. He then spent the rest of the meal watching us eat with a vague half smile, as if he expected us to announce our engagement as soon as our bowls were empty. Of course, there was no announcement. Instead Phineas talked more of balls and parties and his suggestions for how he, personally, would have treated King George's madness had he been given the chance (if I remember correctly, it involved electrocuting the poor man's brain via his nose).

After we had eaten, Phineas excused himself to set up his scientific demonstration. Father and I remained at opposite ends of the dining table until summoned. Father's face was still hopeful.

'Well?' he said, once Phineas was out of earshot.

'Well what?'

'What happened on your morning ride? Did you apologize?'

'He said there was no need.'

'Bede.'

'But yes,' I lied. 'Of course I did.'

'Good. And?'

'And *what*?'

'How did you get on?'

'We got on passably, Father.'

'Only passably?'

'I do not like him, Father. The smiling, the compliments . . .'

'Why must you be so negative in your disposition, Bede? Listen to you! Is there really anything so awful about smiles and compliments? Have you not considered the possibility that he might simply be a *good man*?'

I considered and dismissed it.

'He's after something.'

'He's after your hand in marriage.'

'And the rest.'

'What do you mean, "the rest"?'

I folded my arms and didn't say anything. I did not want to mention Herbert for fear of enraging Father again. Besides, I was not sure myself what Phineas wanted, or how much he already knew about our family's past.

'You see?' said Father. 'You can't even say why you dislike him!'

After a few minutes Perkins called us through. He would not meet my eye. I poked irritably at the breadcrumbs on the tablecloth and thought I might feign illness to avoid Phineas' little show, but then decided there might be something of interest in it. It might, I thought, even reveal something of his intentions regarding Uncle Herbert.

All the curtains in the ballroom had been drawn and the candles had been lit. Phineas had arranged a semicircle of chairs as if for a considerably larger audience than the one assembled, and in front of it he stood at a table with his apparatus, grinning.

'Come in! Come in! Make yourselves comfortable! I apologize if this all seems a little modest. It is something of a dry run. The scholars will get something rather more elaborate.'

It appeared he would only be using a fraction of his equipment for this particular demonstration, and there were many unopened boxes under the table and in the darkness behind him. On the table was an oil lamp, and next to it stood a column of metal discs perhaps three or four feet tall. The discs were contained within three rods of equal length, wires protruding from the top and bottom. I had seen a similar instrument on a visit to the Literary and Philosophical Society lectures at Bath, though this specimen was larger and more clumsily put together. Father was intrigued and peered at the equipment as he passed. Mr Elmet and Mr and Mrs Gilly, who had apparently also been invited, leant forward in their chairs and muttered to each other about what they thought they might be about to witness.

Phineas began in his loud tenor without any kind of preamble.

'How many of you have watched the skies in the midst of a thunderstorm and felt the curious mixture of wonder and terror at the power of the heavens?'

He spoke as if addressing an audience of hundreds. There was a pause. No one seemed sure if they should answer.

'And how many,' he went on, 'have wondered if such a power might be harnessed and put to good use in our towns and cities? In our homes?'

Again there was no answer. I doubted anyone here had wondered any such thing. Especially not Mr Gilly, whose whole existence revolved around picking up heavy things and putting them down again.

'Well,' said Phineas, 'I have here the very instrument which might bring the thunder and lightning we see in the sky into this very room, and allow it to be wielded – safely – by anyone who has been correctly instructed.'

Father looked at me to check I was sufficiently impressed.

'This is an invention of my own devising—'

'No,' I said, 'it is not.'

The others looked at me. Phineas smiled and blinked.

'I beg your pardon, Miss Wellrest?'

'That is a voltaic pile. It was invented by Alessandro Volta.'

'Correct!' he said, as if he had been testing me all along. 'Originally the pile was designed by the Italian gentleman, but I have made several modifications to vastly increase its electrical output.'

Father then put up a hand. It seemed he was trying to compensate for my rudeness with his own interest.

'Tell me Phineas, what exactly *is* electricity? I have heard it spoken of so many times but I have no idea where it comes from or what it *actually* does . . .'

There followed a lengthy, tedious, occasionally inaccurate description of the nature of electrical charge and Galvanic cells. I stopped paying attention. I was preoccupied with the specifics of Phineas' research. If he was interested in electricity, then it made sense that he would try to track down Herbert Wellrest, who, so the stories said, had been well ahead of the Italians in his own discoveries. The 'spark of life' had ever been his obsession.

When I came out of my ruminating, Phineas was busy dismantling the voltaic pile and showing Father and the servants the discs of zinc and copper. He let Mr Gilly touch them with his finger and taste the brine that they were soaked in. Mr Gilly found it very agreeable and commented that it was 'very like Mrs Gilly's ham hock soup'.

Phineas reassembled the equipment and then placed the two poles together in front of the stack of discs. He donned a pair of gloves and smeared his nose in some kind of protective paste.

'Now, watch closely!' he said.

I knew from experience that this was, in fact, the last

thing we should do. He pulled the two metal rods apart very slightly and a small but intense blue-white light appeared between them. I squinted. Father shielded his eyes. The servants cooed and gasped.

'This,' said Phineas, 'is what is known as an *electrical arc*. It allows us to see the kind of power that may be harnessed in what I call, if I may be so bold, the Mordaunt cell.'

He patted the top of the voltaic pile.

'What may it be used for?' asked Father.

'Why, all sorts of things. To create light. To create heat. To create motion.'

'Motion?'

'Oh yes. Did you know, it is electrical impulses that move the very muscles in our bodies?'

I was surprised that he had not resorted to Luigi Galvani's twitching frog experiment. By then it was practically a parlour game for wealthy families to gather round and watch some poor dead amphibian being mysteriously returned to life with an electric current.

Thinking on this, it occurred to me what Phineas might be meaning to do.

'Now,' he went on, before I could say anything, 'this is only a very small arc. But I have been able to significantly improve the output of this cell and create a much larger spectacle for you all. Bede, would you care to help me?'

I knew I should refuse but I was too curious for my own good. I got up and stood by the table. He offered me a pair of gloves but I was obviously still wearing my own and declined.

'Take the negative pole,' he said. 'It is quite safe.'

I picked it up from the table and saw for the first time that it was connected to a long spool of wire. Phineas picked up his own. The blue arc of electricity grew between the two nodes, splitting into thin veins that shivered between Phineas' hand and mine. I felt the hairs on my arm standing to attention, and those on my head tried to loosen themselves from their hairpins.

'With the power in the Mordaunt cell we can walk to opposite sides of the ballroom and the arc will not fail!'

I took a step back and he took two in the opposite direction. The arc remained, and even grew in brightness, quite outshining the candles. I will admit I was impressed. I had never seen so much electrical charge focused in one place – it really was as if he had brought a thunderstorm into the room with him.

I saw Perkins skulking in the shadows behind his master and remembered what I wanted to ask Phineas.

'So where does the chicken come in?' I said.

He frowned.

'The chicken? What chicken?'

'Bede,' said Father, and had to raise his voice over the crackling of the arc, 'please stop distracting him with your silliness.'

'I thought perhaps you might pass the electricity through it. Make it dance and cluck upon the table.'

'Well,' said Phineas, 'that is a very fine idea. Unfortunately, I do not have one to hand!'

'Perkins does.'

His smile failed him and he turned to look at his manservant. I was so intent on observing his reaction I didn't smell the fumes from my burning gloves until it was too late. The pole had become incredibly hot, too hot to hold even through thick velvet, and I yelped. Phineas' head snapped back around.

'Don't drop it!' he yelled.

I knew that, of course, but sometimes one's animal instincts know better. Before the pain had even registered in my fingers I let go of the metal rod and it fell to the floor, and it was with a strange calmness that I watched it roll back and nudge the side of my foot. It touched my skin through a gap in my slipper, and I was thrown halfway across the room, first into exquisite pain, and then into utter darkness.

XIII

ŒBEDE

When I woke I was back in my bedroom. The curtains were drawn and there were candles lit at my bedside but there was daylight coming from the edges of the window. My joints still held a feverish ache and there was a kind of effervescent sensation in my fingers and toes that may simply have been the memory of the electric shock. I was in the same gown I had worn to lunch, now damp with sweat, and there was a faint smell of burning hair in the room.

At the foot of the bed I saw, through half-closed eyes, two men. They had their backs to me but revealed themselves when they spoke. Father and Phineas.

'I do not know where to begin with my apologies, Gregory,' Phineas was saying. 'I have performed the same demonstration quite safely a hundred times or more!'

Father put a hand between his shoulders.

'An accident, my boy. Nothing more. If Obedience had not distracted you, I am sure the entire enterprise would

– 106 –

have proceeded without mishap.'

Yes, Father, I thought bitterly. *All my fault.*

'I will not hear of it,' Phineas protested. 'The responsibility lies with me. I must make amends when she wakes.'

'You have already made amends in your care for her.'

Phineas sighed theatrically and shook his head. 'My heart gave me no choice at all. It has been the most exquisite honour to stay at her bedside. She is such an *extraordinary* young woman.'

'An apt choice of words, my boy. She is certainly not ordinary, in any way. I hope you will be able to curb her more reckless tendencies in future.'

'She is spirited, Mr Wellrest. That is all. A quality to be admired, surely.'

'I'm glad you think so. Old Mrs Hickson was less complimentary. She hardly knew where Bede was most of the time. Leaving the house to wander the grounds at the most uncivilized hours. Riding to Oxford without permission. *Twice* now she has been to London and back, to watch the proceedings of the Royal Institution. Once to Bath. And always unaccompanied! It beggars belief!' He sighed. 'I only wish she cared for her safety as much as I do. But since her mother died . . . Sometimes I think she has half a mind to join her.'

I lay as still as I could to listen to them, but on hearing this my eyes began to prickle and I was forced to blink.

'Ah! She is waking!'

Phineas came to my bedside and tenderly took my hand. His face and nose loomed over me.

'We are here, Obedience,' he said. 'Do not exert yourself.'

He smiled.

I sat up in bed and squinted at them both. To add to the pain in my extremities, I felt a great heaving ache in my stomach, but it was nothing to do with the electric shock. My books. I could not see any of my books. Someone had taken them.

Father came to the other side of the bed and put the back of his hand to my forehead.

'My love, we were so worried!' he said. 'How do you feel?'

'Cooked. I feel as if I have been on Mrs Gilly's rotisserie for an hour.'

He laughed.

'Well, it seems your mental faculties are intact. Can you move?'

I clenched my fingers and toes and it sent little spasms of pain up and down my limbs.

'My muscles ache something rotten,' I said. 'But everything seems in order.'

'I'm not sure I'd say the same for your hair.'

I raised a hand and found it floating in a static cloud around my head. He smiled again.

'Thank God Mrs Hickson is not here to see me so unpresentable,' I said. 'She must be turning in her grave.'

Father seemed to think this was in poor taste and a frown darkened his face. He got up and opened the curtains and then fetched a hairbrush from the dressing table and left it on the bed beside me.

'Mr Mordaunt has been at your bedside since the accident.'

I turned to him.

'Thank you, sir,' I said.

'It was a very great pleasure,' he said.

I squirmed.

'How long was I unconscious?'

'It has been almost twenty-four hours, Miss Wellrest. But here you are. Back from the dead!'

He leant slightly further over the bed and squeezed my hand. I looked over his shoulder at the dressing table and the bureau. There were no books there, either. And what about the diary? What if Phineas had found that? I had hardly taken any pains to hide it, since I so rarely had visitors to my room.

'I shall go and inform the servants,' said Father. 'They have been as worried as the rest of us. Get lots of rest, Bede. And do what Mr Mordaunt asks of you – he is a natural philosopher after all, I'm sure he knows exactly what your body needs to recover.'

I wanted to point out that it was Mr Mordaunt who had nearly killed me in the first place, but I was too tired to argue.

Father brushed some wayward hairs out of my eyes, kissed my forehead, and left me alone with Phineas. We sat in silence for a while. The pigeons cooed and clattered in the roof overhead.

'A natural philosopher is it, now?' I said. 'I thought you said you were a chemist.'

'Chemistry is my specialism,' he said. 'But I have a passing interest in all branches of natural philosophy. Just as you do, it seems.'

I withdrew my hand from his.

'You were far too coy when you spoke at dinner,' he went on. 'I had no idea your reading habits were so eclectic. I hope you don't mind me borrowing a few of your volumes?'

So, he had taken them. I struggled to compose myself.

'It might have been more courteous to ask instead of helping yourself,' I said. 'And perhaps you could have left one or two books for my own study?'

His face became a mask of self-reproach.

'Forgive me, Miss Wellrest. Only we were not sure when you would awaken. My presentation for the university is very soon indeed, and many of your volumes were simply too tantalizing to ignore!'

What exactly was he hinting at? I looked again at the bureau. The diary had been there in plain sight. He could not have missed it.

'I find it quite astonishing,' he said, 'how closely our interests align. An extraordinary coincidence.'

'Quite extraordinary.'

'I think we might make a fine partnership, you and I. It is rare to find a woman who might be my intellectual equal, and I intend to make the most of our acquaintance.'

I began to feel trapped in the bed: somebody had tucked the sheets around me far too tightly and I could not have run away even if I were fully recovered.

'You have already taken my books,' I said, irritably. 'I'm not sure what else I might offer.'

'Oh, I think you know,' he said.

'I'm not sure I do.'

'Your father would like us to be married.'

'Would he?'

'I would like us to be married, also.'

With some effort I freed myself from the sheets and sat up a little higher. I turned away to look out of the window. He took my fingers in his.

'What would you say, Miss Wellrest, if I were to ask for your hand?'

'I would say that I hardly knew you. That I was unsure of your intentions. And that I was too young by at least ten years.'

'Ten years!' He laughed. 'In ten years' time, my dear, you will be practically a spinster.'

'Then I will accept that as my fate. I have more important concerns than finding a husband. I certainly would not marry for the sake of practicality.'

He looked unconvincingly shocked.

'My dear, there is nothing practical about it. I am, quite simply, in love with you.'

'I don't believe it.'

'Might I perhaps convince you of my affections with a favour?'

He reached into the pocket of his tailcoat and produced a ring. The band was the same colour as his nose, and upon it was a diamond so huge it looked like he had broken it off from a chandelier.

'That is very beautiful, sir. But I cannot accept.'

'Please,' he said, and raised my hand, 'at least try it on one of your lovely fingers.'

'No.'

'If you might remove your gloves.'

'*No*, sir.'

'Now I think of it,' he said, undeterred, 'I don't believe I've ever seen what your hands look like underneath them.'

'Nor shall you.'

'I am sure they are as fine as Wedgwood china!'

He began to tug at the fingers of the gloves. I slapped him, hard, across his face. I must have caught his brass nose in the process because when he looked back at me, red with rage and embarrassment, it was slightly skewed. I caught a glimpse of the wound it concealed. He quickly adjusted it, pocketed the ring and stood up.

'Your father shall hear of this,' he said.

'I don't care if he does.'

'And while I am at it, perhaps I shall also tell him about what you have been reading.'

'Father knows what I read.'

'And does he know about Herbert Wellrest's diary?'

I said nothing. We were both of us breathing very hard. He looked down at where I lay on the bed and smiled, and for the first time it was his true smile: cruel and full of triumph.

'Yes, my dear,' he said. 'I know you have it. Well – *I* have it now.'

I tried to bluff, though my heart seemed to be shaking the bedframe.

'Then show him. He will not understand the cipher. He will think it a puzzle, or a game of some kind.'

'Perhaps the cipher will elude him. But the diagrams are very easy to understand, are they not? He will be perfectly horrified. His darling daughter, filling her head with such unnatural things. I'm sure a wife's duties will seem to him a perfect solution to your idle and wayward mind. Wouldn't you say?'

I had no reply to that. He made for the door and just before he left he turned around and his old, false smile was back on his face.

'Make sure you get lots of rest,' he said.

He bowed and withdrew from the room, and his receding footsteps seemed so light I could have sworn he was skipping.

XIV

ꓳEDE

In the hours that followed I lay in bed and considered how I might make my escape. It was plain, now, that it would take more than blunt words and a stubborn disposition to remove Phineas from the house. Simply running away was out of the question, though – I wasn't sure I could stand in my current state, and even if I could, a man with Phineas' resources would surely be able to find me in no time at all.

I waited for my father to visit me in a rage, but he never came. Afternoon turned to evening and the windows turned black and showed only the reflections of the candle flames within. I could hardly think straight for the incessant flapping and scratching of the pigeons above me. It sounded like they had found a way inside the attic.

At seven, Mr Gilly brought me a supper of thin soup. I did not know if this was designed to punish me or aid in my recuperation.

'Good evening, miss,' he said. 'It is good to see you well again. Quite a fright we had, down in the ballroom.'

He laid the tray on my lap. The bowl and spoon looked like things from a doll's house in his huge hands.

'Thank you, Mr Gilly,' I said.

He went to the door. I remembered something suddenly.

'Mr Gilly?'

'Yes, miss?'

'Yesterday morning I saw you and Mr Mordaunt in the stable yard.'

'You did, miss?'

His tone was uncertain, as if he thought he might yet deny the whole thing.

'I did. A little after ten. Before we took Victor and Clerval out.'

'Yes, of course, miss.'

'What was he talking to you about?'

'Oh.' He looked at his feet and presented me with the gleam of his bald head. He was none too bright and it seemed to take him several minutes to think of a good lie. 'He was asking for another warming pan, miss,' he said eventually. 'He complained of a chill in the night, you see.'

'Ah yes. I see.'

There was a pause.

'Will that be all, miss?'

'Yes. Thank you, Mr Gilly.'

He bobbed his head again and retreated very quickly from the door. Everything was very troubling. In a matter of days Phineas had claimed all that I held dear. My father. The servants. My books. The diary. This last was perhaps the only reason why he was so adamant about our union. He suspected that I could help him understand Uncle Herbert's cipher. Which, of course, I could.

The soup was already cold but I was famished and finished it quickly. I still received no word from Father, and neither Mr nor Mrs Gilly came to collect my tray. I dozed. When I woke, however many hours later, the din of the pigeons had moved to a different corner of the ceiling. I could not quite believe that they were capable of so much noise. It sounded like something much larger. A fox, perhaps, or a badger, though that hardly seemed likely given it was up in the roof.

The uproar kept me awake and soon it occupied my every thought. I followed the sounds as they criss-crossed the roof, the patter of clawed feet interspersed with an occasional short, sharp *crack*, as if a woodpecker were searching for insects in the floorboards. For several minutes the noises disappeared entirely and I attempted to return to my plan for evading Phineas. But then they returned, louder, closer. They were now coming from somewhere on the landing, the same frantic, irregular scratching and pecking. I assumed one of the pigeons had found its way through one of the many holes in the house's frame.

And then there was a scream.

It was not a human scream. It seemed too high and thin, like it came from a much smaller pair of lungs. There was a slight gurgle behind it. From where I lay in my bed it seemed to be coming from the floor, rather than from the height of a human head and shoulders.

I eased myself out of bed. Standing up brought with it

the sensation of having several hot needles thrust into the soles of my feet and softness behind my knees. I closed my eyes, breathed, composed myself. I took a candelabra in one hand, shuffled like a crone to the door, opened it slowly, and stepped out into the corridor.

I took a few paces and came across it quite suddenly. The source of the sound. Beyond the edge of the candlelight all was utter darkness, and the thing was illuminated so quickly I could not at first tell what it was. A shapeless, fleshy thing that looked as if it had been amputated from another creature.

The chicken hardly looked like a chicken at all, since it had been completely plucked and its head was hanging at a grotesque angle where its neck had once been broken. It strutted unsteadily around my feet and then staggered to the door of one of the empty servants' rooms. There it smashed its crooked head several times against the skirting as if trying to put itself out of its own misery.

I had no idea what to do with it. Should I wring its neck for a second time? There seemed no guarantee that this would put it to rest.

I put down the candelabra and crouched down to grab it in both hands. It let out its horrible, gurgling scream, wriggled from my grasp and ran along to the end of the landing. It scrabbled and fell down two flights of stairs and then, as far as I could hear, ran into the ballroom.

I followed the monster, little though I wanted to. In the ballroom the candles were lit, just as they had been when Phineas had given his demonstration. The wax dribbled thickly at their bases, suggesting he had been at work for some time, though the man himself was nowhere to be seen. There was far more equipment on display than there had been the previous day, and it was a good deal more complex. There were copper kettles and spirit lamps, flasks of both coloured and colourless solutions, Leyden jars and several voltaic piles of the kind Phineas had demonstrated. Everything seemed connected to everything else with spools of wire or lengths of brass tubing.

The chicken skittered wildly among the legs of the benches and disappeared into a corner where it slumped and clucked plaintively. For a few moments I was distracted by the extent of Phineas' apparatus. It was as impressive as anything I had seen at the Royal Institution. I traced the course of the wires and tubes with a finger and then came upon Phineas' desk, scattered with books and papers. I looked for Herbert's diary but could not find it. I did find something else, however.

The man's nose was in the desk's drawer. By which I mean his original nose. It was preserved and suspended in a jar of greenish liquid. I held it up to the light. It looked like a little unborn animal.

'You are searching for this, I imagine?'

Phineas stood at the ballroom door, face half in shadow. He took Herbert's diary out of his inside breast pocket and waved it in the air. I paused a moment, still holding the jar.

'What about an exchange,' I said. 'Your nose for my book.'

'An exchange? Why, my dear, I would be delighted for

– 118 –

you to have it as a keepsake! Then a piece of me could always be with you.'

'I cannot think of anything more romantic.'

He laughed and strode towards me quite confidently. I could not back away with the workbench behind me. He reached me and snatched the nose-jar and put it back in the drawer without comment.

'Have you considered my offer at all?'

'There is nothing to consider.'

He sighed.

'And here I was thinking you were sleepless with love for me.'

'I am sleepless because your experiment found its way into the attic above my bedroom.'

'My experiment?'

'Your bird. It is hiding in the corner over there.'

His eyes widened.

'Ah! This is wonderful news!'

He shouldered me out of the way and went into the darkness to look. He found the chicken tangled in the bottom of the curtains. The clucking turned again to screaming and Phineas came back to his apparatus holding the creature at arm's length. It writhed and flapped as if its bones were not properly bound to each other. He bundled it into a large copper pan, rather like a kettle for steaming fish, where it continued to flap and squawk. Then he took up a syringe of something, injected it through the gap between the pan and the lid, and the noise stopped immediately.

He placed the kettle under the bench and stood up.

'I suppose I should thank you,' he said. 'My most successful result in years; she escaped before I could sedate her! You can imagine my frustration.'

'Successful is a generous description, I think.'

'Yes, yes, I know it is only a small step forward. But an important one!'

'So this is the aim of your research?' I nudged the kettle with one toe. 'Spontaneous animation?'

'Oh, my dear, you say it with such distaste! I should remind you that *you* are the one who has been poring over Herbert's book with such enthusiasm.'

'Not with the aim of reviving the Sunday roast.'

'Then with what aim?'

'I have no aim. I told you, I am more interested in theory than practice.'

He brought himself a little closer to me. I was always disappointed by how pleasant his smell was. Today it was wine and cinnamon.

'Yet another reason,' he said, 'why you and I would make such a fine pairing.'

'So I might do the research, and you can take the credit? Is that what you mean?'

'What I *mean* is that you seem to have the patience and the erudition to make sense of this little book.' He patted his pocket. 'I also suspect you know a good deal more about Herbert and his theories than you are letting on.'

'We do not need to be married to work together, if that is what you wish.'

'After your behaviour earlier,' he said, rubbing his cheek as if it was still stinging, 'I hardly think I can trust you to work with me voluntarily. No, my dear, I need certain re-assurances. A union would make more sense.'

'I shall not marry you. You cannot force me.'

'Your father can.'

'He can, but he would not.'

'Why not?'

'Because he loves me.'

Phineas laughed.

'Don't you see?' he said. 'It is because he loves you that he is *bound* to force the marriage on you. He wants you to be safe and financially secure. I do not see many other suitors sniffing around this dunghill, do you?'

I went to slap him again but this time he was ready and caught my hand. I kicked him in the groin and he cried out. While he was doubled over I reached into his jacket and snatched the diary back. I tried to flee but my joints and my feet were still aching from the electrical shock and I found running an agony. He quickly caught me and we fought over the little book until someone else entered the room at the double doors.

'What the devil is going on here?'

I turned. Father stood with his own candle and the foot-man, Mr Elmet, at his back. He looked so old and so silly in his nightcap and slippers. While I was distracted Phineas took possession of the diary and marched over to the door holding it in an outstretched arm. He knew exactly what he was doing. He was a clever man, in a conniving sort of way – I will grant him at least that much.

'Mr Wellrest,' he said, 'I am *so* glad you are here. Something most disturbing has taken place.'

'What is it?' He looked at me, and there was fear in his eyes. 'Bede? What have you done?'

'I have not done anything!' I said. 'Mr Mordaunt has—'

'She must have come down to try and use the equipment,' Phineas interrupted. 'I'm glad I found her when I did, the danger to the inexperienced is really unspeakable . . .'

'Even after what happened yesterday, Obedience? After the accident? What on earth were you trying to do?'

'Father, please—'

Phineas cut me off again.

'I fear to tell you, Mr Wellrest, for you know I love you as a parent and I would not want to break your heart.'

'What is it? What did she do?'

'Don't listen to him, Father!' I cried out, but Phineas again went on regardless.

'I found her in possession of this,' he said.

He handed over the diary and wrung his hands. There was an awful silence while Father thumbed through its old pages. I caught glimpses of the pictures and diagrams as he brought the candle to each one. A body, flayed; a brain, sliced in half; a pair of lungs, opened out and flattened. Father did not bother reading to the end. He closed it and looked at me sadly.

'Is this yours, Bede?'

'It is not actually *mine*, no.'

'Then whose is it?'

I opened my mouth but at first no words came. Phineas helpfully spoke for me.

'I believe the notes were made by your ancestor, Herbert. They are more macabre than I thought possible. And the symbols, well, I don't know what they might be. I would be tempted to say they were some kind of magic spell—'

'Nonsense!' I interjected.

'This is very disappointing, Obedience.'

'He is *lying*, Father.'

'Please, do not make any more of an embarrassment of yourself.'

'But he is! He is the one who wishes to use the book!'

'A book such as this is good for one thing only,' said Phineas, taking the diary from Father's hands. 'And that is lighting the stove.'

'Mr Mordaunt is a thief, Father. He stole it from my room earlier.'

'Obedience!'

'I admit, I did,' said Phineas. 'I was most disturbed that it should be in your possession.' He paused. 'She struck me when I tried to remove it.'

There was a long silence.

'Is this true?' said Father.

When I did not reply he simply sighed and turned to Mr Elmet.

'Robert,' he said, 'please escort my daughter to her room.'

'Really, Father? You would trust this noseless big-head over your own daughter?'

He stamped on the floor and Phineas' glassware shook.

'That is enough!' he said, raising his voice in a way that I had not heard since before Mother had died. 'I do not know what has happened to you. I do not recognize you, Obedience. I do not recognize my own daughter.'

Nobody spoke for a moment. Phineas had gone back to his desk. I watched him place the diary carefully in the desk drawer, alongside his jar.

'The feeling is quite mutual, Father,' I said, and took myself back to my bedroom without any help from the servants.

XV

BEDE

The rest of the night was spent thrashing in my night-dress, plagued by terrors and frustrations of every kind. After an hour or two I decided to put my sleeplessness to good use, and by dawn I had settled on a plan to deal with Phineas. First of all I would need to take a walk into the village, but when I got up from the bed and tried the door I found it locked. I suppose I must have fallen asleep at some point in the night. I had not heard anyone turn the key.

I am not ashamed to say I raised hell. I hammered and hollered, tried to pick the lock with my hairpins, and when that failed, attacked it with the poker from the fireplace. Eventually I heard someone arrive on the other side.

'Who is that?' I yelled. 'Is that you, Mr Gilly? Open the door, for God's sake! Am I to be a prisoner in my own house?'

There was no reply.

'Mr Mordaunt? If that is you, I swear on my mother's life that I shall—'

'It is your father, Obedience.'

His voice resonated through the wood, as if his head was resting against it.

'Did you do this, Father? Did you lock this door?'

'I have been speaking with Phineas.'

'Oh! Poor you.'

'He has been *most* patient, and *most* forgiving. He suspects the accident with the electricity may have affected your judgement.'

'*My* judgement? What of his? Stealing from young ladies' bedrooms!'

'He has agreed to forget the incident last night. And he has proposed a date.'

'A date? For what?'

'For the marriage.'

There was a long pause. I stepped back from the door.

'What wonderful news. And who, may I ask, is he marrying?'

'Listen to me, Obedience.'

'Please pass on my apologies. I would dearly like to attend but unfortunately somebody has locked me in my bedroom.'

'*Listen* to me.'

I did listen, but only with one ear, and as he spoke I took up the iron poker again and went to the window.

'I know you have been suffering,' he said. 'I know you have been carrying a good deal of grief. But I have, too. And I do not wish to lose a daughter as well as a wife. Do you understand? I have no wish to be estranged from you. But if you continue behaving the way that you do . . .'

The window looked as if it should slide upwards, but it had been painted shut and no one had ever opened it. I forced the hooked end of the poker under the frame.

'Obedience?'

'I understand, Father,' I called from the other side of the room.

'We cannot spend our lives simply doing what we please. We have responsibilities, to ourselves as much as to anybody else. And this means sometimes doing things that are perhaps not what we wish to do, but which are good for us nonetheless.'

Luckily this window was in as poor a shape as the rest of the house, and the wood was spongey and rotten. I scraped and stabbed until the bottom of the frame was all damp splinters but the window would not open. Thankfully Father was pontificating so loudly he could not hear me at work.

'Your marriage to Mr Mordaunt is the kind of blessing we might never have hoped for. He will look after the estate, when I am gone. He will look after both of us, financially. He will give you children. And if you are determined to continue in your . . .'

I stopped what I was doing to hear how he was going to phrase it.

'. . . hobby, he will be able to point you in more meaningful directions. A marriage to Mr Mordaunt will give structure and *purpose* to your life. I really do not see anything about that which you could call disagreeable.'

I tried digging the poker into the side of the frame and

levered with all my strength. Without warning the entire lower half of the sash window came free, leaving a gap large enough to climb through. I managed to catch it as it fell, but at the same time dropped the iron poker, which clanged to the floor.

I waited a moment, expecting my father to fling open the door and see what all the noise was about. He did not.

'Obedience?' he said.

I gently placed the broken window frame on the carpet and leant it against the wall. I waited a little longer, so I would not sound too breathless when I answered.

'I understand, Father,' I said, eventually. 'I know I have been foolish. And rude. And I am sorry if I have caused you any embarrassment.'

He sighed.

'I am glad,' he said. 'Then perhaps you might join us for breakfast, and we can discuss the wedding in a little more detail. You might even start to feel excited, if you give it proper consideration.'

I looked at the window.

'Obedience? Will you come down, if I unlock the door?'

'Yes, Father.'

'There's a good girl.'

The key clicked heavily in the lock. I opened the door only a fraction, so he could not see the broken window. His face was grey and unshaven and very tired.

'Are you dressed?'

'Not yet, Father. I shall find something suitable and join you in a minute or two.'

He found a weary, uncertain smile, blinked very slowly, and walked away down the landing.

As soon as the sound of him had gone I went back to the open window. I got up on to the sill and squirmed through.

The dawn air was chilly and bracing. I crouched there on the edge of the precipice for some time. The cobbles of the stable yard below seemed to get further and further away as the sun lit them. I imagined, with a strange detachment, how my bones and flesh would look after a fall from such a height. I turned back to the room. I took off my gloves and held them between my teeth and began to shuffle along the window ledge, hanging on to the guttering above my head.

When I reached the drainpipe I clung to the cold lead and began to shimmy down. I was halfway to the ground and outside the drawing room window when I heard Father and Phineas in conversation.

'She is dressing and will be joining us shortly,' said Father. 'No doubt she wishes to wear something that will impress you.'

Phineas immediately launched into loudly recounting my many virtues, none of which I actually had. I could still hear him singing my praises when my feet touched terra firma and I made my escape, from breakfast, from my marriage, from my life as it had been dictated to me.

XVI

NED

I had finished my nightly vigil and the sky was starting to blush when she appeared at the gate. She was in a pale nightdress that wavered slightly, as if she were underwater. It made her look even more ghostly than she had in her mourning clothes. More beautiful, too.

At first I stood quite stupidly on the path, listening to my heart thumping and thumping. It was a few moments before I realized that she wanted me to open the gate. Reverend Biles had not yet arrived to unlock it.

I straightened my hat and came down the path. Mosca's buzzing had changed to a pitch that seemed mocking, somehow.

'Good morning, sir,' she called out, before I had reached the gate.

'Good morning, Miss Wellrest,' I said. I came to the iron bars and stopped. There were dark rings around her eyes and her skin had an oily sheen. She looked as if she had not slept since I had last seen her.

'I was wondering if I might speak with your grandfather.'

'You mean Pa?'

'I mean the old man.'

She looked behind her quickly, as if she feared she was being watched, or followed.

'Yes,' I said. 'Of course. I'll fetch him for you.'

'Can you not open the gate?'

'No.'

'No? You are the sexton here, are you not?'

'Yes, but our keys . . .' I stopped. I did not wish to explain it all over again. I just said: 'I do not have the key.'

She looked at me, and then at the wall either side of her, and then disappeared from the gate. There was silence. I assumed she had gone, and I cursed myself for wasting such a precious opportunity to speak with her. I heard a little grunting, the scrape of her slippers on the brickwork, and her head reappeared at the top of the wall. She swung up a leg and rolled over and jumped to the ground. I watched her brushing the dirt from her nightdress. She looked up and there was a pause between us.

'Well?' she said.

'Excuse me?'

'Are you going to take me to him?'

'Oh. Yes. Follow me.'

We set off down the path with the sky brightening overhead and the birds starting to chatter. We walked in silence for a while. At first she seemed more tense, and less friendly than I remembered, and I naturally assumed this was my fault.

'I am sorry about the magpies,' I said.

She looked at me askance.

'What about them?'

'They're always gossiping. Don't pay them any attention.'

She looked ahead. I had a feeling she was smiling but I was too nervous to check.

'You are quite the strangest young man I have ever met,' she said.

I smiled too. I have been called strange many times, but in this instance it sounded like a compliment.

We fell into silence again. I tried to think of something to say. I thought about mentioning her fiancé, the handsome man with the golden nose who had visited a couple of days earlier. But I preferred to pretend that he didn't exist.

'What do you want to speak to Pa about?' I said.

It was another few paces before she answered.

'Your garden.'

'Really?'

She nodded. 'I couldn't help noticing it last time I was here. Now my governess has passed on and I have so much time on my hands, I would very much like to learn how to cultivate certain plants and herbs.'

'From us? Surely you have a gardener at the manor house.'

'Mr Gilly is less a gardener and more a beast of burden. Besides, there are some very particular plants in your garden that I would like to discuss with your grandfather. Very rare, I think.'

This all seemed quite beyond belief. Pa never received

visitors besides the reverend. Neither of us did. We certainly never entertained anybody looking for horticultural advice.

When we got to the cottage, Pa was sitting on the step cleaning the mud off his boots with a butter knife. He saw us and stood up and put the knife in his pocket.

'Miss Wellrest came back,' I said.

'So I see,' he said. 'How can I help you, miss?'

'She wants to talk about our garden.'

'I think she would like to speak for herself.'

'Yes. Of course. Sorry, miss.'

She looked at both of us and smiled, as if there was some joke only she was privy to.

'It is, indeed, your garden that brings me here,' she said. 'If you have the time, I would like to discuss the plants that you grow at the back of your cottage.'

Pa looked suspicious.

'May I ask why?'

'They have medicinal properties, do they not?'

'Most of them, yes. You have a keen eye for plant species, miss – it sounds as if you already know a good deal.'

'I know a little. But I was wondering if you might show me exactly what it is you are growing. And perhaps you might let me take a sample or two back to the manor.'

'It would be my pleasure. Although . . . May I ask what you intend to use them for?'

She smiled her secret smile again.

'That will require a little more explanation. Perhaps I might come in, and we can talk in private.'

'Very well, miss.'

Pa pushed through the door and Miss Wellrest followed. When she had stepped inside she suddenly stopped and turned to me.

'I'm sure your grandfather will be quite able to assist me. You must have all sorts of important tasks to do.'

She did not move. My heart sank. She did not want me there.

'Oh yes,' I said. 'There is always something that needs attending to.'

'Very good. My father may come looking for me. Or one of the servants. Or someone else. Perhaps, if you see them, you would be so good as to tell them I am not here.' She paused. 'That I was never here.'

I blinked and nodded.

'Of course, miss.'

'Bede.'

'Beg pardon?'

'Call me Bede. We are the same age, are we not? Or near enough. No need to stand on ceremony. I have enough of that at home.'

'Very well.'

I turned to go, and then, just as she was about to go inside, I turned back. The door was almost closed and she very nearly trapped my nose in between it and the door frame.

'If it is plants that interest you,' I said, 'you might like to read Darwin.'

She looked surprised, and then smiled even more broadly.

'Darwin?'

'Erasmus Darwin. The book is called *The Botanic Garden*. Pa has a copy. It is quite beautiful. Both the words and the pictures.'

'A sexton and a scholar,' she said. 'How extraordinary. I thank you for the recommendation.'

She closed the door, and the last thing I saw was Pa's face, contorted with a deep frown.

I went for a walk around the church wall to clear my head. It was turning into a very fine day and the insects were singing in the warmth. I tested myself on the names of the flowers that grew around the path and among the headstones. Burdock, cornflower, columbine, kingcup. *Caltha palustris*. My head grew hot with the frustration of being shut out of the cottage – Pa had taught me well enough, and I had read many of his books, so I had as much of a right to be part of the discussion as he did. I could teach Bede everything I knew, if she would let me. I put my case to Mosca, but he was enjoying the warm weather and did not seem terribly interested.

Bede. What a strange name that was! But then, all names seemed strange to me back then, because I hardly knew any.

I was talking to Mother and Father when I heard the church gate groan on its hinges. I went to see who it was and saw Reverend Biles, key in hand, talking to Miss Wellrest's fiancé. He spotted me among the headstones and snapped his fingers.

'Boy! Come here!'

I made my way over to them and could already feel my face getting warm. I knew what they would ask of me. I was not good at lying. There had never been any need for it.

'This is Mr Mordaunt,' said the reverend. 'He was wondering—'

Mr Mordaunt interrupted him at once.

'Have you seen a young woman come through here?' he asked.

'A young woman? What kind of young woman?'

'Mr Wellrest's daughter. She is slight. Pale. Very dark hair. She may have been wearing a nightdress.'

'I do not think so, sir. No.'

'You do not think so?'

'I have not seen anybody this morning. And besides, the gate has been locked until now.'

'If she can climb down from a third-storey window, then I am quite sure she can scale a church wall.'

He scanned the graveyard and his nose flashed this way and that. He, like Bede, seemed less agreeable than he had when we had last met.

'I have not seen her,' I said. 'I assure you.'

He seemed unconvinced and began stalking down the path towards our cottage. My heart flipped like a fish on a line.

'Let me ask my grandfather,' I said. 'Perhaps he knows something of her!'

I ran ahead of him and reached the cottage and hammered on the door. There was no reply. I heard murmuring at the rear, and I went around to find Pa and Bede in the middle of our kitchen garden. Bede was collecting leaves and seeds and putting them in a small glass jar that Pa had given her.

They both looked at me, a guilty air about them.

'Ned, Miss Wellrest told you to keep watch!' he said.

'I was. Miss – I mean, Bede – your husband—'

'I do not have a husband.'

'I mean, your fiancé—'

'I don't have a fiancé either.'

I paused, in confusion at first, then in an absurd wave of relief. She was not to be married after all!

'Well,' I said, 'there is a man at the gate who is looking for you. He *says* he is your fiancé.'

'Ah. Phineas. Yes. He says a lot of things. I doubt if one tenth of them are true.'

'Miss – I mean, Bede – there is no time. He is coming down the path even now.'

'Did you tell him I was not here?'

'I did. He did not believe me.'

She laughed.

'It seems he knows me very well. Perhaps we would make a good pairing after all.'

I was about to impress upon her, again, the urgency of the situation, when she screwed the lid on to the jar and turned to Pa and said: 'Here, before I forget.'

She took a locket on a chain from around her neck. It was silver and bright and very delicate. She held it out for Pa, one gloved hand to another, and he took it. He gave me a glance and seemed uncomfortable that I had witnessed the exchange.

'Thank you, sir,' she said to him. 'I hope we meet again soon.'

I could hear Mr Mordaunt's footsteps on the gravel, now. Bede gave us both a quick nod and then climbed over the broken section of the wall and disappeared into the woods. Her fiancé – or whoever he was – arrived moments later. I turned and spoke too quickly to be convincing, I think.

'My grandfather says he has not seen her, either.'

'We have had no visitors this morning, sir,' said Pa. 'We've had no visitors this past year, in fact, save the reverend.'

Mr Mordaunt smiled, but it did not reach his eyes. So different, I thought, from the man who had saved us two days previously.

'Then I beg your forgiveness,' he said. 'I must have been misinformed. One of the villagers said that they had seen her heading towards the churchyard.'

'Perhaps she went on, down to the watermill?' I suggested.

'Perhaps. I do hope she has not gone far. We are all worried for her safety and her sanity.'

'Sanity?' I said.

He did not answer. He looked around the garden, as if Bede might have been crouched somewhere in the bushes, and without asking went around to the front door of the cottage and went inside. Pa and I looked at each other and followed.

'I can assure you,' said Pa, 'there is nobody here but us.'

Within we found him examining the remains of the horse liver.

'Now there is a surprise,' he said. 'Where did you find this?'

Neither of us spoke.

'It is a very fine specimen. If a little old.'

'Only the remains of our supper. I am sorry, you must think us very slovenly.'

'Where did you get it?'

'There is a woman,' said Pa, slowly. 'She collects dead animals, for glue and hair and such. But many of them are still quite edible.'

'Ah yes,' Mr Mordaunt said, 'I know of such people.'

He seemed annoyed by something. Perhaps, I thought, he had been the rival bidder that the Meat Maid had spoken of? No, it did not make sense. A gentleman of his standing was surely used to eating far daintier things.

His eyes continued roving the cottage and lighted on a book that was on Pa's bed. He went and thumbed a few pages.

'Erasmus Darwin? You are very well read for a gravedigger!'

He laughed but at the same time fixed Pa with a stare that seemed to expect some kind of explanation.

'The nights are long here, sir. I read a little for pleasure. A little for self-improvement.'

'I think there are few who would take pleasure in a book like this. Though Miss Wellrest would no doubt enjoy it immensely.'

Pa met his gaze and the inside of the cottage seemed to grow suddenly, unbearably hot.

'You seem greatly preoccupied with her,' he said. 'I am sorry we cannot be of more help.'

There was a pause, before Mr Mordaunt smiled and his face changed completely, yet again.

'No, no!' he said. 'Do not worry. I am sorry to have interrupted your morning. If you *do* see my beloved, please escort her home. We are all so dreadfully worried for her.'

'Of course, we shall,' said Pa. 'Good day to you, sir.'

'Good day to both of you.'

We bowed to each other. Mr Mordaunt took one last glance at the plate of liver, corrected the angle of his hat, and made to leave. Perhaps he did not realize I was watching him so closely, but his smile turned to the most thundery kind of grimace before he had even reached the door.

XVII

NED

'What did she want?'

Pa stood on the doorstep with his hands on his hips, staring down the avenue of yew trees. The sun was strong and in the shadow of the branches the path was blue and striped like the skin of a mackerel. He did not reply.

'Pa? What was she collecting in the jar?'

He abandoned himself to a coughing fit and spat into his handkerchief. Then he took a long, fluttering breath and cleared his throat.

'Miss Wellrest is having trouble sleeping,' he said. He still had his crooked back to me.

'Oh,' I said. 'Was that all?'

He nodded and was silent. More secrets, I was sure of it. The whole business seemed more cloak-and-dagger than a simple request for a sleeping draught.

'I wonder why she did not want anyone to know she was here? And I do not understand who Mr Mordaunt is. Are they to be married or not? He seemed very eager to find her.'

'Not as eager as you might think, actually.'

'What do you mean?'

'He is still in the graveyard. Look.'

I got up and went to the door. Far in the distance, beyond the trees, Mr Mordaunt was making a slow circle around the Nameless Grave. We both watched him for a minute or two, and eventually he went on his way.

'Now then,' said Pa. 'Why do you think he might be taking an interest in that?'

My whirling mind stilled and several very disparate recollections suddenly took on a single shape.

'I wonder,' I said, but then found no more words would come.

'You wonder what, Ned?'

Again I sifted my memory.

'Perhaps this is all fantasy,' I said. 'But he seemed very interested in the liver, didn't he? He called it a specimen.'

'He did. Go on.'

'When we met him the day before last, he said that he was a man of science. And that he was well connected with the doctors at the university. And he knew all about resurrection men. When I was listening to the man and the woman who stole our keys, the woman said something . . .'

I recalled it very clearly.

'Said what, Ned?'

'She said, "be glad he's not asked us for a body this time". I did not know who she meant by "he". But they were going by boat, and upstream, too, so he could not have been far away.' I paused. 'Maybe he was Mr Mordaunt.'

Pa seemed to weigh this up for a long time. The birds looped and tweeted in the shade of the yew trees. Eventually he shook his head, but I did not know if this was in disagreement or resignation.

'I do not know what to make of it all,' he said. 'But whatever his intentions, I think we should keep a very close eye on that grave.'

'All right. You won't tell me what it contains, will you, Pa?'

His good eye looked at me and he said: 'No.'

He went back inside and settled into his armchair. He poured a cup of tea from the lukewarm pot and sat massaging his temples with his fingers. His skin was so loose it looked as if it would come off entirely if he rubbed any harder.

'I never thought,' he said, 'that there would be quite so much drama in this place. I thought the dead would make quiet neighbours. But look at us. Disturbed graves. Thievery. And now this business with Miss Wellrest and Mr Mordaunt.'

He took out the locket Bede had given him and placed it on top of the stove, its chain curled around it. I thought he was going to elaborate on their meeting but instead he just looked up and said: 'I am sorry, Ned. I wanted a quiet life for you, too. It would seem the church wall is not as inviolable as I once thought.'

I went and joined him in the opposite chair. One of its legs was wobbly since the break-in and I cast around for something I could fold and put underneath to keep it stable.

At the foot of the chair, where I presumed she had been sitting, there was a handkerchief. I picked it up between thumb and forefinger. The initials 'O.W.' in one corner. I caught that distinctive floral scent.

'Oh!' I said. 'She forgot this!'

Pa was still lost in thought. He looked up but did not reply.

'I should return it to her,' I said, hopefully.

'I don't think she will miss it, Ned.'

'She is a lady. Of course she needs a handkerchief.'

'Ned, don't be ridiculous. You can't just go and knock on the door of the Wellrest house.'

'Why not?'

'You *know* why not.'

I looked at the handkerchief and put it to my nose and breathed deeply. She had been gone less than half an hour but the scent already brought with it a strange feeling of both loss and anticipation. I wanted to see her again. I *needed* to see her again.

I stood up.

'If I go now, I might still catch her.'

Pa sighed.

'Ned, I know . . .' He paused to find the words. 'I know she *interests* you, but you cannot go chasing after her now. Her life is complicated enough as it is, and the last thing she needs is another suitor.'

'Complicated how?'

'She does not wish to marry Mr Mordaunt.'

I smiled in spite of myself. There was hope, then!

'But the marriage is being forced upon her. That is why she is having trouble sleeping, Ned.'

My heart immediately shrank several sizes, as if pricked with a needle.

'Oh.'

'So. I think it best if you leave her be.'

I sat back down in the chair. I folded and refolded the handkerchief. I looked at Pa, and he smiled sympathetically. I liked Bede, yes, very much – but thought there were other reasons why I should pay her a visit. I suspected there was more to her meeting with Pa than just collecting herbs to help her sleep. There must have been some other reason for their talking in private.

'As you wish,' I said. 'I am sure she has plenty of handkerchiefs, anyway.'

I poured myself some tea and sipped the cold dregs, less because I was thirsty than because I wanted to conceal whatever expression was on my face. As I have said, I am not a good liar.

XVIII

NED

I climbed the broken wall at the back of the cottage a good hour after Bede had left. Neither Mosca nor I was able to pick up her trail. I found some churned footprints in the mud and leaves but soon realized that they were my own from several nights back. I asked a passing robin if he had seen anything of her, but he was proud and irritable and seemed to suggest that it was not his *job* to keep track of every person who came and went through that part of the woods.

I searched fruitlessly for most of the morning and then decided it would be best to wait for her at the manor house, since she was bound to return at some point. I did not much fancy another run through the village, so I followed the path of the river and cut up through the woods until I was back on the road and opposite the long driveway that led to the house.

It was clear that the Wellrest family had fallen on hard times. The gateposts were entwined in ivy, and in the gaps, the stone was pale and crumbling like stale cheese. The gates themselves were flaked and furred with rust and one had come off its hinges entirely. They did not close properly, so it was quite easy for me to slip through the gap and into the estate.

I made my way up the weed-choked drive to where the manor house sat slumped and silent. It seemed derelict and I wondered if perhaps circumstances had changed and the family did not even live there any more. Its roof was crooked as an old nag's spine. Its walls bowed outwards and in places looked like they had been pummelled with cannon fire.

As Pa had said, I could hardly go and knock on the front door, so I went around the back of the house to the stables. In the stalls were two old and thoughtful-looking horses. I asked them if they had seen Bede return, and one of them shook his head, though this meant little since horses will shake their heads at almost anything.

I heard the crunch of feet on the gravel. It did not sound like Bede. I already thought I would be able to recognize her footsteps anywhere. Hers were light and measured; these seemed frantic. I vaulted the stable door and landed in the hay alongside the older of the two horses. I watched the yard through a crack in the boards.

It was the tiny woman who had stolen from our cottage. Her accomplice was nowhere to be seen, and I was glad of that, but the sight of the woman was still enough to bring out the gooseflesh on my arms.

Mosca flew back from the pile of dung he had been

investigating and straight into my earhole, as if he were the first to spot her.

'I know, I know!' I said. 'Keep quiet! You're not making me any calmer!'

The little woman had both of her hands thrust into her apron pocket and she loitered nervously on the cobbles looking this way and that. She seemed to be expecting somebody. After a minute or two there were more footsteps and the man with the golden nose, Mr Mordaunt, strutted smartly around the side of the house, beaming.

'No need to look quite so anxious, my dear!' he said.

He spoke very loudly. She winced and looked over both shoulders. He laughed.

'There is nobody here to spy on us,' he said. 'Apart from your husband, and I hardly think he is planning on betraying you.'

'Couldn't we have met somewhere else?' said the little woman. 'If Mr Wellrest were to find out—'

'Mr Wellrest is out looking for his daughter with the others. Your secret is safe, Mrs Gilly.'

She looked towards the stable I was crouched in and he followed her gaze. I pulled my face away from the crack. I was sure they had seen me. I heard a click.

'Would you like me to shoot the horses when we're done?' he said. 'In case they are the loose-lipped sort?'

'No! For goodness' sake, sir—'

I turned back to my spyhole and saw the gentleman pointing a pistol directly at the stall. I nearly cried out myself. He seemed stranger and crueller each time we met.

He laughed again and lowered his arm.

'A joke, Mrs Gilly! Your nerves, good grief. You must lie down while the house is empty. Enjoy an hour or two of relaxation.'

'I can't relax *because* the house is empty, sir. I'm doing three times as much work since everyone else is out looking for Miss Wellrest.' She clicked her tongue. 'You ask me, someone needs to put a leash on that young woman.'

'Perhaps someone will.' He grinned. 'Well, then, if you have so much to do we should get this over with. Do you have them?'

She nodded. She brought her hands out from her apron pocket and handed over a clinking set of keys. I had to put both hands over my mouth to stop myself from gasping.

'Wonderful!' Mr Mordaunt said. 'I am sure this means nothing to you, but you have done a great service in the name of scientific progress.'

'You know what they're for, then?'

'I have my suspicions, Mrs Gilly,' he said.

She sighed.

'Will that be all, sir?'

'For now,' said Mr Mordaunt.

'And the other gentleman? If he asks?'

'If he asks, by all means point him in my direction. He is welcome to haggle with me for your services, but I doubt he will be able to pay you half of what I can. Which reminds me.'

He took out a purse and counted a handful of coins and gave them to her.

'That should buy you a few more chickens, should it not?'

She counted the coins herself and made a small curtsy. As she did, the great apeman appeared in the kitchen door at the rear of the house. He was as large as I remembered but now, in the daylight, looked expressionless and unthreatening. He did not step out into the stable yard; it seemed to me he could not have fitted through the door frame if he had tried.

'Yes, Mr Gilly?' said Mr Mordaunt.

'She's back,' the apeman said. 'Obedience, I mean.'

Mr Mordaunt sighed.

'What must I do to get a *moment's* peace around here?'

He marched back to the manor and Mr Gilly withdrew his huge bulk to let him past. For a while Mr and Mrs Gilly just looked at each other and seemed to be exchanging words without moving their lips. Then they followed him inside.

XIX

NED

I was a long time in the close, warm darkness of the stable. It was small and comfortable and the horse was good company. I did not wish to leave. I thought perhaps I could make a new life for myself there in the hay, and the rest of the world could go on without me, and I would never need to worry about the things I had seen and heard.

But worry I did. Some things were very clear to me, others were not. I knew that Mr Mordaunt now had the keys to the graveyard, and to the Nameless Grave. I knew that he had paid Miss Wellrest's servants to do the job, and it was a fair assumption that he had paid them to dig up the bodies, too. If the whole business had not been so horrifying, I would have felt quite proud of myself for guessing at the truth in my conversation with Pa.

But there was also much I did not understand. I did not know why Mr Mordaunt had done such a thing. I also did not understand why Mrs Gilly was only now handing him a set of keys she had stolen three days earlier. She had mentioned some 'other gentleman' she had been afraid of offending. Someone else she had promised the keys to? Surely there were not yet *more* resurrection men to contend with?

Hours passed. Outside the stable the day darkened and the sky took on the appearance of a sodden blanket. My stomach whimpered at the thought of how many meals I had missed. I heard raised voices inside the house and a lot of marching up and down stairs and then, I thought, the sound of hammering in one of the top windows.

I was considering returning to Pa to tell him what I knew when the glow of candlelight appeared in that same window, followed by Bede's unmistakable silhouette. Just a glimpse of her made me feel that things were not as bad as I had thought. Yes, I would tell her about Phineas and Mrs Gilly first. It made more sense, since I was here. And I still had her handkerchief!

Mosca laughed at me and I told him to go back to his dung pile.

I could hardly stand in the open yard and throw stones at Bede's window, so I waited until it was fully dark and then crossed to the drainpipe that led all the way up to her room. Mosca had his reservations but I began to climb anyway. I have always been a good climber, of walls and trees and church steeples. I have always been proud of it, too. Proud to be a strange, skinny, sneaking sort of person.

When I was halfway up, Mrs Gilly came out of the kitchen and emptied a bucket of something into a drain. I clung in the darkness and my forearms ached and burned.

She stood in the yard for some time, sighing. She seemed very troubled. Eventually she went back inside and I resumed my climb.

At the top of the drainpipe was a narrow stone ledge. I hauled myself up and shuffled along until I was outside Bede's window, and squatted there like a gargoyle. The window was open – missing its bottom half, in fact – but somebody had nailed crude wooden bars horizontally across the inside, a couple of hands' width apart.

The room looked empty at first. Then Bede appeared from behind her grand four-poster bed and sat down at a desk in the corner. She produced a little glass bottle from inside her glove and held it to the candle flame in her thumb and forefinger with a look of great concentration.

I watched for a minute and then cleared my throat. She looked around and stared at me as if completely unsurprised. She got up and came over and my heart began to thump ten times faster because I realized I had not planned a single word of what I would say to her.

She stood behind the wooden bars and crossed her arms and waited for me to speak first.

'Hello, miss,' I said, and immediately cursed myself for not using her name. If we were to be friends I would surely have to dispense with formality.

'Hello,' she said. And that was all. She squinted at me through the gaps. I must have looked a little odd, squatting there, my knees up around my ears. It started to rain.

'Perhaps you do not remember me,' I said.

'We saw each other only a few hours ago.'

'Oh. Yes. Of course we did.'

'Are you quite safe out there? You are not holding on to anything.'

'Oh, yes miss – I mean, Bede – I am quite safe. I can crouch like this for hours. I am very good at crouching.'

There was a long pause.

'Forgive me for being forward,' she said, 'but what are you doing here?'

'I came to tell you something.'

'I see.'

Another pause.

'Well? Quickly, please. Someone may overhear us and then we shall both be ruined.'

'Yes. Quickly. Of course.' I tried to gather my thoughts. 'Well, firstly, I wanted to tell you that you left your handkerchief at the cottage.'

I took it out of the pocket of my jerkin. It was balled up and damp and it had somehow got dirtier since I had put it in there. I put my hand through the bars and she looked at it for a moment and then took the handkerchief from me. She was not wearing her gloves and her fingers touched my own. It was the first time I had seen her hands uncovered. They were a mess of burns and scars.

'You are hurt!' I said, without thinking, and she quickly snatched them back and concealed them in the folds of her dress.

'What of it?'

'What happened? Are you in pain?'

'It is nothing. I thank you for your concern. Was that all?

You have come a very long way to return a handkerchief.'

It was a moment before I stopped worrying about her fingers.

'No,' I said. 'There is something else. Something important I have learnt only recently.'

'If it is about plants, your grandfather told me all I
needed to know.'

'No, it is not about plants. It is about your fiancé.'

'I have no fiancé.'

'I mean the man who wishes to marry you. Mr Mordaunt.' I leant in closer to the window. 'He is not who he
seems.'

'Oh, I do not know about that,' she said. 'He both *seems*
and *is* an arrogant and duplicitous bastard.'

I was stunned for a moment by her cursing. I swallowed
hard, as if the word itself were a piece of gristle, and
went on.

'There is more than that,' I said. 'He has been mon-
strously abusing the graveyard.'

She raised an eyebrow.

'Has he now?'

'He has been digging up the bodies. Not personally.
He has been asking somebody else. It gives me no great
pleasure to say this, Bede, but he has been paying your *own
servants* to do his work.'

I waited for her to reply but she simply narrowed her
eyes.

'Mr and Mrs Gilly. I saw them myself. They have stolen
the keys to the churchyard, too, and just now I saw the

woman accepting coins from Mr Mordaunt, in return for the keys, in your own stable yard!'

I pointed behind me and nearly lost my footing, and snatched at the window frame. Bede's hand shot through the bars and held on to the front of my shirt.

'Careful,' she said. She waited until I was steady again and then withdrew her hand. 'You saw this? You are sure?'

'I saw it all,' I said. 'Just before you returned. And now you are here, locked in the house with all three of them. I do not think you are safe at all. The man is, as you say, quite untrustworthy.' I was thinking of a tactful way to phrase my next thought, but the words came without warning. 'I don't think you should stay here. I think you should come back with me to our cottage. It is small, but comfortable enough. And you would be safe in the grounds of the church, while someone deals with all this horrid business. Mr Mordaunt is dangerous, Bede. You must not marry him.'

She stared at me a long while and I thought I had over-stepped the mark.

'Of course I will not be marrying him,' she said at last. And then: 'Does anybody else know what you have just told me?'

'No. Not apart from your servants. I think they are dangerous too.'

She put a long finger to her lips.

'Interesting. Very interesting. I thank you for risking life and limb to tell me.'

'You are most welcome. What will you do?'

'I don't know. Yet.'

'Would you like to stay at the cottage?'

I was hopeful for not more than a few seconds.

'No,' she said. 'But thank you. Even if I wanted to, I have no way of leaving this room. And besides, there is business for me to finish here.'

'Very well. But if there is any way I can help you, you must tell me.'

I was aware of a slight desperation in my voice. She looked at me and half closed her eyes for a moment. I wondered if she had fallen asleep standing upright. Then she pointed at me.

'Now you mention it, I think you might be able to do something for me.'

'Of course!' I said. 'Anything at all!'

She smiled with only one half of her mouth.

'Yes. You're absolutely perfect.'

I did not know what to say. I gripped the window frame hard and it took all of my concentration to hear her through my blushing ears.

'If you are happy enough to climb all the way up here,' she said, 'you should have no trouble at all sneaking into the ballroom.'

'Oh yes,' I said, 'I am as good at sneaking as I am at crouching!'

She laughed. A warmer laugh than I had ever heard from her.

'Outstanding. I assumed as much.'

'Where is the ballroom?'

'On the other side of the house. On the first floor. The

oriel window – the large one, in the middle – is always slightly open to let out Phineas' noxious fumes.'

'His fumes?'

'From his experiments.'

I wondered, again, what these experiments might entail. I began to feel the first twinges of regret for my enthusiasm. But then, I was quite prepared to do anything at all for her.

'We will be having supper shortly. It is perhaps the only time when Mr Mordaunt leaves his work unattended. You will be able to climb the rose trellis and enter the ballroom through the window.' She suddenly held up a finger in warning. 'Do not touch *anything*, once you are inside.'

'I would not dream of it.'

'Somewhere in that room you will find a little book. It is most likely in a desk drawer, though Phineas may have been reading it and left it elsewhere. It is easy to recognize, though. The covers are charred, and it is bound together with string.' The finger shot up again. 'Do not open it.'

'I will not,' I said. 'I promise.'

'Good.'

She gave me a hard look and did not speak for a few moments, as if she was considering, or perhaps reconsidering, the whole plan.

'What *shall* I do with it?' I said. 'Shall I bring it to you?'

'No,' she said. 'Absolutely not. Take it away from here. Give it to your grandfather. Tell him I shall come to collect it from him in due course.' She paused again. 'In fact, speaking of your grandfather, perhaps you could also look for his keys. I suspect Phineas will have left them in the ballroom along with everything else.'

I was about to voice my support for this idea when she turned abruptly.

'Somebody's coming,' she said. 'You need to go. My thanks . . .' She frowned. 'What is your name? I do not believe you ever told me.'

'Nedric,' I said. 'I mean, Ned.'

'Thank you, Ned.'

'You are most welcome,' I said. 'I do hope this sorry situation can be resolved. And I hope you are able to sleep soundly once it is.'

She cocked her head.

'Why do you say that?'

'Pa told me you wanted ingredients for a sleeping draught,' I said. I pointed at the phial of amber liquid on her bureau. She turned to look and turned back.

'Oh, do not worry about that,' she said. 'Tonight I shall sleep very well indeed.'

XX

BEDE

Everything that the boy had said left me feeling more than a little discomfited. It would not change anything of the plan, but the news was still unexpected, and left me feeling less in control of events than I would have liked. And perhaps just as discomfiting was the boy himself. Such an odd creature, but so eager to please, and a friendlier soul I had not met since I was a child. He was handsome, too, I admitted to myself – in a bony and angular and most unusual sort of way.

The key turned in the lock of my bedroom door and I quickly put on my gloves. Father opened it but did not come inside. He looked more exhausted than ever. I could have told him I was attempting to summon the devil himself, and Father would not have reacted with anything more than a weary indifference.

'What are you doing?' he asked. 'Why are you by the window?'

'I wanted some air,' I said.

'Mr Elmet said he heard you talking.'

'I was talking to myself. Or are you going to deny me my own company, as well as the company of everyone else?'

Neither of us wished to argue any more, and the exchange failed to gather any heat.

'Mr Mordaunt requests your company at dinner.'

'How wonderful.'

'He wishes to discuss the details of your wedding day.'

'Very kind of him to invite me to be a part of the preparations. I assumed I would simply be carried into the church bound and gagged.'

'That is all I came to tell you, Obedience. Come.'

'Now?'

'Now.'

He waited. I waited. I glanced at the phial on the bureau. It lay in plain sight for me, but Father would not see it so long as he did not enter the room.

'May I at least change into something more respectable?'

Father sighed.

'You would try this ruse again, would you? Mr Gilly nailed those bars to the window quite firmly. And we have taken all the tools from the fireplace.'

'I do not mean to escape, Father,' I said. 'I wish to make amends. Perhaps you might send up Mrs Gilly.'

'Mrs Gilly will be cooking the dinner.'

'I'm sure whatever strange concoction she has on the stove will survive being unattended for a few minutes. I will need somebody to tie me into my corset.'

Father relented.

'Very well. But hurry down as soon as you are ready.'

He turned and went out into the corridor. As soon as he was gone I hid the glass phial in one of the bureau's little drawers.

Mrs Gilly arrived a few minutes later. She was very quiet and said not a word as she entered the room. She practically radiated guilt, but of course I could not discuss the matter with her openly.

I thought it a good idea to keep her occupied while Ned was finding his way into the house, so I was most unhelpful when she came to dress me. I squirmed and complained and did everything I could to make the process take as long as possible. Eventually she grew impatient. She roughly yanked the laces of my corset – a feeling like being punched in the kidneys – and tied them in a knot. She bobbed a small curtsy and left. I went to follow her, then came back to the bureau, secreted the phial in the front of my bodice and went to meet my husband-to-be for dinner.

Phineas was all smiles and courtesy when I got to the dining room. He was at the head of the table. Father was not present. Presumably this was at Phineas' request.

'My dear,' he said, pulling out a seat next to him, 'I am so glad you decided to join me.'

I sat down in a different seat, opposite his own, and stared down the length of the table at him.

'You look quite recovered from your excursion! I have not been so worried in all my life. Where on earth did you go?'

I did not reply. He laughed.

'Another secret? It is no matter. Let us not dwell on what has already happened. This evening, I would very much like to talk about our future.'

'If you are intending to discuss our wedding day, Mr Mordaunt, I have nothing to say on the matter. Hold the ceremony in Westminster Abbey, for all I care – I will not be attending.'

He steepled his fingers and smiled.

'This is uncharacteristically naïve of you,' he said. 'Yes, that is what I told your father. But nothing could be less interesting to me than wedding preparations.'

'Then why am I here?'

'We are alone, Obedience. We know much of each other's research. Too much, perhaps. So, then. Let us talk openly and truthfully of our desires and ambitions.'

I waited a moment or two before I answered.

'You know my greatest desire already, Mr Mordaunt.'

'I do?'

'I hoped you would. Perhaps you have not been paying attention.'

'Enlighten me.'

'I would like nothing more than to take you to the top floor of the house and push you out of an open window. How does that align with your ambitions?'

Mr Gilly knocked and entered and we both fell into silence again. He poured a glass of wine for each of us. Phineas thanked him and looked at me over the rim of his glass, his eyes like hot coals.

Mr Gilly lumbered away and closed the door behind

him. Phineas took a sip.

'I meant what I said the other day,' he said. 'I think we could be truly formidable, if we worked together. There is much you could learn from me, and I from you. My practical expertise and your theoretical understanding. We might change the course of human history, Obedience. The two of us will be remembered for as long as there are men upon the earth. Which, if our research is successful, could be a very, very long time indeed.'

'Herbert Wellrest thought that too,' I said. 'It got him killed and buried in a nameless grave.'

'Ah, so you *do* know where he is buried!'

I felt my face flush. Such a foolish, simple mistake!

'Yes,' Phineas went on, 'I found it too. Such a dreary place! I was disappointed to find it so robustly protected, but luckily for us I think I have the solution.'

He watched me carefully for a reaction. Outside the wind gusted and threw raindrops against the window like handfuls of stones. There was a distant murmur of thunder.

'I do not know what you mean,' I said.

'Please, Obedience,' he said. 'I think I deserve a more convincing performance than this.' He drank his wine again. 'I have deciphered what I can of Herbert's diary, though I am sure I have only understood a fraction of what you know. Quite fascinating, is it not? Such a strange commixture of the rational and the muddle-headed. But this is precisely why, I think, we cannot disregard it. So many men who would call themselves natural philosophers are too narrow in their thinking. It seems Herbert was open to a great many ideas. Like myself.'

'If you wish to return to principles that were abandoned centuries ago, then do what you will,' I said. 'To me his work seems to be utter nonsense.'

'Then why were you studying the diary in the first place? And why are you so anxious to have it back? There are no secrets here, Obedience. There is no shame. There is a great deal we can learn from his diary, I have no doubt about that. But it does not contain everything he knew, does it?'

I did not reply.

'No,' he said. 'I have several of his letters to other alchemists – acquired through great perseverance, and at great expense – in which he claimed, repeatedly, that his greatest secrets would go with him to his grave. Going by the lengths he went to conceal his burial place, and to protect it, it would seem he meant that quite literally!'

Then came the biggest smile of all, lit by a great flash of lightning outside the window. The thunder followed a few moments later, louder than any that had come before. The panes shook and the candle flames quivered and the whole dining room convulsed as if the storm had somehow taken up residence in the house. In fact, the harder I listened, the more it seemed the thunderclap had come quite specifically from the ballroom.

XXI

NED

The rose trellis was much easier to climb than the drain-pipe, even in the rain. The wood was soft and spongey and in places it was rotten all the way through, but it held my weight. Not for the first time I was glad to be as skinny as I was. At the top I was able to stand upon the pediment of the manor house's front porch, and from there I slith-ered through the half-open window into the ballroom.

It smelt of dust and damp and obviously had not hosted a ball in a very long time. It did not look like it would any time soon, either. Bede had told me that Mr Mordaunt had constructed his laboratory in here, but I was not prepared for how enormous and complex it would be. It had the appearance of a miniature city from some fantastical dream – spheres and cones and cylinders built of glass and metal. In the centre of it all was a single oil lamp that cast its light over the walls and the ceilings in a hundred broken rainbows.

'Someone has been here recently,' I said to Mosca. 'Bede

said it would be empty . . .'

There were voices out on the landing and I withdrew into the darkest corner of the room and hid behind one of its damp, heavy curtains. Someone began speaking just outside the door. Clipped and articulate. Mr Mordaunt, I thought. The door suddenly slammed shut. He locked it and walked away, whistling.

'I'll look for the book,' I said. 'Mosca, you find the keys. I'm sure you remember what they smell like.'

He flew off into the darkness and I approached the mountains of scientific apparatus. I wormed my way around the delicate labyrinth of bottles and tubes and towers of glass. They all converged on a large brass plate stained with something that looked very like blood. It reminded me of the serving dish Pa had used to carve his liver.

On the far side of the room a desk was pushed up against the wall. Above it hung a gloomy oil painting of someone whose very serious face did not match his very comical way of dressing. I spent a little too much time looking at it – something about the face seemed familiar. Perhaps it reminded me of Bede, since he must have been a relative. To tell the truth, I was seeing her face everywhere. I could have found her features smiling at me from a bowl of porridge.

More voices brought me back to myself. I hurried round to the desk and took the oil lamp with me. It was piled high with books and papers. I looked at every single one, and while some of them reminded me of Pa's books, none of them matched the description that Bede had given me. They were too big; too thick; the wrong colour. There was nothing small or burnt or tied together with string.

I went through the drawers, as Bede had suggested. More papers, more diagrams. Pictures of arms and legs, sinews and bone. This, then, was the nature of Mr Mordaunt's research. For all I knew I was looking at sketches of the residents themselves. The man was a ghoul.

And then, in the last drawer I searched, two pieces of luck.

I saw the keys first. They were very familiar to me since I had spent my whole life looking at them hanging from a nail above the stove. I lifted them out of the drawer carefully so they would not clink against each other, and fingered each one: church gate, church door, cottage, belfry. And, yes, one other, whose use I had never questioned. The key to the Nameless Grave. I hung the iron ring upon my belt.

Underneath them was the book. I took it out and held it to the oil lamp. It seemed exceedingly old, and the cover flaked beneath my fingertips, as if it had been rescued from a fire. It gave off a very strange smell. It had been bound shut with a new piece of string, and despite what I had promised to Bede, it took all my willpower to stop myself from loosening the knot and leafing through its pages.

I tucked it into my jerkin pocket and went looking for Mosca. He had been buzzing around the apparatus and not helping in the slightest. Now all I heard was rain on the glass and distant thunder.

'Mosca?' I whispered. 'I've found them! Where are you?'

There was a noise, not from the window, but from under

one of the workbenches. A *thump* like somebody falling down some stairs.

'Mosca?'

I took the lamp from the top of Mr Mordaunt's desk and went back to the apparatus and listened. Another grumble of thunder. Another *thump*. Beneath one of the tables was a small wooden chest with a brass clasp. Everything else in the laboratory was arranged very fastidiously, but this box was lying on its side. Mosca was crawling around on its surface as if he was the one who had knocked it over. He agitated his wings but did not take to the air again.

I picked up the box and righted it and something soft and heavy flopped about inside. There was a noise a lot like a chicken clucking. I placed it on the workbench and undid the clasp. I raised the lid slightly and peeked inside. The light from the lamp reflected from a black and beady eye.

'Oh, hello . . .'

There was a sudden flash of lightning and the thunder seemed to shake the walls of the manor. I am not usually scared by a storm, but I was already very anxious and exhausted from all my climbing, and I dropped the box. It hit the floor and the lid fell open. Its contents rolled at my feet.

For a brief and horrifying moment I thought I might have been looking at a human child – some terrible progeny, lying there naked and plump and pink as a newborn. But no, there was the beak, there were the claws. The chicken had been plucked but it was very much alive. It scrabbled about on the floorboards of the ballroom and could not right itself. I had never seen a more wretched thing.

I did not know what I should do. I knew that I wanted to throttle Mr Mordaunt and I was surprised at the feeling, a great red wave of anger that I had not felt towards anybody before. But I did not know how I was to deal with the bird.

I crouched down and tried to soothe it. There was another, even louder crash of thunder and it nipped me hard with its beak. I cried out and dropped the lamp and staggered backwards into the bench behind me. I turned. Mr Mordaunt's apparatus wobbled. I watched it for what seemed like hours. It was a slow and inevitable catastrophe. The whole thing fell in a glittering cascade, the metal twisting and groaning, the glassware shattering into a thousand pieces across the floor.

I looked at the devastation. The chicken was flapping wildly in the middle of it all. There were footsteps along the landing outside. Somebody unlocked the door.

For a moment I considered taking the bird with me, but there would be little chance of me escaping so encumbered. It seemed beyond saving anyway. Poor, wretched creature. I ran to the half-open window and climbed out on to the slate roof of the porch. There I crouched beneath the windowsill and watched as Mr Mordaunt opened the double doors and stormed into the room.

He stood in the centre of his ruined apparatus and turned fully around, once, twice, three times. He put his hands on his hips and his chest heaved in fury, in disbelief. He picked up one broken piece of equipment, then another, and threw them both to the floor. Then he came back to the chicken.

He stood over it for a moment and shook his head, as if disappointed with a wayward child. I realized that in running away I had foisted the blame for the disaster on to its plucked head – it looked as if it had charged chaotically through the whole laboratory.

Mr Mordaunt's brass nose twitched. I watched, even though I knew what was coming. Watched *because* I knew what was coming. Forced myself to, as a kind of penance for letting it happen.

In the sliver of light from the ballroom door, Mr Mordaunt raised one polished leather boot and brought it down again with all his might, and the sound that followed was not the harsh crack of heel on wood.

XXII

BEDE

I could hear Phineas thumping around in the ballroom, even though it was three rooms further along the landing. Moments later the servants rushed past the door, followed by Father. I ignored them. I worried the boy had come to some harm, but in truth I was also glad for the confusion. There were yet more pressing matters than the diary, or the stolen keys.

I took a large mouthful of wine and removed the phial from my bodice. I looked at the tiny glass bottle. So much depending upon so little. The rest of my life contained in those few teaspoonfuls. I hoped I had measured the ingredients correctly.

I was still rolling the bottle in my thumb and forefinger, lost in thought, when Phineas marched back into the room. I closed it in my fist and put both of my hands in my lap.

At first Phineas could not look at me. He came back to the table and picked up a napkin and began scrubbing at one of his boots. When he threw the white linen back on his plate it was covered in what seemed to be blood.

I felt a great, cold lurch. Surely it was not the boy's? No, it could not have been. Not even Phineas could be so monstrous. Besides, the blood did not look like it belonged to a human. It was thick and dark and stringy as tar.

'Is something amiss?' I asked, trying very hard to sound unconcerned.

Phineas stared at me, his nose sharp and hard and aggressive, like the beak of an ancient warship. For once he was not smiling.

'You let it out,' he said. 'On purpose.'

'Let what out?'

He made no mention of Ned. The relief must have showed quite plainly on my face.

'Look at you,' said Phineas. 'You cannot conceal your pleasure! I can read you like a cheap novel, Obedience. I know it was you. You let it out, on purpose.'

'I do not understand.'

'The bird! It has run amuck through the whole laboratory!'

'Oh dear.'

I smiled openly. Yes, Ned had done extraordinarily well. Phineas stormed to my end of the table.

'Do you have any idea how much this will cost to replace? How much you have set back my research? The scholars from the university will be here in a matter of days! And I shall have nothing to show them!'

'Nothing? Did the bird escape, then?'

I glanced at his bloody boot. He pointed a finger at me.

'You are a wilful, idiotic, childish little witch.'

'Careful, Mr Mordaunt. My father is just down the hall.'

'Your father agrees with me. You wait until I tell him this was *your* fault. He will not tolerate any more of your nonsense. He will be glad to be rid of you. He has said as much himself. I have no doubt this will prove to be the last straw. The act of disobedience that finally pushes you into my arms.'

He took another step towards me. I clenched my fist around the glass bottle.

'We shall be married, Obedience Wellrest. And when we are, you will have to do what I say. I will keep you in the cellar until you tell me what I want to know. You will tell me what Herbert wrote in his diary. And when we dig him from his grave, you will help me decipher any other secrets he was buried with. I know that you know more than you say. And I will get answers from you at knifepoint, if I must.'

'You can threaten me all you like,' I said. 'I assure you, death does not frighten me in the slightest.'

He regarded me carefully, as if weighing up how much truth might be in this remark. There was a long silence. Too long. I heard the sounds of sweeping in the ballroom, of Mr Gilly letting another piece of equipment slip through his clumsy fingers.

'Why are you sitting like that?' said Phineas.

I felt a rush of hot blood to my face and could do nothing to recall it to my heart.

'Like what?'

'What do you have in your hands?'

'Nothing.'

'Show me.'

I raised my hands above the table and as I did the phial rolled from the chair's cushion and dropped between my feet. There was no carpet in the room and the floorboards were very hard and I may as well have fired a gunshot.

Phineas sprang forward and shoved both me and my chair to one side. I fell painfully on to one hip and sprawled on the floor. Phineas swept around with his hands and stood up with the bottle in one fist and a quite manic look of victory upon his face. He held the poison to the candlelight and uncorked and sniffed it. He swung around and stood over me, his legs a little wider than they needed to be, the pose of a conquering hero. He tutted.

'Dear oh dear oh dear, Obedience,' he said. 'I knew you were troublesome, but *a murderess*?'

'Phineas, listen to me.'

'You would kill me before handing over Herbert's secrets? I am afraid, my dear, that will only whet my appetite. They must be very great indeed, if you would go to such lengths.'

'This is not at all what you think, Phineas.'

He shook the phial a few inches from my face, taunting me like a kitten with a ball of string.

'It seems you are more of a practical chemist than you let on, does it not? Well, fortunately, so am I. And I am very well acquainted with the appearance and the odour of all sorts of poisons. This one is a compound of gelsemium, is it not?'

I was surprised. Perhaps he was not as stupid as he

seemed. I lay there a long time, on the brink of telling him the truth. I took a deep breath.

'It is,' I said.

'Not just any poison, but a truly horrid one! Seizures and paralysis and God knows what else. Shall I explain this to your father, too? Or shall I take it straight to the magistrates in Oxford? Do you know what the penalty is for murder?'

'I do, but I have already tried to explain: I have no fear of death.'

I kicked back the chair and it clattered into his shins. He bent over and I snatched the phial from his hand, quickly uncorked it, and drank its contents down to the last drop. Phineas looked at me. His face was suddenly ashen. I was aware of the voices down the corridor growing slightly less distinct.

'Now,' I said. 'Try explaining *this* to my father.'

And the room began to swim.

XXIII

NED

I ripped my clothes to shreds climbing down the rose trellis and a few feet above the ground I caught my thigh on a stray nail sticking from the wall. It tore a dirty great hole in my trousers and the skin beneath them, but I limped on regardless. Behind me there were more voices and more lights being set in the house's windows but I hurried down the driveway and through the puddles and dared not look back.

When I reached the broken gates I stopped to catch my breath. For a minute or two there was nothing to hear except my lungs and the irregular patter of rain from the leaves. And then, drifting all the way down the avenue of trees from the manor house, there was a howl. The sound of utter grief and desolation. I froze.

'Mosca? What was that?'

He perched on my ear and stayed as still as I was. I waited. A lower, longer groan and then nothing. Bede's voice? No, it had sounded too much like a man's. It was probably Mr Mordaunt again, distraught at the loss of his equipment. Well, let him be distraught, I thought – and I was more than a little thrilled at having caused my adversary such upset.

I listened a little longer but the night was silent again. I checked that Bede's book was still safely stowed in my pocket, and the keys were still hanging from my belt, and set off back to Pa and the graveyard.

The road through the village was a mire and the going was very slow. By the time I had arrived at the churchyard wall I looked abominable: soaked and tattered and smeared with mud. I used the keys I had recovered to unlock the gate, and went on down the waterlogged path to our cottage.

Pa looked even more haggard than usual when he opened the door. He gazed at me for a moment and then pulled me into a tight embrace. I felt the curious looseness of his bones under his clothes. He released me and held me at arm's length to take all of me in.

'I thought the bodysnatchers had got you, Ned,' he said. 'Where the devil have you been? You look as if you've been dragged through a hedge backwards. Several hedges.'

'Forgive me, Pa,' I said.

'For what?'

'For running away.'

'Is that what happened? Where exactly did you run away to?'

'I went to see Miss Wellrest.'

I caught just the faintest hint of amusement in his face.

'Yes. Of course you did. Was she glad to have her hand-kerchief back?'

'She was. Very glad.'

'And did she invite you to supper? You have been gone for hours.'

'Not to supper, no.' I wiped the mud and rainwater from my eyes. 'Pa, I think I have done something very stupid.'

His bad eye rolled up into his head until it was all yellowish white.

'It sounds like I might need to be sitting down for this,' he said.

He put an arm around my shoulders and we both hobbled back to the stove and pulled up our chairs. I dried my hair and face with an old shirt. Pa already had a goblet of tea resting on the floor of the cottage. He took a few sips and watched me closely.

'I found our keys,' I said.

I took the ring from my belt and laid it on top of the tea chest. Pa sat forward and his whole face split into a smile. He picked them up and counted them off.

'Ned! This is not stupid at all! How on earth did you find them?'

I told him all I had seen and all I knew of Mr Mordaunt. I told him about visiting Bede on her window ledge, and the task she had given me. Pa listened carefully and his brow and the corners of his mouth sank when I got to the part about the laboratory, and the book, and the unhappy fate of Mr Mordaunt's chicken. When I was finished he said: 'This is troubling, indeed. You saw nothing else in the laboratory?

Nothing besides the bird?'

'What do you mean?'

'I mean, you didn't see the bodies he might have stolen?'

'No. I found *pictures* of bodies. In amongst Mr Mordaunt's papers.'

'And this book. You found it with those same papers?'

'Yes.'

'May I see it?'

I took Bede's diary out from my pocket and laid it between us. Pa sat up and both of his eyes came suddenly into focus.

'Bede told me to give it to you,' I said. 'She said she would come here to fetch it in a few days.' I paused. A delightful thought came to me in the midst of my tiredness. 'I wonder, when she does come, perhaps we could invite her to stay for dinner? If we found some more money we could buy some steaks from the Meat Maid. It will be expensive, but I do not think Miss Wellrest is the sort of person to eat liver or kidneys or calf brains.'

Pa did not reply. He looked up at me, and then back at the book, and began to slowly unwind the string that held it shut. I reached out and put my hand on his.

'She told me not to look inside,' I said.

He went on regardless. The string fell away and he thumbed the pages. He was clumsy with his thick gloves on, and for a moment I was reminded of Bede's scarred fingers. He held the book very close to his chest so I could not see what was written there. He shook his head, then opened the iron door to the stove, and tossed the book inside.

I leapt up.

'Pa! That's not yours!'

He poked at the glowing and fluttering remains with a poker and crushed the book to brittle embers.

'Miss Wellrest should not be in possession of this book,' he said. 'Nobody should.'

'But she wants it back! I told her she would get it back!'

'Then I shall explain myself when she comes to fetch it.'

'Explain yourself now!'

He looked up in surprise. I was trembling with rage and exhaustion. All of my efforts, for nothing. And what would Bede say? She would probably blame me for its destruction, and then there would be no repairing our friendship at all.

'I cannot,' he said.

'You can,' I came back at him. 'You *must*.'

'Ned, listen—'

'I am not a *child*, Pa,' I said. 'Stop treating me like one. You're keeping things from me. And I hate it.'

I felt as if the words had been in me for some time. I felt as if I had been brooding on them, like a bird perched on top of its eggs, waiting to speak them aloud.

'I know I am, Ned,' he said quietly. 'I know.'

'Then tell me.'

'I cannot,' he said again. 'Not yet. Believe me when I say: this was a bad book. An evil book. Not fit for anybody's eyes. You will understand in time.'

The rain had eased by now and all I heard was the fizz and spit of the pages as they settled into the fire. I felt, in some way, like I was the book – white-hot and paper-thin and delicate to the slightest touch.

Pa stared into the embers and shrugged his old, sagging jacket back on to his shoulders.

'Have a wash,' he said, 'and go to bed. You must be tired. I shall do the rounds alone.'

I watched in frustration as he took the lamp from its nail and lit it with a taper from the fire. He limped to the door and opened it and went outside. For the first time in my life I had no urge to follow him whatsoever.

XXIV

NED

I slept badly, visited by half-dreams of Bede and Pa and Mr Mordaunt, all of them displeased with me in some way. Pa did not return from his vigil all night and the cottage felt very lonely. Only a week ago our world had been intact and uninterrupted, a quiet little garden within the walls of the churchyard. I did not understand how everything could have collapsed so quickly and so completely.

The sun was barely up when my grandfather finally came back. I watched him from under the covers as he quietly went about stoking the fire and tidying the cups and saucers and pots and pans. I was breathing very quickly, half of me furious about what he had done to the book, the other half desperate to make reparations. If I did not have Pa, then who did I have? Not Bede, certainly.

'You should get up and dressed,' he said, without turning to look at me.

I stayed where I was and pretended to sleep. He came over to the bed.

'Quickly now, Ned. You will need to be out of here in an hour or two.'

I threw back the blanket.

'Out?' I said. 'Why? Do you want me to leave? You do, don't you. It's because of the things I said last night. I didn't mean them, Pa. Really, I didn't.'

But I *had* meant them.

'Leave?' he said. 'For good? No, Ned, of course I don't mean that!'

'Then what?'

He lowered himself creaking on to the end of my bed.

'I have been thinking. If what you said is true, and Mr Mordaunt is the one who has been pillaging the graves, then we need to let somebody else know.'

'Who?'

'A magistrate. A man of the law. Somebody with authority. You will have to go to Oxford.'

My heart leapt into the dome of my skull.

'*Oxford?* But I have never even left Withy Bottom, Pa!'

'You said last night that you did not want to be treated like a child any more. And you were quite right. I have no desire to keep you imprisoned here. It is time you went and joined the rest of the world. You can start by going to the city to report Mr Mordaunt to the authorities.'

'But, Pa . . .' It took me a moment to get all my conflicting thoughts into some kind of order. 'While I do not wish to be a child any more – and, yes, I would like to see more of the world, I think – I would like a little more time to get used to the idea.'

'What idea?'

'The idea of being grown up. Of being a man.'

Pa smiled sadly.

'So would we all. But I'm afraid there is no more time. Mr Mordaunt must be stopped at once. Today. Not just for the sake of the churchyard and the residents. If we can remove him from the Wellrests' house, Bede will not have to go through any of her—' He paused. 'Discomfort.'

'But, Pa,' I said, and I realized how much I *did* sound like a child, despite all my protests. 'I have no *proof* that it was Mr Mordaunt. And no one will take my word over his, surely? He is a gentleman. He is respected. You and I, Pa, we are just . . .' I did not finish my thought and did not need to. 'Besides,' I said, 'Mr Mordaunt was not the one who did the digging, or who stole the keys – it was the two servants from the house. He paid them to do it.'

'Then that is good news for us. If we have more parties involved, then we have more witnesses.'

I sat up in bed for a moment, trying to envisage myself walking through the streets of Oxford. Trying to converse intelligently with men of the law. If I could not even pass from one end of the village to the other without being mocked and cursed, how would I fare in a crowded city?

There were footsteps on the path outside. Pa and I looked at each other. The visitor paused and there followed a very slow, very loud knock on the door that seemed to shake the whole cottage.

Pa endured another of his coughing fits, dabbed at his mouth, and then got up and smartened his jacket and collar. I stood and went to the cottage window, half intending to leap out of it if pursued. Pa lifted the latch and opened the door.

The man on the other side was shorter than Pa, but not as stooped, so their faces almost met. I did not recognize him. He wore a top hat and greatcoat, both black and pristine but somehow old-fashioned-looking. His face was serious and unsmiling, but not unfriendly. There was an air of melancholy about him, which always warms me to people.

'Good morning,' he said, and removed his hat. His hair was thin and grey underneath.

'Good morning, sir,' said Pa. 'Can we help you?'

The man's nostrils flared at the sight and smell of my grandfather. It is the usual reaction of any new acquaintance. Bede had been an exception, of course – she had not minded at all. Another reason why I had liked her.

'I was looking for the reverend . . .' He waved a hand back in the direction of the church. I realized that, after taking all the trouble to reclaim our keys, I must have left the front gate unlocked.

'It is early, sir,' said Pa. 'Reverend Biles will not be here for some time. Is there anything we can do?'

'Well, yes,' said the man. 'I suppose you are precisely the men I should be speaking to.'

The man sighed again. He slowly raised a finger to the corner of one eye, a motion so deliberate and dignified I hardly realized he was crying at all. I looked over his black clothes again, and felt a terrible premonition.

The man composed himself and said: 'Perhaps you do not know who I am, tucked away in here. But then, I rarely go into the village myself. Perhaps you knew my wife. I think you may have buried her.'

'I believe I did, sir,' said Pa. 'I know who you are.'

I did not know. But I had my suspicions. The deep-set eyes. The heart-shaped face. Bede's features were recognizable even in a middle-aged man.

The visitor nodded and fiddled with the brim of his top hat.

'I am very sorry to say that we have need of your services. Up at the manor house.'

'I am sorry to hear it,' said Pa. He turned to look at me but I was frozen, waiting for the man to continue.

'There has been another death in the family. Last night, the angels . . .' He took a long, shuddering breath. He started again. 'My Obedience. My Bede. My poor, sweet Bede. She is dead.'

He began to cry in earnest.

At this point a sexton might have removed his hat as a mark of respect, but Pa never removed his hat, just like he never removed his gloves. He guided Mr Wellrest into the cottage and sat him in my chair, where he stayed, hunched and sobbing. I would have done the same, had I not been so utterly paralysed in body and soul. My every thought protested the truth of it. This was some act, surely. Some ruse engineered by Mr Mordaunt. Or perhaps this man was speaking of a different Bede. Yes, that was it! He could not be speaking of *my* Bede – if he were, then life could not go on, and from where I stood it did seem to be going on much as it always had.

I watched the man's shoulders shaking. In the time it took him to snatch a dozen gasping breaths I did not take one.

Pa sat opposite him with his hands folded awkwardly.

'We are sorry for your loss,' he said.

'Forgive me,' said Mr Wellrest. 'A gentleman should not . . . even in front of a . . .' He paused and took a deep breath and rubbed vigorously at his nose. 'She is to be buried in the family plot,' he said. 'We will need you to prepare her resting place. Tomorrow morning.'

The thought of it was too much to bear. Bede, my Bede, laid into the cold, cold ground. Food for worms and flies and fungus. I had spent my whole life watching men, women and children being buried and it had never unsettled me in the slightest. But then I had never known them when they were alive. And I certainly had not loved them like I loved Obedience Wellrest.

'We will of course do whatever is required,' said Pa. 'Though I must say I am somewhat infirm of late and a walk across the grounds of your estate may be beyond me.'

Mr Wellrest frowned.

'It is not far,' he said, sounding a little annoyed.

'It is my rheumatism,' said Pa. 'I can barely get from one end of the graveyard to the other. But my grandson, Ned, he is young and vigorous and will be able to prepare the plot in half the time. Ned? Would you assist Mr Wellrest in his request?'

I heard my name but the rest of his words came to me as

if I were underwater.

'Are you sure she is dead?' I said.

Mr Wellrest looked to Pa, and then back to me. His confusion turned slowly to anger.

'What kind of impertinence is this? Am I *sure* she is dead?' There were tears in his eyes again. 'Her heart has stopped and her skin is blue and not a breath issues from her lips. Even now she is lying in her bed. A waxwork of my own daughter. Yes, I am *sure* she is dead.'

'May I ask, sir, how she died?'

He looked for a moment as if he might be furious with me again, and then slumped into his chair and looked at his hands.

'Her death was very sudden. Her heart simply stopped beating. Can you imagine? Mr Mordaunt says that it may have been something that she ate, but we do not know for sure. I suspect he is trying to spare my feelings.' He was quiet for a while. 'In the end, I suspect it is my fault.'

'I am sure, sir, this is not true,' said Pa.

'You would contradict me too, would you?' Mr Wellrest snapped. He took a couple of breaths. The flame of his anger died as quickly as it had flared. 'No. I am to blame. Bede was so distracted after her mother died. I should have looked after her myself. I should have shown her a father's love. But instead I handed her over to a governess and only worried about my own grief. And then I tried to force a husband upon her, when she was still so young. Still a child. Still a child.' He shook his head. 'Is it any wonder her heart broke?'

He started to cry again.

'You are too hard on yourself,' said Pa. 'Sometimes the Lord takes souls earlier than we would like. That is the way of things. The fate of your daughter was in His hands, not yours.'

'You are kind to say so, but I do not deserve such generosity. I was a bad husband, and now I have been a bad father.'

There was a pause.

'Can I offer you a cup of tea, sir? It might perhaps calm your nerves.'

The man shook his head but Pa filled his communion goblet anyway.

Mr Wellrest looked up in surprise and said: 'Thank you.'

He took the tea, sipped, scowled. He paused and then swallowed another mouthful and it seemed a little colour returned to his cheeks. 'This is an invigorating blend,' he said quietly.

Pa smiled and inclined his head. 'An old herbal remedy.'

Mr Wellrest finished the rest of the cup quickly. He took several deep breaths and seemed calmer.

'Listen to me, talking and talking. I should be going. I have imposed on your hospitality quite enough, I think.' He turned in his chair and looked up at me. 'Come to the house early tomorrow. One of the servants can show you to the cemetery.'

Who did he mean? Mr or Mrs Gilly? I did not relish the prospect. I swallowed and nodded but no words came. Mr Wellrest turned back to Pa.

'Are you sure he is quite capable?'

'Oh yes, sir,' said Pa. 'Be assured. I taught him myself. He will take every care.'

Mr Wellrest sniffed hard and sat up straight and smoothed the front of his greatcoat, as if by neatening himself he might convince us that he had not been crying after all.

'Very well,' he said. 'Thank you for your help. Forgive me for taking up so much of your time. And thank you for the tea.'

He leant forward in his chair and balanced the goblet on top of the stove. He stiffened, his arm half extended. Pa and I realized what he had seen at exactly the same time. The locket that Bede had given to Pa was lying there in plain sight.

'Pretty thing,' said Mr Wellrest. He picked up the locket by its chain.

'It is the only thing we own of any value,' said Pa quickly. 'I should really put it somewhere safe.'

He reached out to take it back but Mr Wellrest stood and withdrew from both of us towards the door. Pa and I looked on in horror as he opened the locket and looked inside. He turned it around to show us. In the two opposing oval frames, a pair of miniatures: one of Bede, the other of an older woman who looked very like her.

When Mr Wellrest spoke again, his voice was very quiet.

'Would you care to explain,' he said, 'how you came by this?'

'It was a gift,' said Pa.

'A gift? From whom?'

'To tell the truth, sir, from your daughter.'

'Really? Then perhaps it might surprise you to learn that this particular item was buried with my wife over two years ago.'

Both men regarded each other steadily, the only noise in the room the gurgle of Pa's lungs.

'It does surprise me, sir. I am not trying to deceive you. Your daughter gave it to us.'

'And why would my daughter – my Bede – think it a good idea to hand over her mother's jewellery to the village gravedigger? Why would she even come here in the first place? Why would she even talk to you?'

Pa hesitated a moment too long. Mr Wellrest kept on.

'There are two competing explanations here. The first is that my late daughter – God rest her soul – has robbed her own mother's grave, and then handed a most precious family heirloom over to a complete stranger.'

'Sir, if I may—'

'The second is that the village's two sextons, who have been witness to every burial in the last decade or more, and who have recently been dogged by rumours of grave robbing, have made use of their *very* specific knowledge to enrich themselves.' He paused, trembling. 'Now, which of those seems the more plausible?'

'I understand, sir,' said Pa, 'why you might come to this conclusion—'

Mr Wellrest stamped on the ground.

'There is no other conclusion! Not content with pilfering from your own churchyard, you have now decided to go roving abroad and stealing from private cemeteries! It is beyond belief. It is beyond all decency. It is the work of the devil!'

He whirled around and opened the door to the cottage. Before he left he turned back and pointed at both of us.

'This will not end well for you. When the villagers get wind of this, I can tell you: prison, the scaffold, these things will seem a mercy!'

He put his hat back upon his head and stalked off into the shadowed gallery of yew trees.

It was a long time before either of us spoke. Eventually Pa got up and took down the sack that I had used to carry the liver and pulled out another that he had rolled up under his bed. He handed the first to me. It was still a little damp and pink-stained.

'Get packing,' he said. 'Take only what you need.'

He started to collect up his books and place them in his sack. In with them he put a few sprigs of the dried herbs he used to brew his tea. When I had not moved after a moment or two he stopped and looked at me.

'Ned? We really don't have time to waste. If we are quick we might be able to make two trips.'

'We're not leaving, are we?'

'Of course. You heard what he said.'

'But we've done nothing wrong!'

'Do you think the rest of the village will care to listen to us?'

'What about Bede's funeral? I can't leave before that!'

'We can think about Miss Wellrest later. I do not wish to face down a mob.'

'Where will we go?'

'We can go into the woods for the time being.'

'And then what?'

'I do not know. I will think of something.'

'We cannot stay in the woods, Pa. You are not well!'

'I will be quite all right. I have done it once before, in fact. You might even enjoy it.'

That was news to me.

'When have you done it before?'

'Oh, a long time ago. Before you were born.'

He went back to packing.

'We will be able to come back though, won't we?'

'Enough questions, Ned. The villagers will be here with pitchforks and firebrands before long. I do not wish to be in this cottage when they arrive.'

'But Pa—'

'Ned!'

I went miserably about the place, stuffing the bag with my only other pair of trousers, a different shirt, a blanket, Mosca's jar. I could not stop thinking of Bede. I did not want her buried at all, but if it must happen I at least wanted to do the digging myself.

XXV

NED

The mob came sooner than expected, heralded by Mosca, who had followed Mr Wellrest into the village. He came flying through the window buzzing and babbling. I went to the New Quarter with my bag in hand and found half of the village was already outside the gate, brandishing rakes and hoes and rolling pins and other sorts of unpleasant implements. Mr Wellrest was front and centre. The Hickson brothers were either side of him. They saw me and the weight of their hatred fell like a savage and thunderous downpour.

'He's making a run for it!'

'Look! He's got all his loot in that there bag!'

'Bet you've got my mother's wedding ring in there, haven't you?'

'Probably got her ring *finger*, too. Probably got all her fingers and toes. Made them into a right pretty necklace.'

I was gone before I could hear the rest. Back at the cottage Pa was collecting plants and herbs from the garden but abandoned his task when he saw me running.

'They're here,' I said, and he just nodded.

We set off together, over the allotment and through the brambles, sacks slung over our shoulders like a pair of vagrants. I could hear the crowd at our backs like the roaring of some distant sea.

Pa was very slow. Every step was an effort for him and we had not reached the broken wall before he was coughing and spluttering. I helped him over the tumbled, mossy brickwork and we started down the wooded slope to the river. The villagers reached the wall themselves and they laughed and jeered from the top of the ridge. I heard the whistle of stones and clods of earth as they flew past my ears, the clang and clatter of things being knocked about in the cottage.

'What are they doing, Pa?' I said. 'We left, didn't we? They don't need to break anything in our home!'

He could not reply for wheezing. His head jerked suddenly as a rock hit it from behind. He dropped his bag and slumped forward and I was forced to take his whole weight like the yoke of a plough.

We skidded and slithered through the leaves until we reached the water's edge and the cries of the villagers faded. From there I dragged him upstream for what seemed like miles. Eventually I came upon a clearing, set back a little from the riverbank, and we collapsed in amongst the roots and the new, green bracken and lay there. Pa's lungs sounded like a pair of broken bellows. I propped myself on an elbow and leant over him.

'Are you all right?'

He said nothing. His bad eye rolled queasily in its socket.

'Pa?'

He just lay there. Bees and birds went about their business and they buzzed and sang like nothing at all had happened.

My first thought was to fetch him some water. We had not packed any pots or pans and I scanned the clearing for anything I could use as a vessel. The only thing that came to hand was Mosca's jar, and I knew he would not forgive me for getting it wet.

I looked at Pa's feet. His boots were enormous. They could have held a gallon or two of water, I thought, and the leather was surely watertight, given that he wore them day in, day out. Yes, they would work. I took it upon myself to remove one of them without his permission.

I slipped off the left boot as gently as I could. He was not wearing any socks. I wish he had been. His foot was quite the foulest thing I had ever seen. The skin – what little there was clinging to his bones – was dark and cracked like old leather, and dissolved into a yellow ooze around the toes, of which only four remained. Worse than the sight was the smell, so thick and pungent I could almost see it spreading through the air like the spores of some sulphurous and putrescent fungus.

For a long time I just stared at it. Even Mosca seemed unwilling to investigate more closely. Pa was obviously far, far more unwell than he had wanted to let on. I was amazed he could even get out of bed in the mornings. Mixed in with the pity and, to tell the truth, the nausea, was not a small amount of shame: all the time I had been obsessing over Bede I should have been looking after my grandfather.

I put the boot back on. I looked at his hat and his gloves, neither of which he had ever taken off, and preferred not to think about what he looked like underneath. I went to the river and cupped my hands in the shallows and came back dripping through the trees. Half of the water had already leaked through my fingers by the time I returned but I threw the remainder on to Pa's face. His eyebrows twitched but he did not wake. I made a second trip, and a third, tried to pour a little between his blue and flaking lips, but he remained unconscious.

I left him and Mosca and I retraced our steps into the woods and found the bag he had dropped. I could still hear voices further up the hill. They were mocking and triumphant. And then, beneath their chatter, I heard a crackle of flames. I smelt the smoke before I saw it.

I hurried back to Pa.

'They've set fire to it, Pa!' I said. 'They're burning our cottage!'

I shook his shoulder very gently where he lay. Still he did not respond. Before long a brownish cloud was drifting above the treetops. Sometimes a fleck of ash would settle on Pa's coat or get trapped in my eyelashes. Maybe this fragment was part of my bed, I thought. Maybe that used to be Pa's footstool.

I spent a good part of the day fashioning a long, low shelter from branches and ferns and I hauled Pa's body inside when it was finished. I did my best to make a kind of paste from the herbs in Pa's bag and a few handfuls of river water, but I could not make him swallow any of it.

I read to him from his books, as best I could. There were a fair few words I could make no sense of. I read to him from Darwin, from Galen, from Albertus Magnus. He had a small book by a certain Mr Crosse which contained a section about flies, which Mosca enjoyed. When it got too dark to read I just sat and talked to him, but I felt like I was back in the graveyard talking to the residents. I knew he could hear me but apart from his gurgling breath he gave no indication that he was alive at all.

That was a long and sorrowful night. A thick cloud concealed the moon and the stars, the smell of smoke and charred wood pooling in the clearing. No home, no Pa, no Bede, and my fly my only company.

Day crept up on the world without me realizing. I had been awake for some time, staring listlessly at the woven roof of the shelter, before I made a decision about what to do that morning. I heard the church bell ringing but I lost count of how many tolls there were – nine or ten. Far too late to be in bed, at any rate.

I decided to see Bede.

I rolled over and looked at Pa. He was still breathing but his eyes were closed and his eyelids quivered as if he was dreaming a very vivid dream.

'I'm going to go up to the manor, Pa,' I said.

He did not reply, of course.

'I think I would like to see Bede's funeral. It doesn't seem at all right to let her be buried without one of us being there. I won't let anybody see me. And maybe I can correct any mistakes, if I wait until it's dark. I don't know who they will ask to dig her grave, but I'm sure they will make a mess of things.'

I waited a little longer. Part of me hoped he would protest and tell me I had to stay to look after him.

'I will come back. I promise. And when I do, we will talk about where we might live. We can go anywhere in the world now!'

I did not wish to live anywhere, though, apart from the churchyard at Withy Bottom.

I changed my clothes and tramped through the woods at the edge of the village. It was a dreary day, befitting all that was on my mind. Three or four times I thought of Pa and considered going back. Either decision was the wrong one, it seemed.

When I reached the manor I did not dare go back through the gates and up the driveway, but skirted the wall until I found a section I could scramble up on to. From the top I could see the family cemetery, perched on the hill at the rear of the estate, surrounded by an iron fence and the dark silhouettes of cypress trees. I climbed down from the wall into the park and set off through the long, untended grass.

I could hear someone at work before I reached the top of the hill. I came up the back slope and crept behind a small but very smart mausoleum that stood at the centre of the cemetery. I thought that Bede, of all the Wellrests, had surely earned a place inside – but presumably it was full of much older, more venerable ancestors. When I peered around the corner I saw the apeman roughly shovelling the earth under a cold and leaden sky.

'Well,' I whispered to Mosca, 'at least they have chosen somebody with a little experience.'

I watched him digging for a few more minutes and then he climbed out of the grave and mopped his shining brow with a rag. He muttered something to himself and set off back towards the house. He left his shovel at the graveside.

Mosca warned me not to, but I could not help stealing out from my hiding place to inspect the man's work. It was a disgrace. It was not even deep enough! I checked to see if I was alone and took up the spade and spent the best part of an hour smartening the edges and flattening the floor. I did not even consider how reckless it was, to be out there working in broad daylight. I thought only of Bede's satisfaction. When all was correct – though, I should add, far from perfect – I made my way back to the mausoleum and waited for her arrival.

The funeral took place in the early afternoon. The sky still had not lifted and the clouds made a half-hearted attempt at raining as the mourners appeared in slow procession from the manor house. I retreated to the back of the crumbling tomb and took off my hat and watched the whole thing as if it were a dream that would vanish if I simply willed it hard enough.

I was obviously not the only one who loved her. Most of the village accompanied the coffin, including many who had spent the previous day demolishing my house and trying to kill my grandfather. They plodded up the hill led by Reverend Biles. Mr Wellrest was the first of the pall-bearers, along with Mr Gilly and a few others whom I did not recognize. Mr Mordaunt, the scoundrel, did not deign to help. He loitered behind with the rest of the mourners and every time I glimpsed him he was either scowling at his shoes in boredom or scowling at the sky in annoyance, as if he could not believe the sky had the barefaced cheek to rain upon him.

The burial did not take long at all. I imagined most of the service had taken place in the manor house. The vicar murmured through the usual liturgy, the one that I had heard so many times I could recite it from memory. It was not fair. It was not right. Bede deserved more. Her funeral should have been accompanied by a beautiful, sorrowful song, a choir, an orchestra, poetry composed by Lord Byron and Mr Shelley specifically for the occasion. But she had none of these things and had to content herself with some half-heard words from the King James Bible.

I chewed my hat to stop myself from crying as she was finally lowered into the ground. When the mourners began to throw earth upon the coffin, I turned away completely.

I sat in the grass for a long time after the sorry business had finished. I knew I needed to get back to Pa but I thought Bede needed my company just as much as any other resident in the graveyard, especially since it was her first night in her new home. So I stayed. It was such a dark and grey day that I barely marked the slow change from afternoon to evening.

Just before nightfall I checked that there was nobody left in the cemetery and came out from my hiding place. Even in the gloaming I could see that Mr Gilly had done as bad a job filling the grave as he had digging it.

'I'm so sorry, Bede,' I said. 'I wish I could have helped you. I wish I had known what was wrong. You looked well enough when we spoke through the window!'

I could not help wondering if Phineas had been responsible in some way. From his behaviour during the service, he hardly seemed concerned by her death. But, surely, even a man like Phineas was not so much of a devil!

I removed the wreaths from the grave and smoothed out the mound of soil that had been piled on top.

'I should have been the one to do this. I wanted to. But they drove us out. Your father did. And the rest of the village. Your father found the locket, you see. The one you gave to Pa in return for the herbs . . .'

I stopped. A terrible thought had occurred to me. I sat back on my heels and put a hand to my mouth.

'Oh, good God! Was that what did it? Was it our fault? Did you poison yourself with something from our garden?'

I shoved the heels of my hands into my eyes, ground dirt into the sockets, shook my head over and over. Of course. What other explanation could there be? She had made a mistake with the sleeping draught. She had mixed it wrongly, or drunk too much.

I thumped the ground in frustration. I squirmed on my belly in the dirt and howled Bede's name again and again to the sky and to the earth. But she was dead. Dead, dead, dead, and it was Pa and I who had helped her on her way.

XXVI

BEDE

I was a long time coming to my senses, and when I did, I could not even be sure it had happened – there seemed little to distinguish between sleeping and waking, between having my eyes open or having them closed. The darkness was absolute. It seemed to have seeped into my skull through my nose and ears.

Life returned to my body from the top down, as if somebody were injecting it into the crown of my head. There were a few minutes when my mind was alert but my limbs were as limp as dead fishes. I had expected as much, but it still took all of my reason and willpower not to panic. I took tiny breaths. I kept my eyes closed. *Nothing at all to worry about, Bede*, I told myself. *Nothing that you have not foreseen and planned for.*

I felt new, warm blood tingling in my fingers and was able to focus a little better. I groped around in the stinking, suffocating darkness, as far as I was able with the coffin pinning my elbows to my ribs. I felt about on one side, and then the other. In front of me, behind me. There should have been a string, but it was not there. If there was no string, I could not ring the bell. Which meant I could not tell anybody I was awake. Which meant I was trapped under six feet of earth and fated to die a second time, but this time without anybody knowing.

And then, regrettably, I *did* panic.

It is impossible to prepare oneself for being buried alive. I had tried. The coffin felt much smaller than I had anticipated. The air hotter, more stifling, and less of it than I had hoped. I had thought I might be able to roll from side to side, or knock on the inside of the wood, but there was no space. Under the weight of the earth the lid of the coffin pressed upon my breastbone, and my galloping heart sent vibrations through my tiny prison.

I tried to scream. Not a sound came from my mouth. I have experienced such a thing in my dreams, my nightmares, but in those I had at least been woken by my own terror. Here, the cold, black wave of dread rose and rose and did not break.

I imagined I heard footsteps overhead. Very distant. I assumed I was already hallucinating.

I tried shouting again. A small sound came, but not enough to be heard by the outside world. The sweat poured from me in rivers and seemed to pool in the bottom of the coffin. I am ashamed to say I began to cry. I gulped at what little air remained. The temperature rose. I felt as if I were being boiled alive in one of Mrs Gilly's disgusting soups.

I managed to turn my head a little to one side and

discovered what seemed to be a fresh pocket of air by my left shoulder. I took as deep a breath as the coffin would allow and cried out with every fibre of my body.

The distant thumping seemed to get more agitated and then disappeared completely. I shouted once more but now there was barely enough air to half-fill my lungs. I scratched feebly at the coffin lid, still weak from the effects of the poison. I heard nothing but my own pulse. I closed my eyes and prayed for a swift death.

The thumping returned, and closer this time. It was followed by a sharper sound. A shovel in earth. I lay listening for what seemed like hours. I had been deprived of my senses for so long I was not even sure if the sound was real or imagined. Perhaps, I thought, I was already dead and this was how one entered into the world beyond.

Something hard and metallic struck the lid just above my navel. The noise was terrifyingly loud. A tiny crack appeared in the wood, admitting a few grains of dirt into the coffin. I wriggled and managed another hoarse shout. A pause. The clang of the shovel near my head. A shudder down the length of my body, the sound of wood splitting, then a mixture of soil and sweet fresh air flooding into the coffin with me.

Whoever had been digging pulled away the fragments of the lid. The world got no brighter, but colder and slightly bluer. The night sky above me, only faint and fleeting glimpses of the stars through the torn clouds. I fell in love with the world again in those moments. Fell in love with life. I gasped and gasped.

Somebody reached in and hauled me out by the armpits and I slumped against them. We held each other, there in the bottom of the grave, while I got my fill of clean air. I knew it was Ned – from his bony arms, the mess of his hair. I felt his heart beating strongly through his thin ribs and threadbare shirt.

'Bede!' he said.

'Yes?' I said.

He let me go and I sat back against the wall of mud and we looked at each other. His face was no more than a pale smudge in the darkness. He paused as if thinking of what to say next. Eventually he simply said: 'What are you doing?'

I laughed. I could not help laughing. The question seemed entirely sincere.

'What am I doing?' I said. 'Well. The list is long, but I suppose my first priority is getting out of this grave.'

'Oh,' he said. 'Then I would be glad to help. More glad than I can say.' He paused again. 'I thought you were dead.'

'I *was* dead,' I said. 'For a day or so.'

'But now you're not.'

'I don't think so.'

He frowned but said nothing else. Of course, the boy had known nothing of my conversation with the old man. In fact, I had specifically told the sexton not to involve Ned at all. I had assumed that, when faking one's own death, it is better for as few people as possible to know the truth of the matter.

I tried to lever myself out of the coffin but it felt as if I had never used my muscles before; as if I had been born anew.

'Steady on,' said Ned.

He tentatively, awkwardly got his arms around my waist and lifted me up on to the graveside. I had thought him a very slight young man but his arms were strong and sinewy. I suppose a lifetime of digging will do that for you.

He stood beside me and waited for me to speak but I had nothing to say. I looked around the cemetery but it was too dark to see anything of my ancestors' graves. In the far distance there was light spilling from a few of the windows of the manor house, and beyond that a dim glow from one or two houses in the village.

'What time is it?' I asked.

'I don't know,' said the boy. 'I haven't heard the church bell. I think, perhaps, eleven o'clock? Or slightly earlier.'

I allowed myself to feel a little pride in that. Only one hour short! I had intended the poison's effects to wear off at precisely midnight. Given how quickly I had been forced to work on the concoction, an error of one hour seemed more than acceptable.

'Where is your grandfather?'

'He is in the woods.'

To him this seemed self-explanatory.

'Why?'

'We were evicted from the churchyard.'

'Evicted?'

He nodded.

'Your father saw the locket you gave Pa. He thought we

had stolen it from your mother. The rest of the village hardly needed any encouragement to come and get rid of us once and for all.'

'The locket!' I struck my head. 'Blast! Then it was my own stupid fault!'

'Oh, no, Bede, not at all! Pa had left it out for all to see. He should have hidden it in his boot.'

'Still. I could perhaps have foreseen this. Then your grandfather was not the one to oversee my burial?'

'No. It was Mr Gilly. Though, I made the finishing touches.'

'On your own?'

'Yes.'

'Why?'

'I wanted to make sure it was done properly.'

I was quite unexpectedly touched by this. I did not know why I deserved such attentiveness, especially given that he had known nothing of my plan.

'Your grandfather did not come here with you, then?' I said. 'Did he have something more important to do?'

I could not keep the bitterness from my voice. It was not really the time to be casting blame but the old man had not kept his side of the deal, and there had been no bell, and my experience of the evening so far had not been a pleasant one. Ned just looked at me and then glanced down at his hands and shook his head.

'He is sick, Bede,' he said. 'Very, very sick indeed. I knew he was not in the best of health, and then after we were forced into the woods . . .'

'And you left him there?'

'I left him to come here! And it is a good thing I did, isn't it?'

He spoke with a sudden heat that I had not heard before.

'Forgive me,' I said.

I sat and thought about the old man and a jumble of memories took on clearer shapes. I handled each of them one by one.

'Does your grandfather have the diary?'

'The diary?'

I corrected myself.

'I mean the book. The one I sent you to find in the ball-room. Did you get it?'

'Oh, yes, yes, the book. I did. I found the book.'

'And you gave it to him?'

He shifted on his feet for a moment.

'Oh, yes. Pa has the book. The book is safe. Certainly.'

'Excellent. What about the keys?'

'Yes, I found the keys. He has those, too.'

That buoyed my spirits. It seemed catastrophe had turned quite unexpectedly to triumph. If I could keep the diary and the keys out of Phineas' hands and escape without him knowing, then all would be well. There was the matter of Ned and his grandfather, and what they knew, but the more time I spent in their company the more I wondered if we might not be of help to each other in the future. And Ned – well, I had not had any friends my own age for several years. I had certainly never had a friend who seemed as lonely; none who might understand all the strange and sad corners of my soul.

He cleared his throat suddenly, as if dislodging a peach stone.

'Forgive me, Bede . . .'

'Yes?'

'But could you possibly tell me what is going on? Why are you here? You shouldn't be alive.' He spluttered. 'I mean, of course, you *should*. We all *want* you to be alive, and it is *right* that you should be alive. Wonderful that you are alive! But I don't understand *how*. Your father seemed quite sure that you were dead. He said you were a waxwork. Blue and cold to the touch.'

'He said that did he?' I grinned into the night. 'That is most pleasing!'

'Pleasing?'

'It seems that the poison was even more convincing than I had hoped.'

'I don't think I understand.'

I looked at him. His face glistened in the starlight, white and quite guileless. Yes, I decided he could be trusted.

'We should go and find your grandfather. I will explain on the way.' I looked back at the grave and picked up the shovel. 'But first we should make sure that poor Obedience Wellrest gets the burial she deserves.'

XXVII

ꞴEDE

When the grave was filled we made our way back through the estate to the stables. My knees and elbows still felt like the inside of one of Mrs Gilly's pork pies – all jelly – but my head was a good deal clearer. Yes, we needed to find the old man, but we would also need the horses if we were to stand any chance of getting shot of Phineas – we could hardly stay in the village, or the woods for that matter, and I was not planning on criss-crossing the country on foot. It would also be easier to get to the wind-mill on horseback, and the windmill was a necessary part of the itinerary. I had not yet mentioned this detail. I thought it was something my companions would better understand once we were actually there.

While we crept back to the house Ned kept a few paces behind me and did not say a word. He was so quiet I kept having to stop and look behind me to check that he was still following. When I did, I invariably ended up with an intense buzzing in one ear.

Coming past the hedge maze I heard the boy say: 'Mosca! Leave her alone!'

I stopped again, just beyond the dim glow of the house's windows.

'What?'

'I am sorry, Bede. I know he keeps annoying you. I can see you flapping your hands.'

'Who keeps annoying me?'

'My fly.'

I paused.

'Yes. Your fly. I remember. He came with you, did he?'

'He comes everywhere with me.'

'And you speak to him?'

'All the time. He was the one who told me about you making all your racket.'

'He told you? Your fly?'

'Well, he didn't need to. He was on top of your grave and I could tell something was amiss from the way his legs were quivering. He can feel all sorts of things that people can't. So I put my ear to the ground where he was, and I thought, yes, I *could* hear something. If there was any chance you were still alive, then I thought it better to err on the side of caution . . .' He paused. 'But really it was Mosca who saved you.'

I laughed but I was not sure if he was joking or not. He did not seem the joking sort. So earnest and so honest and so very, very strange. We went on.

We waited on the edge of the stable yard long enough for all the lights in the manor to be snuffed out. Last of all was the candle in the kitchen, and I heard either Mr or Mrs Gilly turn the key in the kitchen door and make their way up the stairs. The yard was plunged into blackness again, and I had to find my way to Victor and Clerval's stable by touch alone.

I found the bolt and slowly, silently drew it across. I was about to warn Ned that Victor could be skittish around strangers, but he strolled in and patted my horse on the nose and said, in a quiet voice:

'Hello old thing.'

I turned to him in astonishment.

'You know each other?'

'Oh, yes,' he said. 'We spent the afternoon together the day before yesterday.'

Victor seemed perfectly happy to be handled by the boy while I went and fetched the tack. A good sign, I thought. Perhaps he *could* talk to animals. I saddled the horse and stuck my head out into the courtyard to make absolutely sure, again, that nobody was awake.

The house was silent, the windows blank and dark as eyeless sockets. I thought of Phineas, trying to piece together his equipment and searching frantically for the lost diary. I thought of Father, tossing and turning in his bed, or perhaps not in his bed at all, perhaps on the edge of it, his head in his hands.

There had been no other option, I told myself. He would know the truth, in good time. He would understand. And once he understood, he would forgive me. Or so I hoped.

'Do we need a horse?' Ned whispered. 'The woods are not far. I came here on foot quite easily.'

I went back inside the stall. The horses were starting to paw restlessly at the straw.

'Your grandfather is in the woods, yes. But my future lies a long way from Withy Bottom.'

'You're leaving?' He could not disguise his disappointment. 'Where are you going?'

'I don't know. Not yet.'

'Are you going alone?'

'That is up to you, I suppose.'

I did not admit to myself, much less to Ned, that his company would be very much appreciated.

I tethered Victor and Clerval together and led them both out into the courtyard. With any luck Phineas and Father would assume that someone had simply left the stable door open. With all the comings and goings of the funeral it was not unlikely that the servants would be remiss in their duties.

'Tread lightly, please,' I asked the horses.

They did not. The sound of their hooves on the cobblestones was like cannon fire. I pulled myself up into Victor's saddle as quickly as I could — which was not very quickly at all, after the hours spent in the coffin — and held out a hand to the boy.

'Quickly,' I said.

'But I have never—'

I did not wait for the rest of his protest. I hauled on his arm and draped him like a wet towel over Victor's rump. I dug my heels in the horse's bony flanks and we clattered out on to the grass with Clerval beside and slightly behind us.

I was sure we had woken somebody, and I did not wish to risk a long and noisy canter down the driveway, so we cut back through the deer park and the orchard to a section of wall I knew was broken. I could hear Ned squirming to get upright behind me. For reasons known only to himself he found it preferable to hold on to the sides of the saddle rather than my waist, and sat there rather stiffly.

We crossed the rubble of the wall and took the long way around the village. The cloud parted slightly as we trotted through the farmers' fields and revealed a thin, bright fingernail of moon. Ned had gone very quiet again.

'What do you think, then,' I said.

'About what?' he said.

'About coming with me.'

He seemed to hold his breath.

'I would like that very much,' he said. 'But I can't leave Pa.'

'You should both come.'

'But he is so sick, Bede.'

'I am quite sure I can help with that.'

'You can?'

'I think we can all help each other, a great deal.' I paused but decided I should not go into the specifics of it all – not yet. 'Besides,' I added, 'it would hardly be wise for me to leave you here in the village, given that you are the only people who know what has happened.'

'In truth,' he said, somewhat cautiously, 'I still *don't* know what has happened. I wish you would tell me.'

'Of course,' I said. 'You deserve that much, at least.'

We rode on a little way before I continued. I wondered

how much to tell him. He would learn much more when we reached the windmill – I decided the full truth could probably wait until then.

'As you know,' I said, 'on the day of Grammy Hickson's funeral I noticed the plants in your garden. I have always had a passing interest in botany, and I recognized a handful of them. Opiates and poisons and all sorts. After the arrival of Mr Mordaunt, I wondered if I might make use of them, if my situation at home became unbearable.'

'You mean your marriage?'

'To Phineas. Yes. Unfortunately for him, I know a good deal more about chemistry than he does – or thinks he does. Some time ago, in the course of my research, I read of a toxin that allows one to simulate death for several days before its effects wear off and warmth is returned to the body. The stuff of stories, you probably think, but quite possible with modern scientific methods.'

'*Atropa belladonna*,' he said.

I pulled Victor to a halt and turned in the saddle.

'Yes,' I said. 'Yes, that is one of the ingredients in the solution. How on earth do you know that?'

'I read Pa's books.'

Both Ned and his Pa seemed remarkably learned, for men whose business was corpses. We started trotting again.

'When I met your grandfather, I explained what I wished to achieve and he agreed that he would tell no one. He said he would come to dig me up at midnight – once I had regained my senses and rung the bell.'

'The bell? What bell?'

'Well, exactly, Ned! He was *supposed* to have organized a special kind of coffin and headstone for me. They are quite common, with so much cholera around. It is not unheard of for someone who is still very much alive to be buried by accident. So they are buried with a string attached to their finger, or toe, or some such, and the string runs to a small bell above the grave.'

'But there was no bell. When you awoke.'

'Correct. A minor inconvenience.' I paused. 'To own the truth, I have not been so scared in all my life.'

'I am sorry, Bede. And I am sure Pa is sorry, too. It was not his fault. He is very sick. When we were evicted from the cottage he took a stone to the back of his head. He would have helped you if he had been able.'

We had reached the edge of the woods by this point. Victor and Clerval stood snorting in the silent road, the stars arcing overhead. I turned in the saddle again.

'You are sure your grandfather is *alive*, Ned?'

'Yes. Of course he is.' He thought for a moment, and then added, quietly, 'At least, he was when I left him.'

I tried to reassure him with a smile, but I could not tell what expression my face made in the darkness. I gently prodded Victor with my heels and we disappeared into the trees, towards the river, towards what remained of the old man.

XXVIII

NED

We spent hours searching the woods but I could not find the paths I knew by starlight alone. By the time dawn began to creep into the sky, I was quite beside myself with worry. It was hard to feel any kind of relief or joy in Bede's salvation while Pa was still suffering somewhere in the wilderness, alone on his bed of leaves. What if he had passed away in the night, while I had been digging Bede's grave? Surely the world was not so cruel – that I should have to lose one of them to save the other.

We reached the river and wandered upstream and downstream with the horses several times. The edge of the world brightened. In the half-light I began to recognize trees and stones and the burrows of animals, and the way back to Pa revealed itself by the broken stems and flattened leaves I had left the day before. I delved into the murky undergrowth and behind me I heard Bede say: 'There. Is that him?'

It was. We came upon the clearing quite suddenly. The shelter I had made of branches and saplings was still there.

Pa's boots were poking out of the entrance. While Bede tethered the horses to a sturdy bough on the edge of the clearing, Mosca flew ahead of us and looked inside. When he returned he seemed in a despondent mood. His wings made a low drone, as if he was carrying some grievous burden.

I crossed the clearing and got down on my hands and knees and stuck my head into the shelter. Pa was as I had left him, on his back. I could not tell if he was breathing. There was a smell in the enclosed space not unlike spoilt meat.

'Pa? Pa, can you hear me? I came back. I know you must think I abandoned you – but I have Bede! I saved her! And she told me everything!'

He let out a long wheezing groan, such as I had never heard from him before. He seemed in terrible pain. I could hear fluid in his lungs and his eyelids fluttered erratically.

'Your tea, Pa! Would you like your tea?'

He did not reply.

I crawled out from the shelter and looked for Bede. She had secured the horses and was crouching in the mossy roots of an oak tree. She had found one of our hessian sacks and was examining a few of the herbs and plants that Pa had rescued from the garden. She seemed quite absorbed and did not look up.

'He is not well at all,' I said. 'I don't know what I should do. He's never gone so long without his tea, but I don't know how to make it.'

Eventually she stood and went to the shelter herself and

put her head inside. She spent a minute or two with Pa and then returned to the bag of ingredients.

'Did you bring these from the cottage?' she said, holding a fistful of roots.

'Yes. They're part of the recipe. I tried to make a paste with them, but he wouldn't swallow it.'

'Even if he did, it would do him no good. They should be gently animated with heat.'

She rummaged deeper in the bottom of the sack and pulled out Mosca's jar.

'This will do very well,' she said. 'Do you have flint? Or kindling?'

'I don't.'

'What about back in the churchyard?'

She swatted lazily at Mosca, who was buzzing about his home with a noise that sounded like outrage.

'We had a stove. But it's all gone, Bede. They burnt it all.'

'Burnt? Well, then, there is a good chance that the embers are still warm.'

'Perhaps. But—'

'But what?'

'But I don't want to see what's left. And I won't leave Pa again.'

She looked at me for a moment and said: 'Stay with him. I will see what I can find. If we can boil the solution he may yet revive.'

I shook my head in disbelief. Was there no end to Bede's gifts?

'What is it?' she said.

'How do you know this?' I said. 'Are you a physician?'

She paused and made a strange face, almost of embarrassment.

'Of sorts,' she said, and then took off in the direction of the village and the church.

Not half an hour had passed before she returned with a blackened, smouldering bough in one hand. A beam? Part of my bedframe? I did not want to think about it.

She set about her task without a word, working with the ease and swiftness of somebody who had done the same thing one hundred times before. Despite Mosca's protests she went to the river and filled his jar with water. She collected kindling and a few larger sticks and placed them in the centre of the clearing, and then tore strips of material from her dress and unpicked the threads to use as tinder. She blew upon the smoking timber to enliven it and before long we had a small fire crackling on the damp earth. She left us again, this time in the direction of the horses, and when she returned she had cleverly dismantled Victor's stirrups to create a kind of sling, which she used to suspend the jar above the fire.

She sat cross-legged on the ground and began poking leaves and stems into the boiling water. Still not a word passed between us. She seemed in a state of great concentration and I had no desire to disturb her. Mosca, on the other hand, was happy to make his feelings known, as the bottom of his jar darkened with soot. Bede did not notice, or simply ignored him.

Eventually she got up and removed the concoction from

the fire. She was, even now, wearing her gloves, and was quite able to handle the hot vessel. I remembered her scarred and blistered skin from when we had talked at the window and thought, suddenly: perhaps she *has* done this a hundred times before.

The tea certainly seemed the right colour. She blew upon it a couple of times and took it to Pa. Several agonizing minutes passed. Mosca and I paced in circles around the shelter.

'What if it doesn't work?' I said. 'What then?'

I heard gasping inside. I came to the entrance, and the branches and leaves of the frame shuddered as Pa sat up and banged his head on the roof.

I scrambled inside to look at him. The three of us sat in the gloom, Bede still holding the steaming jar. Pa peered at me through the vapours as if he did not recognize me. When he spoke, his voice was like the wind through dried leaves.

'Where am I?' he said.

'In the woods.'

'Am I dead?'

'No, Pa! You are quite alive, thanks to Bede. I mean, Miss Wellrest.'

'Oh.'

'You are very welcome,' said Bede. 'I would say that I was just returning the favour, but that's not quite how it turned out, is it?'

Pa looked confused. He closed his eyes and took several long, hoarse breaths.

'How do you feel?' Bede asked him.

'I don't really feel anything,' he said.

'Well. I suppose that is better than excruciating pain.'

'What is that?' He pointed to the jar she was holding.

'This? I would call it a concentrated analgesic solution with slight stimulating properties. I believe you would call it a cup of tea.'

Pa reached out a gloved hand, took the jar, sniffed it.

'Remarkable,' he said.

He passed it to me and I put my nose to it. It smelt very much like Pa's tea, only more intense. Bede took it back from me.

'May I suggest,' she said, 'that we go out into the open air? It is a little stuffy in here.'

Once we were outside Pa got very slowly to his feet, every piece of his spine clicking and clacking as he tried to straighten himself. He wavered where he stood for a moment, as if the breeze might blow him back down again. His bad eye settled on me, his good one on Bede. He frowned.

'Miss Wellrest? I am glad to see you but . . . How is it that you are here?'

'Ned dug me up.'

'Ned?' He turned to me. 'But I never told you anything of our plans! What were you doing in the Wellrest cemetery?'

Mosca landed on Pa's shoulder and all three of them seemed to be waiting for an answer; waiting for me to proclaim, publicly, that I was hopelessly in love with Obedience Wellrest, that her death had devastated me more than words could say, and that I'd had half a mind to jump into the grave and be buried with her until Judgement Day.

In the end, I simply said: 'I thought it respectful to attend the funeral of a good friend.'

'It was eleven o'clock when you opened the grave,' said Bede. 'The funeral had finished hours ago.'

'I was just keeping a vigil. I always keep them, for every resident. Tell her, Pa. Is that not the truth? It's nothing out of the ordinary.'

'Yes,' said Pa. 'Well. Sometimes, you do.'

'Well, I am very glad I did this time, because otherwise Mosca would not have heard Bede shouting, and she would still be in the cemetery, and you would not have your tea, and—'

Bede laughed. 'I am teasing you, Ned. I am very glad for your concern.'

Her gaze lingered on me a moment and I felt the heat rise in my cheeks. At last she turned to Pa, and it was a relief when she did.

'I am glad for your concern, also. And I am sorry you were unable to follow through with what we discussed. I understand my father played a part in your eviction.'

Pa sighed, as if only just remembering what had happened at the cottage.

'It is regrettable, miss. I am afraid your locket gave the game away.'

'So I heard.'

'I am curious to know how you came by it. Your father said it was buried with your mother.'

Bede rolled her eyes.

'Yes. That was what he thought. And what he wanted.

Because, of course, he always knows best. But at the time I was sure my mother would have thought quite differently. She would much rather I kept it to remember her, than have it thrown in the ground for the worms to admire. What would be the sense in that?'

'You took it from her?' said Pa.

'Yes. On the day of the funeral. While she lay there in her pauper's coffin.' The memory seemed to trouble her only for a moment, and when she looked up there was a fierceness in her eyes. 'And I am glad that I did,' she added.

Pa nodded and it was a while before he spoke again.

'Then I have failed you a second time,' he said. 'Your father took back the locket when he found it.'

Bede opened her mouth but before she could reply there was a distant sound of barking. The three of us stiffened to hear it. It was difficult to pinpoint where it was coming from, or how far away the dogs – and their owners – might be.

'Is somebody looking for you?' said Pa.

'I should hope not,' said Bede. 'It must be a farmer out hunting for rabbits.'

She seemed unconvinced by her own explanation.

'Even if it is,' said Pa, 'it would not do well for him to find you. For him to find *any* of us.'

'Indeed,' Bede said, quickly. 'We should be on our way. Do you have the book?'

'The book, miss?'

'The diary. Which Ned gave you.'

A second tide of worry rose on top of the first and my head grew very hot. There was no escaping the truth now.

Even if Pa wanted to conceal what had happened, he would not be able to sustain the lie for long.

'Ah, yes,' said Pa. 'I remember now.'

'Do you have it?'

'I do not.'

'Why not?'

'Because I burnt it.'

'You didn't.'

'I did.'

'I don't believe you.'

'It is quite, quite lost.'

Bede's face became unrecognizable, flushed and contorted with anger.

'Why on earth would you—'

The sound of the dogs was suddenly closer. Bede glanced over her shoulder and then back at Pa.

'What about the keys?' she said. 'Tell me you have those at least?'

Pa frowned and patted his hips. The iron ring clinked beneath his thick coat.

'I do,' he said. 'Though, I do not know why that should interest you.'

She just looked at him. Her chest heaved and I thought the colour in her cheeks cooled a little. She said nothing.

'Bede?' I said.

The hunting party was very close. There were voices, now, as well as the barking. Mosca was extremely agitated.

Bede heaped the wet earth on to the fire and dismantled the shelter, scattering the sticks around the clearing. She retrieved the scorched leather stirrups and then went to fetch the horses. She stopped on the edge of the clearing and made wide eyes at us both.

'Well?' she said. 'I do not intend to discuss this here and now. We will go to the laboratory. There, perhaps, we can all explain ourselves.'

I looked at Pa but this seemed to come as less of a surprise to him than to me.

'Laboratory?' I said. 'Surely we are not returning to the manor house?'

'Not Phineas' laboratory,' said Bede. 'Mine.'

A hundred half-formed questions arose but the dogs were nearly upon us. She helped Pa and me on to Clerval's back, then mounted Victor herself, clicked her tongue, and led us at a canter towards the river.

XXIX

NED

We followed the riverbank upstream, forging through the hot clouds of our breath. Bede rode ahead in silence. She seemed lost in thought, and though we were behind her I could see her jaw working, as if she was talking to herself. Pa clung to my waist and did not speak either. He seemed as preoccupied as Bede and was perhaps still in pain. So I sat between the two of them, unsure of who to side with, and unwilling to interrupt either of them while their moods were so foul.

When we were well clear of the village and the woods we came upon a meander in the river and a shallow, sandy bay where cattle came to drink. Bede led us straight into the water. I was on the verge of protesting but even in the middle of the stream the ripples only wetted the horses' bellies. We rode across and when we reached the opposite bank Mosca suddenly launched himself from the tip of Clerval's ear. He had spotted something interesting among the reeds and the bullrushes. A rowing boat.

'Oh, very good Mosca!' I said. 'We've seen that before, haven't we?'

It had been a long time since anyone had spoken and Bede jerked upright in her saddle.

'Seen what before?' she said.

'The boat. It's the one your servants used, the night they stole our keys.'

'How do you know? Wasn't it dark?'

'Yes. But there can't be that many boats on this section of the river.'

We trotted past the upturned hull but Bede did not care to look at it.

'I wonder what it's doing here,' I said, and I thought of Mrs Gilly. I remembered her talking of 'the usual place' and 'the other gentleman'. Was this where she and her husband had been heading?

'There will be time for wondering later,' said Bede shortly. 'Hunting dogs can swim, you know.'

I held my tongue and we all went on in silence again.

Ahead of us the land rose gently and on the brow of the hill I could see the silhouette of the old windmill, slumped against the grey sky. I had seen it many times from the top of the church's bell tower, though I had never been there. I was glad I had not, given the rumours that parishioners passed between themselves every Sunday morning.

We tramped through sodden fields and tangled thickets and entered another wood that seemed older and denser and darker than the one we had left. The ground became steeper and Bede wound her way quite confidently through the ancient trunks until I lost my bearings completely. Then all of a sudden the trees stopped and we were exactly where I had feared we might be.

The windmill seemed like the ruin of some great fortress, besieged and burnt and now inhabited only by the ghosts of its defenders. The morning was well upon us by now but there was no birdsong in the branches, no rustling of woodland animals.

'This is it?' I said. 'This is your laboratory?'

'It is,' said Bede, dismounting. 'My home from home.'

I slithered off Clerval's back and helped Pa to the ground. His body was heavy and loose as a sack of potatoes. Bede led the horses to a stone trough at the base of the windmill. I was not so happy about going further. Even as we stood there, the clouds seemed to descend to just above the treetops and brought with them a hard, cold rain.

'I am not superstitious by any means,' I said. 'But . . . they say this is a place of ill omen. They say it is haunted.'

'It *is* haunted,' said Bede. 'By me.'

I looked back at Pa. He was wheezing terribly and his face was as dark as the blackened heap that stood before us.

Bede pushed on the charred remains of the windmill's door and it opened quite easily. Pa and I followed her inside. The lowest level was lit by a tiny, square window that showed a mess of broken cogs and cracked millstones. She went to the far side of the room and felt around the wall and removed a loose brick, which seemed a very bad idea since the entire structure was already threatening to collapse upon our heads.

She produced a single rusted key and proceeded up a short flight of steps to a trapdoor. She unlocked this and heaved it open with her shoulders. She went up to the floor above and Pa and I followed without a word.

If there were any windows on this level of the mill they were boarded up or curtained off. Bede went around lighting spirit lamps with a taper and it was as if the sun were rising on a new and strange world. I gasped.

'Good heavens,' said Pa.

The circular room was filled, from wall to wall and floor to ceiling, with vast mountains of scientific apparatus and paraphernalia. Whereas Phineas' equipment had seemed expensive and exquisite and fastidiously put-together, there was a distinctly home-made feel to Bede's laboratory. There was the same range of glass bottles and copper pans and strange towers of metal discs, but nothing was the same size as anything else. It looked as if she had stolen every piece of apparatus from a dozen other chemists, if not from the kitchens of Wellrest Manor. There was a chafing dish and several saucepans of varying dimensions, various wine bottles and vases for flowers, all slightly modified for their new uses. Two umbrella stands held herbs and coloured powders. In the few nooks and crannies where there was space, there were piles of books and papers and bundles of clothes. The centrepiece of the whole laboratory was a silver serving dish and upon it she had left half an apple and a piece of bread, both apparently gnawed by rodents.

Bede lit the last of the lamps and turned to rest against

a workbench. She folded her arms and seemed to wait for our appraisal.

'Oh, Bede,' I said. 'This is marvellous.'

'Thank you,' she said. 'I am rather proud of it.'

'You made all this yourself?'

She nodded. 'Piece by piece.'

'When? How?'

'I started after Mother died. And I have been making improvements ever since. Two years spent scavenging like a magpie. Mostly from rich men like Phineas when they give their demonstrations. They are usually so busy enjoying the adulation they do not notice when something goes missing.'

Pa went about the room silently, inspecting every piece of equipment. He stopped beside a particularly large vessel that looked like a copper bathtub.

'This,' he said. 'What is it?'

She turned to look.

'That is a bathtub.'

'What is it for?'

'It is where I take my baths.'

She seemed to think this was obvious, but it was a strange thing to have in a laboratory. I wondered if perhaps the question was not so foolish, nor the answer so straightforward.

The three of us stood some distance from each other — I next to the trapdoor, Bede at the centre of the room, Pa next to the copper tub. Mosca drifted around the ceiling, probing the cracks in the beams.

'Well, then,' Bede said. 'Here we all are. I have admitted

you to my inner sanctum. We are quite removed from the world and can speak our minds freely. Perhaps you would like to start by explaining why you have destroyed my most valuable heirloom?'

Pa coughed and caught his breath.

'I thought your most valuable heirloom was your mother's locket,' he said.

Bede's face darkened and it was terrifying to behold.

'You are not answering the question. Why did you burn my book?'

'It is not *your* book, strictly speaking.'

'And what, may I ask, do you mean by that?'

'It belonged to Herbert Wellrest.'

A slight smile crept on to Bede's face, though the darkness remained.

'How would you know such a thing?' she said.

'It is not so great a mystery, miss. His name is written on the first page.'

'In his own cipher, yes. I am surprised you could understand it.'

She eyed him curiously, but Pa did not reply. I watched him, too. I was as eager for answers as Bede was.

'You're right,' she said. 'It *did* belong to Herbert Wellrest. Once upon a time. But he died over two hundred years ago, so I think I am within my rights to claim it as my inheritance.'

'Where did you find it?'

'Is that important?'

'It might be.'

'It was in a fireplace, in the empty servants' quarters. Brittle and half-burnt, but still readable, for the most part.'

'I see,' said Pa. 'Then you must know that Herbert himself tried to destroy the book?'

'Somebody did. Not necessarily Herbert himself.'

'Well, then, I was only finishing what that person intended.'

'You still have not answered my question. Why would *you* burn it?'

'Because it was a record of abominable things,' said Pa, and in raising his voice he fell into another coughing fit. Bede watched him, somewhere between fury and concern. He wheezed for a moment and went on.

'Unnatural things. Experiments in alchemy and natural philosophy that should never have been performed. And God help you if you or Mr Mordaunt or anyone else has been using it as some kind of commonplace book for their own research.'

'How would you know? How would a gravedigger possibly understand the smallest fraction of what is written in the pages of that book?'

For the first time since I had known her, I felt the smallest pang of displeasure at the way that Bede was speaking. I had hoped that she, unlike every other villager, did not assume us to be dumb beasts. But in her anger the old prejudices seemed to rise to the surface.

Pa replied quite calmly.

'I know a good deal more than you about such things,' he said. He looked around the heaps of scientific apparatus.

'And there is much in this room that disturbs me, miss.'

There was silence in the windmill. The wind picked up and howled through the gaps in the old stones and set the laboratory shivering.

'Please, Pa,' I said. 'Bede is a physician. She revived you not more than an hour ago! Surely there is nothing disturbing in that?'

He continued to watch Bede.

'There is also the matter of the keys,' he said. 'I would not be surprised if Miss Wellrest were intending on opening the Nameless Grave herself.'

His face was quite serious. I looked at Bede and back to Pa, and laughed in complete disbelief.

'What a ridiculous thing to say, Pa! Why would she be interested in such a thing?'

But he was already limping across the floor towards the trapdoor, one hand on his hip, as if Bede might try and snatch the keys from him even as he was leaving.

'I have seen all I need to see,' he said. 'Come, Ned. The sooner we are gone from this wretched place the better.'

He started down the stairs. I looked at Bede but could not read her expression. When all I could see of him was the cap upon his head, Pa said again:

'Come, Ned.'

But I did not. He waited only a moment or two, and then he simply sniffed and nodded before he disappeared without asking a second time.

XXX

BEDE

'**A**re you?' said Ned.

'Am I what?'

'Intending to open the Nameless Grave.'

I turned and pretended to adjust a valve on one of the brass pipes. It was not just that I could not answer the question. I also could not bring myself to look upon his pale, clear-eyed, innocent face, which produced a quite intolerable and unhelpful feeling of compassion in me.

'Would it matter to you if I was?' I said.

'It would,' he said. 'One can't simply go around digging up bodies.'

I turned back to him.

'Please, Ned! Is that what you think me? A bodysnatcher? I would not be opening the grave to exhume its owner.'

'So you do wish to open it.'

His expression drew the truth out of me piecemeal. It was no great matter, I thought. He would have to know it all at some point.

'Yes,' I said, 'but there is nothing so macabre in it! I am interested only in his research. I have every reason to believe that there are secrets buried in Herbert Wellrest's grave that he did not include in his diary.'

'Herbert Wellrest? Your ancestor? The Nameless Grave is his?'

'I am quite sure.'

'And the book belongs to him, too?'

'Yes. I could not have achieved half of this' – I gestured around the laboratory – 'without the help of his notes. But, like I say, there is something missing. Something crucial. I believe it to be concealed beneath the mortsafe. So if you will excuse me, I would like to continue this conversation with your grandfather.'

I crossed the floor to the trapdoor. Ned wrung his hands and his thick eyebrows came together, as if in secret conversation with each other.

'What Pa said. About Herbert Wellrest's work. About unnatural things. Is it true?'

I stopped with one foot on the top step.

'No,' I said.

'Then what exactly are you trying to do?'

I spoke carefully, but also quickly – the old man had left the windmill and was probably halfway down the hill by now, still holding on to the keys.

'What is natural and unnatural is very much a matter of perspective, Ned. People talk about nature as if she is quite beyond our understanding – a goddess, sacrosanct, inviolable – but that could not be further from the truth. Nature is a mechanism, like a very complex pocket watch, and with enough probing and tinkering we can solve a great number of problems that we always assumed were simply part of our lot as humans. Injury and disease and death. These are not unavoidable, Ned. Herbert Wellrest knew this. I simply wish to follow in his footsteps.'

'So,' he said. 'You *are* a physician.'

'Physician! Pah! You should have seen the men who attended on my mother, when the cholera took her. Quite, quite useless. Convinced her death was somehow written into the fabric of nature. That it was simply her fate. Or worse still, that it was God's plan for her. I could not believe how easily they gave her up to oblivion! They barely tried to save her! That was when I decided to begin my studies in earnest. To improve the odds, as it were, in our game with Death.'

The knots in Ned's brow seemed as tight as ever. He was quiet for a moment.

'What about Mr Mordaunt?' he said.

'Phineas? What about him?'

'Is he trying to do the same thing?'

I had not been expecting the question. I still needed to catch up with the old man, but again, I could not leave without setting the record straight.

'No. Phineas and I are in no way alike. Not in our methods, not in our motivations. I am trying to *help* people with my research. People like my mother. People who are taken much too soon. Phineas is simply vainglorious. He does nothing that is not designed to improve his fame and his reputation. And, to be quite honest, he doesn't understand the most basic principles of chemistry. He is sloppy. And he is stupid. And we should be thankful that he has neither the diary nor the keys to Herbert's grave.'

I set off down the stairs but Ned called after me one last time.

'But why?' he said. His head loomed above me in the square of daylight. 'What is he trying to do?'

There was an explosion of barking from outside the windmill. I met Ned's eyes and then turned and rushed out into the clearing.

Ned's grandfather was backing up towards the windmill door and two enormous hounds were hectoring him. I knew them well. I had known them for years. They were old now, and grey around the muzzle, but I had fond memories of trying to ride one of them when we were all a good deal younger. Somebody whistled to them from the woods and the pair of them stood to attention, quivering, looking back into the trees. I heard Ned coming down the stairs behind me, but I continued to look in the same direction as the dogs, their noses pointing towards my inevitable destruction.

Phineas stepped out into the daylight, squinting, a duelling pistol in one hand. There was more rustling in the undergrowth behind him and a moment or two later came Mr and Mrs Gilly. Both of their expressions showed the same mixture of confusion and shame.

'Back from the dead, my love?' He laughed. 'It would seem your research is rather more advanced than mine, after all!'

For once, I did not know what to say, and this only gave him permission to laugh harder. Mr Gilly whistled again and the dogs came to his side. They belonged to his brother, I believe. He had brought them on every one of my father's pheasant shoots, and when the hunt was done Mother used to let me play with them in the kitchens.' No wonder they were so accustomed to my smell.

With the dogs subdued, Ned's grandfather got to his feet and stood behind me alongside Ned. The six of us faced each other in the cold shadow of the windmill.

'What are you doing here, Obedience?' Phineas said. 'Have you not heard the rumours that this place is haunted?' He paused. 'Or was it you who started the rumours in the first place.'

'We were sheltering from the rain,' I said. 'That is all.'

'I see. And while you were sheltering, I wonder, did you meet the other resident?'

This wrong-footed me a little.

'What other resident?'

'The gentleman who lives here.'

I swallowed. I could hear Ned and his grandfather shifting in their boots behind me.

'I do not understand your meaning. There is no gentleman. It is a ruin.'

Phineas made a theatrical frown.

'How strange. You see, I have been speaking to Mr and Mrs Gilly here – or rather, they were speaking to each other on the night of my arrival at Wellrest Manor, and I happened to overhear. They did not realize that I keep the same antisocial hours that they do, and there are many secrets whispered in dark passageways after midnight.'

He smiled genially at the two servants and they averted their eyes.

'On further questioning they told me that, given the atrocious wages paid by your father, they were forced to accept work on behalf of a gentleman who lives in this very ruin. A rather *grisly* kind of work. This gentleman – though, I hardly think he deserves the title – sends them unsigned letters, with requests for human remains. If you can believe it! Requests for this kind of body, or that kind, to be brought here and left on the bottom floor, just inside. He requests other items, too, sometimes. A ring of keys from inside the sexton's house, for example.'

Ned suddenly interjected. 'That's not true! She gave the keys to you! I saw it!'

'Only because I was curious about this other gentleman,' Phineas said, without even bothering to look in Ned's direction. 'And because I paid a good deal more for them. It seems their employer can hardly be a man of means, because his wages are quite extraordinarily low! And, curiously, he leaves the paltry sum here for them to collect, rather than handing them the money in person. In fact, they say they have never met the man!'

I looked at Ned, who seemed so indignant on my behalf – something else I did not deserve. I turned back to Phineas and tried very hard to sound unconcerned.

'If this is true,' I said, 'then I am very disappointed in Mr and Mrs Gilly for agreeing to such work. Had I known that members of my household were engaged in such activity, I would have made sure to put a stop to it.'

'Of course, you *must* be disappointed,' said Phineas, and I could tell he was warming to something. 'Especially when you have spoken to me in such glowing terms of their – loyalty.' He made his exaggerated frown again. 'But then, it does surprise me that you did *not* know such a thing was happening. It was under your very nose, Obedience. I discovered one of the gentleman's letters, addressed to Mr and Mrs Gilly, tucked inside one of your scientific journals.'

All the blood seemed to drain from my head, as if somebody had removed a plug at the base of my skull. I felt suddenly faint. I remembered the contents very well. They urged Mr and Mrs Gilly to range a little further afield in their night-time expeditions. In all the confusion of Phineas' arrival I had forgotten to deliver it to them. Foolish, foolish girl!

'How did it get there, I wonder?' said Phineas. 'And why was the gentleman's handwriting so curiously similar to your own?'

Ned spoke quietly behind me.

'Bede? What is he talking about?'

'Yes, *Bede*,' said Phineas, and he positively spat the name. 'Is it not baffling? Well, we are here, now. So perhaps we can go inside and ask the gentleman himself for some answers.'

He raised his duelling pistol and gestured towards the door of the laboratory.

'You do not need your weapon, Phineas,' I said.

'Oh, I'm not so sure about that,' he said. 'He seems a decidedly dangerous fellow.'

XXXI

BEDE

I have ever been proud of my ability to solve problems. Mother always said she could hear the gears and pistons working inside my head when I was thinking hard. I remember reading of Mr Babbage's 'Difference Engine' in the papers of the Royal Astronomical Society, seeing his diagrams and thinking: 'That is me. He has opened up my skull and sketched what he found inside.'

For the first time in my life, my thinking machine failed me. I could not calculate quickly enough to keep up with my own lies. Every person assembled at the foot of the windmill had been told something different. I wondered if there was a lie big enough to contain and conceal all the others. If there was, I did not think I could conceive it; I certainly could not with a pistol in my face.

It was a tight fit for all of us in the laboratory. Mr and Mrs Gilly were forced to wait on the stairs. I wondered why they had come at all — perhaps Phineas was paying them, or, more likely, blackmailing them with knowledge of their shifts in the graveyard.

Phineas took a few moments to survey my equipment and began laughing. It was so loud and mocking I feared it might shake the stones of the windmill apart.

'Good God!' he said. 'Obedience . . . Where did you find all of this trash?'

He could barely get the words out of his mouth. He snorted in between gales of laughter and the air whistled wetly around the edges of his prosthetic nose. I could have killed him there and then. I might have pinned him to the floor and attached him to a voltaic pile and watched as his skin crisped and his hair caught fire.

'I do not know what to think,' he said, wiping one eye. 'Perhaps I have overestimated you after all. This looks as if it was put together by a child.'

I waited for him to compose himself. The ruse of the other 'gentleman' was clearly beyond sustaining, so I did not bother trying. I looked again at Ned. His face was so serious, his eyes so demanding of answers, I could not find my words.

'Unlike you, Phineas,' I said, 'I cannot simply rely upon my inheritance to purchase my apparatus.' I paused. 'Besides, my research has advanced beyond conventional pieces of equipment. I have had to design and build many of my own.'

'And were you drunk when you built them? This looks like the stuff of a lunatic's dream!'

He tapped an ale jug and ran a finger around the inside.

'I assume this is where you made your poison? A very neat trick. Even I was convinced for a few hours. But you rather gave yourself away with all that noise in the stables.'

I felt idiotic again. So much preparation, undone by a couple of thoughtless mistakes.

He continued with his survey of the laboratory. His eyes lighted on a few nosegays I had hung from the ceiling.

'To purge the foul vapours, I suppose?'

I did not answer. I knew what he might ask next. His eyes followed the strings of the nosegays up to the top level of the windmill. On the opposite side of the room to the first trapdoor was a second, and a ladder leant against the wall. My heart hurled itself into my ribs.

'And where do you keep the materials?'

'There is nothing upstairs, if that is what you mean,' I said. 'It is too unsafe.'

'I appreciate your concern.'

He crossed the room anyway, squeezing clumsily between the towers of glassware, tubs of electrolytes, galvanic cells, all of them swaying and shuddering. He pulled out a wooden box and stood upon it and with a couple of shoves opened the other trapdoor.

'I am quite serious, Phineas,' I said. 'As much as I am averse to keeping you safe from harm, that floor is structurally unsound.'

He just looked at me and smiled and propped the ladder up against the open hatch. He climbed a few steps with a spirit lamp in one hand and stuck his head up into the darkness for a moment or two. He paused and his voice echoed dully around the floor above.

'Yes,' he said. 'As I thought.'

When he came back down the ladder he brought the smell with him. I was fairly well accustomed to it, but I had not been up to the top of the mill for many days and it made even my eyes water. I could see the others wrinkling their noses. Of course it did not bother Phineas in the slightest, given that he had no organ for detecting it.

'Well?' he said. 'Are you going to show all of us your results? Why, old Herbert's dream must be so tantalizingly close! I know you have his diary. I presume you have opened his grave. Are you not simply *gasping* to reveal your discoveries?'

'I do not—'

'You do not know what I mean, yes, yes. This is all getting rather tedious, Obedience. There is no need to protest your innocence. Everybody here knows exactly what you have been doing.'

He looked over at Ned and his grandfather and the servants. They seemed baffled, and not a little frightened. Ned in particular. I needed more time, that was all – I was sure he would understand, if I could find the right words.

'Oh, good grief!' said Phineas. 'You mean to say you have been asking all of these poor, honest people to do your dirty work, and you have not even told them your *purpose*?'

Nobody spoke. Poor Ned seemed on the brink of tears.

'Very well, then,' he went on. 'To be plain – Miss Wellrest here has been conducting her research at the very frontiers of scientific discovery. You might even say she has *crossed* those frontiers. Gone *beyond the veil*, as it were. What I mean to say is that she has been searching for the very seed of life itself. As have I. As was dear old Uncle Herbert. All of us hoping to find that vital spark, the animating spirit of the flesh. In short: Obedience is in the business of raising the dead.'

Mr and Mrs Gilly only looked more confused, as if they thought Phineas might be playing an elaborate joke on them. The old man was watching Phineas very intensely. But Ned was watching me. His lips were half-parted, on the brink of saying something.

'So, then,' Phineas said, 'would you like to show us your findings so far? I know you are keeping a few specimens upstairs, but I think it would be fascinating to see how all this equipment works. Yes, that's right, Mrs Gilly! Two scientific demonstrations in one week! You lucky thing!'

I heard the glee in his voice and flared up white and hot as phosphorus.

'Now listen, you whey-faced, bird-witted—'

I advanced on him but he threw me back and I hit my head hard on the edge of the workbench. There was a ringing in my ears and a tinkling of glassware. I blinked and tried to focus. Phineas raised his duelling pistol once more and waved it vaguely at the four people in front of him.

'Obviously, to stand *any* chance of success the body we use will have to be a fresh one. Who would like to offer themselves up in the name of scientific progress?'

I tried to get up and then slumped over. I could feel my pulse behind my eyes. I tried to protest but only an inarticulate groan left my lips.

'Don't worry, Obedience,' Phineas said. 'I will choose

the one who will be missed the least. I am not a cynical man, but just *in case* the experiment is unsuccessful . . .'

And it seemed the decision was made. His arm stopped wavering and he pulled back the pistol's hammer with his thumb and shot the old man through the heart.

XXXII

NED

I remember the sound more than anything else. Not of the gunshot, which was so loud and so violent I felt more than heard it. I mean the sound of the bullet as it punctured his several shirts and entered his flesh and lodged somewhere on the other side of his breastbone. A muted, slightly wet thump, like a blunt knife on a butcher's block. A sound that I thought, even at the time, had no place in the world.

I saw one of Pa's buttons fly quite slowly through the air and then he staggered backwards between the two servants and slumped against the wall. The hole in his chest was very black, as if it went deeper than it should have. He sat there with his eyes half-open, and the wound seemed to grow as the blood left his heart and darkened his clothes.

How long I stood and watched him I could not say. I hardly understood what had happened. I had read about firearms and I knew what they did but had never seen one used in real life. The cramped space of the laboratory was filled with bluish gun smoke which obscured everybody's faces and gave the whole scene the vagueness of a dream.

I cried out into the fumes – perhaps it was his name, perhaps it was not any intelligible sound – and when he did not respond I ran to him. I crouched beside him and put my hand to his chest. It seemed too cold and sticky for a wound so fresh.

'Don't worry, Pa,' I said. 'You must not worry.'

His breath left him in one long, strained whistle.

'Don't try to move. Please. You'll be quite all right.'

He did not reply.

'Don't leave me, Pa. You can't leave. I'm not ready. I can't look after the graveyard by myself.'

I felt between his glove and his sleeve for a pulse. The skin was hard and flaky and there was no warmth there at all.

'Please, Pa.' I begged him, now. 'Hold on. Just a moment. Bede can help you. She is a physician.'

Phineas scoffed behind me.

'She is rather more than that.'

I held Pa in my arms and rocked him as if he were a child. His eyes fluttered slightly, as if to suggest there was life in him yet, but there was no breath and no heartbeat and the hole in his chest only seemed to gape wider and uglier. I looked about me for Mosca, as if he might offer some reassurance, or at least companionship, but he had long since disappeared through the cracks in the ceiling and had not returned. I could not have felt more alone in the world.

'Right then,' said Phineas. 'What comes first, Obedience? We throw the corpse into this, I presume?'

He struck the side of the copper bath with his fingers and it rang out like a bell. Unconcerned. Business-like. Excited, even. The smoke from the pistol cleared and I saw the faint smile on his face and I launched myself across the laboratory.

I clawed and flailed at him, glad for my bony knees and sharp elbows. I could barely see him for tears. I howled like a wild animal and he seemed to find this funny even as he fended off the blows, arms raised to protect his face and his nose above all else. I heard him laugh and snort and at that I only grew wilder.

He got hold of my slim wrists, impatient, now, and we made an ungainly dance around the centre of the laboratory. I caught sight of Bede, her hand at the back of her neck, fingers glistening and ruby-red. Her blood looked nothing like my grandfather's.

'Mr Gilly!' shouted Phineas. 'Would you mind removing this wretch?'

There was a short pause while Mr and Mrs Gilly seemed to share another unspoken word, and then the man came forward and wrapped his huge ape-arms around me. I felt like a barrel bound in hoops of iron. He hefted me up into the air without difficulty and said, very quietly, into one ear:

'I am sorry, lad.'

Phineas rearranged his jacket and ran a clean, pink hand through his hair.

'I don't know why you are so upset,' he said. 'Surely you trust Miss Wellrest's methods?'

Bede's head lolled backwards.

'You are a monster, Phineas,' she said.

He laughed again.

'I think you protest too much, Obedience. I am not the monster here. I have seen what is through that trapdoor.' He pointed to the ceiling and said: 'Put him up there with the others, Mr Gilly. It is a shame you will miss the demonstration, young man. I am sure it will be most illuminating.'

The ape flung me over one shoulder like a sack of flour and I watched Pa's lifeless body recede with each unsteady footstep. He manoeuvred around the equipment to the ladder that disappeared up into the top level of the windmill. What *had* Phineas seen up there? And who were the others? The thoughts flitted vaguely and insubstantially and then my grief returned and quite eclipsed them all.

Bede called out to me.

'Ned,' she said. 'Remember what I said. About my mother. And my work. Please do not think ill of me.'

I did not know what she meant.

Mr Gilly lugged me up the ladder, one rung at a time. I heard a strange droning from above, a sound like Mosca's wings multiplied many times over. Mosca himself, I suddenly realized, was nowhere to be seen.

The ape hefted me through the trapdoor and into the humming darkness. He let go of me and I scrambled away into the corner. He muttered something and, I thought, made the sign of the cross over his heart. Then he pulled the trapdoor closed and there was the snap of a bolt and the sound of his feet on the ladder.

The ceiling on this level of the windmill was very low,

sloping downwards from the centre until it was only a couple of feet above the floor at the edges. I curled up under a beam, face to the wall – cramped spaces have always been a comfort to me. I lay there and thought of Pa and of home, and I cried until I was exhausted and my eyes were swollen and the room was even less distinct than it had been before.

When I had calmed myself a little, or, at least, worn myself out, I dried my eyes and had a proper look at my prison. There were a few slivers of daylight falling between the timbers of the roof, but it was not bright enough to see by. All I noticed was the occasional disturbance against the cracks, like large motes of dust. And there was the noise, of course. That familiar buzzing.

I called out to it.

'Mosca?'

I still had him, at least, even if Pa and Bede and everything else was lost to me.

'Mosca, is that you?'

A pair of flies came cavorting out of the darkness and landed upon my thumb. I held my hand to the crack in the roof. Neither of them was Mosca. Mosca was a bluebottle, *Calliphora vomitoria*. These two were *Sarcophagidae*. Flesh flies.

I shooed them away and looked down at the floor until my eyes grew accustomed to the darkness. Shapes and edges made themselves clearer. In the centre of the room much of the mill's mechanism remained, though the cogs and axles were mostly charcoal. I crawled forward on my hands and knees. The flies came at me in their dozens, now. In clouds.

Curious at first, and then disappointed when they discovered I was not a thing they could eat – at least, not yet. There was the abominable smell of things rotting, too. The kind of smell that, if you caught it on the air in the graveyard, meant you had not done your job properly.

On the other side of the mechanism a shaft of daylight fell upon two feet. They were grey and withered, not unlike what I had seen under Pa's boot. The toes of one of the feet clenched and unclenched. Whilst they were still, the flies clustered upon and between them. Then they would twitch again and the swarm would disperse irritably.

I sat quite still. I had the sensation of cold water dripping on the back of my neck.

'Hello?' I said.

I shuffled closer and the rest of the body came into view, limb by limb. I recognized it immediately. It was Robert Garrick, the man whose grave had been disturbed the night before my birthday. He was lying on top of a grubby shroud. As well as his feet, one of his hands was also moving. His fingers tapped lightly on the floorboards as if he were playing the piano.

I crawled up to his head. In each of his sockets was a yellow, shrivelled grape that had once been an eye.

'Master Garrick?' I said.

Was there a quiver in those eyes? Or had I imagined it? Whatever impulse was in him, he did not respond and I did not call his name again. He seemed neither alive nor dead. I recalled the monstrous chicken in Phineas' laboratory.

I scrambled away from him, into another body, laid face

down on a sheet. I did not care to know who it was, though doubtless I had been present at his or her burial, too. Next to it was a low table on which were placed several surgical instruments and parts of a third resident: a hand, severed at the wrist; a blackened heart; a head, whose features faced away from me and whose long grey hair spilt almost to the floor.

'I'm sorry,' I said, though I knew they could not hear me. I *hoped* they could not, because that was better than the alternative. 'I'm sorry, I'm sorry, I'm sorry,' and I backed away and shut my eyes, not wanting to see anything at all, and when I had reached the far side of the room I tucked myself under a broken axle and wept afresh.

XXXIII

BEDE

Phineas instructed Mr and Mrs Gilly to deposit the sexton's body in the bathtub. He behaved as if he already knew every step of the process. One of them took his feet and the other his armpits and they bundled him in like a sack of old bones.

'Now then,' said Phineas, 'presumably we fill this vessel with electrolytes? And then we shall need to create the requisite electrical charge . . . We must undress him, too, I suppose. Perhaps you, Mr Gilly, would oblige.'

Mr Gilly looked unhappy at the suggestion.

I had nothing to say to Phineas. Even if I had been willing to show him the whole procedure, I was not thinking straight. My head was still throbbing and there was a purple shadow waxing and waning at the edge of my vision. I thought I could hear sobbing coming from the floor above.

'Miss Wellrest? As much as it pains me, I will admit that you are the authority here. You have the diary. You know Herbert's secrets. You will have to tell us where to begin.'

I ignored him and staggered to the opposite bench, where there was muslin and iodine and I set about tending to my injury. Phineas marched over and grabbed my elbow.

'Excuse me, Obedience, but you are well past the point of pretending ignorance, now. Tell me—'

I hissed at him through gritted teeth, more from the stinging pain of the disinfectant than anything else, but it was enough to make him shrink back a little.

'I am not pretending anything any more, Phineas. I do not know how to revive the dead. Nor do I want to. That has *never* been my intention. I seek only to prolong life. To preserve it. To defend it against disease and injury and old age—'

'Then how do you account for the poor fellow upstairs?'

How *did* I account for him? An unfortunate accident, I suppose. That was how I had justified it to myself. If I was to discover a way of prolonging life, I had to understand what life *itself* was – that intangible thing that made the difference between dead flesh and a living being. I had explored that frontier with chemicals, with electricity, with the scalpel. In doing so I had found myself burdened with something that was neither Mr Garrick, nor his body. Even if reanimation had never been the intention, it had been the result, and I thought of it with nothing but shame.

I wound the muslin several times around my skull and tied it tightly at my forehead. Eventually I said: 'I can hardly be expected to understand the human frame without studying it, can I?'

'And your study of the diary? Your attempts to find

Herbert's grave? What about that? You are not fooling any-body, Obedience. You know what Herbert was trying to do. Everybody does. It is everyone's favourite ghost story, round here. It was what got him killed in the first place.'

There was a soft *clang* from inside the bathtub. I looked over Phineas' shoulder.

'Your silence will not excuse you any more,' he said. 'Show me what you know. Show me what you can do.' He came a little closer. 'I still intend to work *with* you, Obedi-ence. That has always been my intention.'

I pointed at the tub. He turned. Mr and Mrs Gilly were watching it too, their expressions equal parts horror, sur-prise, relief. A hand in a moth-eaten woollen glove gripped the rim, then another on the opposite side, and the sexton drew a long rasping breath, so long it seemed his old lungs would not contain it, and suddenly he was sitting upright and the air was leaving him again.

Nobody spoke, not even Phineas. The old man's breath-ing settled and he looked around the inside of the windmill and when his eyes came to rest on us, one and then the other, they showed an ancient and stone-hard sadness.

'Still here, then,' he said.

Phineas turned to me. 'I do not understand.'

'Nor I,' I said.

'Is this your doing?'

I shook my head. He gave an uncertain smile. He did not believe me.

'By God,' he said. 'You have done it. You have *actually* done it!'

'Done what? I swear, Phineas, I am as surprised as you are.'

Phineas looked from me to the sexton and back to me.

'This creature is not the result of your experiments?'

'Of course not! This man has been the sexton in the village for decades! How could he be?'

'If you are lying to me—'

'She is not lying, sir,' said the old man. He coughed and coughed and we waited and waited, all four of us, to see what he might say next. He composed himself and dabbed at the fluid on his chin and then climbed out of the tub and stood inspecting his gloves. The hole in his chest was big enough to fit a fist into.

'Well?' snapped Phineas. 'Explain yourself! How are you alive and breathing? Did she make you?'

'She did not make me, no,' said the sexton. 'Herbert Wellrest did.'

There was a longer, deeper silence. Phineas took a couple of tentative steps towards him. He scrutinized the ruin of the sexton's chest. He put a finger in the wound that he himself had made. It made no sense; and yet, to look at him now, it made perfect sense. Ned's grandfather had always had the complexion of a corpse. And it was no wonder he had sounded so ill all this time. He had been at death's door for years, hovering on the threshold, unable to enter or to go back.

'This is . . .' Phineas looked at the rest of us, lost for words. Mrs Gilly was muttering prayers. 'This is *extraordinary*. May I ask how old you are?'

'I do not recall.'

'But did you *know* Herbert Wellrest? Do you know how you came to be what you are?'

The sexton paused and frowned.

'Where is my grandson?' he asked.

Phineas did not answer him. He walked in a slow circle around the man and said: 'Remove your hat.'

'I would rather not,' said the old man.

'Do it. Let us have a good look at you.'

'I will not, sir.'

'Why?'

'Because I am ashamed.'

Phineas found this funny.

'Ashamed?'

'I do not look like other men.' He paused and then corrected himself. 'Like living men, I mean.'

'That is precisely why we would all like to see you. Hat, gloves, shirt. Off with them.'

'Where is the boy?' the sexton asked again.

'Upstairs. Where he cannot cause trouble.'

'Please release him. I need to see him. To talk to him.'

'And have him running amuck? Now my own laboratory is in pieces, we hardly want this one ruined as well. No. Let him have some time to himself.'

The sexton looked around the equipment.

'Destroying everything might be a good start,' he said.

'And why do you say that?'

'Because, to answer your earlier question, I *did* know Herbert. I knew him very well. And I witnessed every

– 263 –

horror that he committed.'

'You were his student? His apprentice? What?'

'His confidant, you might say. Which was, in fact, the very reason I became a sexton. Once he was gone and his work came to an end, I made it my sole purpose in life to ensure that his crimes were never repeated.'

'If I understand you correctly,' said Phineas, 'are you saying that you are familiar with Herbert's work? That you have seen all this apparatus before?'

'I have. Though, I should say, there are some faults with its construction.'

Phineas crowed.

'Aha! I was *sure* that there were errors here. Yes. Quite certain Miss Wellrest could not be trusted to follow instructions.' He put a finger to his lips, as if considering some new plan. 'I wonder if, in light of all this, you might consider making a deal. This evening I am planning on delivering another presentation to some important gentlemen from the university. It was due to be rather more theoretical than practical, after my equipment was destroyed – but now I have the chance to show them something far more impressive. So, if you would be so kind as to help me with it, then I shall release your boy. And perhaps consider releasing the pair of you. Eventually.'

The old man – impossibly old, I realized, now – looked at me as if to communicate something without words. I did not catch his meaning. In the midst of everything I felt a sharp sting at the suggestion I did not know what I was doing. But I will also admit that I was as intrigued as

Phineas, and quite prepared to learn from someone who had not only seen Herbert's work but had been subjected to it.

He turned back to Phineas, who was looking at him expectantly. He sighed and said: 'Very well.'

Phineas clapped his hands.

'Good. In that case, Mr Gilly, would you mind making your way back to the manor? The scholars from the university will be assembling there later this afternoon. I wonder if you could tell them about the change of plan. We will need the Mordaunt cell, also, and a good deal more candlelight.'

'What is the change of plan, sir?'

'The change of location. Please bring them to the mill. I am sure they would like to bear witness to the extraordinary work that has been going on here. And to meet the genius behind it.'

I did not need to ask who he meant by this.

XXXIV

NED

I was still curled up and facing the wall when Mosca found me. I did not know how many hours it had been. A thousand more could have passed but I swore that I would not turn around. The sound of the flies was incessant, though from time to time it would quieten a little and I would hear the light, irregular tapping of Robert Garrick's fingers on the floorboards and I would clap my hands over my ears once more.

When I was sure the noise and the darkness was about to drive me quite mad, one of the flies landed on the back of my hand and tried to force its way between my knuckles. I knew who it was from the patter of its feet.

'Mosca!'

I spread my fingers and let him into my earhole.

'Have you been here all this time?'

With my ears uncovered I could hear there was a lot of talking going on downstairs. It was muffled and indistinct and I almost convinced myself that I could hear Pa's voice, though I knew it was only the memory of it.

'What are they talking about?' I said to Mosca. He buzzed quietly, three times, in quick succession. 'I need to get out of here. I need to get to Pa. If they do anything to him, and he ends up like . . .'

I put my hands over my face. I did not want to look at Master Garrick, or the others, even in my mind's eye.

Mosca left again as quickly as he had arrived. He returned, and left, returned again, as if asking me to follow.

'If you are asking me to look at what Bede has done, I will not! I have already seen it.'

He would not stop, back and forth, back and forth. Eventually I gave in and followed him around the circumference of the windmill. On the opposite side to the trapdoor he led me directly into a beam at head height. I collided with it and the darkness exploded with colours.

'That's not funny, Mosca,' I said. 'Will you not take things seriously for once?'

I sat and rubbed my head. The beam had once been the axle for the windmill's sails, I thought. I felt it with one hand and found the intense heat of the fire had split it down the middle. I heard Mosca buzzing where the axle met the wall and when I found him I noticed a draught from outside. The wood here was as charred as everything else and came away in flakes in my hand, and then, as I picked at it, in a single large chunk. A gust of cool air blew into the room and the other flies scattered.

'Is this your plan?' I said. 'Are you trying to get me killed as well as Pa?'

He was silent. And then, as if to prove his point, he disappeared out of the hole I had made and out into the fading daylight.

I sat and thought. I would have to escape somehow or other. I wanted to be with Pa, and to see him put to rest. I also needed to find a way of getting to Oxford and bringing the monstrous Mr Mordaunt to justice.

And Bede?

I did not know what to think about Bede. Love is not easily unseated from the heart, but can become so tainted that you wish it would be. I wanted to talk to her, at least. I hoped there had been some misunderstanding, though the evidence seemed clear enough from where I sat.

I looked at the hole I had made in the windmill's frame. The trapdoor was still locked. There was no way out other than via the sails, it seemed. I only hoped that, even in their ruined state, they would take the weight of somebody as skinny and underfed as me.

By the time it was dark outside the hole was large enough for me to fit my arm through and my fingertips were raw and blackened from my efforts. I knew I would need tools if I was to make it any larger. I felt my way back along the beam to the centre of the room and into the swarms of flies. I heard Master Garrick, incessantly tapping his fingers and cracking the knuckles of his toes. I closed my eyes and felt for the edge of the workbench. My fingertips found the heart, cold and wet and leathery, and I gasped and withdrew my hand as if I had been burnt on a stove. I reached out again, slowly, fearfully, until I found Bede's surgical implements. In amongst them was a small bone saw. I took this and returned to my work.

After a good deal of effort I made a gap in the burnt timbers large enough for me to squirm through. I poked my head out into the night and breathed deeply. The air was sweet and cool and smelt of rain. I could have wept with the relief of it, after so long in the stifling darkness. Overhead the first of the stars blazed coldly, and below, in a strange mirror image, I saw a collection of small yellow pricks of light, bobbing out of the woods and towards the door of the windmill.

'Who's that, then?' I said to Mosca.

I shuffled out a little towards the broken sails, clinging to the cross-beam like a sailor to a shipwreck. The wind picked up and nearly took my hat with it. Directly below I saw a handful of wigged and well-dressed gentlemen who had no place out here in the wilderness. Among their grey-haired heads I saw Mr Gilly's shining scalp.

The breeze carried their voices up to me. They seemed to be complaining a very great deal.

'This is perfectly ridiculous!' said one. 'Does he mean to make fools of us?'

'It does not look entirely safe,' said another.

'*He* is not entirely safe.'

There was general laughter.

'He has also not provided us with a dinner,' said the first man. 'Can you imagine? It is past eight o'clock in the evening and I have eaten not a morsel since lunchtime!'

A third chipped in:

'I have heard reports from my colleagues at the Royal Institution that the man is quite talented . . .'

'Nonsense! You saw what he presented at the university at Christmas. Any schoolboy could have produced that demonstration.'

'Let us at least indulge the man,' said the second voice. 'His donations to the university have been most generous. They may be more generous still if we allow him his little . . . performances.'

'I am not sure *any* financial inducement is worth this.'

Then everybody spoke at once. They all sounded alike – each as old and severe and irascible as the others. Mr Gilly attempted to appease them.

'Mr Mordaunt sends his deepest apologies, sirs,' he said. 'But there's things goin' on in this laboratory that he thinks will be worth the trouble.' He paused. 'I seen 'em too, an' if I may say, I think it's worth your while, an' all. Though, I do not think you will be wantin' dinner once you've seen it.'

That was true enough, I thought. The gentlemen conversed among themselves and grudgingly agreed to go inside.

'Perfectly ridiculous,' the first man said again.

When there was nobody beneath me I considered my route down. The least damaged of the windmill's sails was at a forty-five-degree angle to the ground. Its structure was not unlike the rose trellis I had climbed to escape the manor house – a lattice of scorched wood – and I hoped I could climb to the tip of the sail and then simply drop the last few feet to earth.

I touched the frame and a few blackened flakes came away on my fingers.

'Are you *quite* sure about this?' I said to Mosca.

He landed on the sail and began to scuttle up and down it, as if this proved it was safe.

'I am a *little* heavier than you . . .' I said.

He flew to the end and waited for me.

I climbed around to the front of the frame. It creaked slightly but took my weight. It was nothing like climbing up to Bede's bedroom, or into the ballroom – there the house had shielded me from the elements, but the top of the windmill was completely exposed. The wind gusted again and I tensed and clung to the frame like the last leaf of autumn.

I climbed down, inch by brittle inch. The further down the sail I climbed, the more the structure groaned. Just past halfway, and still high enough above the ground to break my back if I fell, the whole thing began to turn. I could hear the gears turning with a gritty, resistant sound. I could climb neither up nor down, and I gripped the frame with all my might, and the sail accelerated in its arc. The ground passed me by and I was left completely upside down with all the blood rushing to my head.

I was dimly aware of voices coming from Bede's laboratory, and then, as quickly as it had started, the sail came to an abrupt halt. A broken cog, or something jammed in the mechanism. I did not know. The sail jerked, quivered, and there followed a sound like a tree being felled. The thickest beam began to split, and then broke off entirely, and the sail and Mosca and I went crashing into the brambles around the base of the windmill.

XXXV

NED

I lay there for some time with the wind knocked out of me, stars both real and imagined circling overhead. There was a commotion inside the windmill, then the sound of many feet on the wooden stairs, followed by the voices of the old men gathering at the open door.

'Mr Mordaunt,' said one, 'we have already suffered the discomfort of travelling to this deserted and godforsaken place. Would you now bring it down upon our heads?'

'Forgive me, gentlemen,' said Phineas. 'I assure you that the structure is *quite* sound. Inside, at least.'

I heard somebody pick up a piece of the sail and toss it into the weeds near my head. I held my breath. It seemed that I was invisible to them, wrapped in brambles and darkness.

There was a lot of grumbling and sniffing.

'I do not understand why you could not have held this demonstration in the comfort of the manor house,' somebody said.

'Or, indeed, the comfort of the university!' said another.

There was loud agreement about this. When Phineas spoke I could hear the faintest air of desperation.

'I assure you, professors,' he said. 'When you see the results of my work you will understand my need for total secrecy!'

Results? Had they, then, already performed some experiment or other upon Pa? Was he alive or dead? Or neither, like poor Master Garrick . . .

'Please, gentlemen, return to the laboratory,' said Phineas. 'I am keen not to try your patience any longer.'

Though, to me, it sounded as if *he* was the one who was impatient.

The men grudgingly went back inside. I extricated myself from the tangle of briars with some difficulty and bent my arms and legs experimentally. Everything seemed in working order, if a little bruised. I crept to the door of the windmill. Victor was still tethered outside, and I patted his nose for good luck and went in.

Overhead there was the sound of coughing and scuffing feet and more unhappy remarks about missed suppers and the unsanitary conditions of the laboratory. I stole silently up the first set of stairs and put my head through the trap-door just a few inches. The group of serious gentlemen – seven of them – were standing with their backs to me. The most elderly of them had been given one of the stools and the rest shifted uncomfortably on their feet. Mr and Mrs Gilly were skulking in the shadows to one side.

The laboratory was ablaze with lamplight. Phineas was

standing before the men making little adjustments to the mass of apparatus, which looked different to how I remembered it. Some of the tubs and bottles had been moved around and there were more of those strange towers of metal discs. And next to Phineas, the strangest thing: somebody was sitting on a chair under a large, dirty canvas sheet, their head slightly bowed. It could not have been Mr or Mrs Gilly. It could not have been Pa, either, because Pa was dead and whoever was under the sheet was breathing steadily, their shoulders rising and falling in time. It must have been Bede.

Phineas turned and neatened his waistcoat and began to address the visitors.

'I must thank you for your patience, gentlemen, and apologize, again, for the discomfort of our surroundings.'

There was further agreement on this point.

'Though, I should add, when I finally present to you my discoveries you will think a cold nose and sore feet a small price to pay!'

He tried to laugh but nobody seemed to find him funny.

'How much of this preamble must we endure?' said one of the old men. 'We have come to witness scientific endeavour, not a night at the theatre.'

'Yes, yes, of course,' said Phineas, quickly. 'I only wish to prepare you for the *magnitude* of what I am about to reveal.'

I had never seen him so flustered. Whoever these men were, all his swagger and composure had quite evaporated under their stern gaze. There was some satisfaction in seeing that.

'He means to show us another electrified worm,' somebody said. 'Only, a larger one.'

They all *did* laugh at that. Phineas looked irritable. His smile quivered with the effort of maintaining it.

'I realize,' he said, 'that you found my demonstration at Christmastime perhaps a little underwhelming. But I assure you that my research has come on in leaps and bounds.'

'Well then? What is it?'

'As you know, sirs, I have been engaged in the study of animation and respiration. The very forces that give life to dead matter. I have looked into the inmost parts of nature to discover what there resides, not only in animals but in the *human* creature.' He licked his lips. 'And there I have found what natural philosophers and alchemists and wise men have wondered at since time out of memory. The essence of life itself. The seat of the soul.'

There was a pause and then a lot of contemptuous muttering.

'The soul?' one of the men said. 'Perhaps, then, Mr Mordaunt, you should have summoned the college chaplain instead of its professor of chemistry!'

'Indeed,' said another. 'I think I have heard enough.'

The pair of them looked as if they might leave and I ducked down through the trapdoor.

'What exactly is your claim, Mr Mordaunt?' said a third, who had not yet made up his mind. 'What is the purpose of all of this, I have to say, *very* strange machinery?'

'I intend to show you a way to generate the animating force I have described! To create it, and instil it into an organic host.'

He had to shout over the rustle and stamp of the men preparing to leave, but as soon as he had spoken the room quietened and the last word hung there, too loud.

'What exactly do you mean by *host*?' said the first man. 'Have you raised a man from his grave?'

There was more laughter at this, but it was uneasy.

'Sirs,' said Phineas, 'that is precisely what I have achieved.'

The men fell into uproar. Seeing that he was about to lose his audience, Phineas suddenly whipped the grubby canvas from the stool beside him. It was not Bede who was sitting there at all. It was Pa. He was alive and breathing, stripped to the waist and missing his hat and his gloves. I am ashamed to say, he was quite the most revolting thing I had ever seen in my life.

There were gasps and a few moments of mute disbelief. I saw Mosca flying unobserved through the gathering. He landed on the crown of my head and I retreated down the stairs. I stared into the darkness, but the image of Pa stayed before my eyes, even when I screwed them shut.

'I do not understand, Mosca,' I whispered. 'What have they done to him? What are they *going* to do to him?'

He did not reply.

'What do we do? I cannot overpower Phineas, or Mr Gilly, or Mrs Gilly for that matter. And I cannot see Bede anywhere.'

He made a long and complicated buzzing, but for once I fancied that I understood him perfectly.

'Friends?' I said. 'What friends?'

XXXVI

BEDE

Phineas had bound and gagged me behind one of the workbenches, so I could not see the reactions of the scholars. I did *hear* them, though. My own reaction had not been so very different. Why Phineas had expected a more positive response from his guests I did not know.

There were groans of disgust, of horror. A little retching. Phineas tried to explain.

'This man,' he said, raising his voice again, 'is able to think and feel in exactly the same way as you or I. And *yet*, he is also resistant to all kinds of injuries and afflictions that would normally be fatal!'

One of the scholars managed to get his words out. His jowls wobbled indignantly.

'In God's name, Mr Mordaunt, what have you done?'

'Well, Professor Collard, I am glad you asked. I intend to show all of you—'

The others joined in chorus against him.

'This man needs a physician.'

'This man needs a *priest*.'

'*Is* he even a man?'

I could only see a part of the sexton's foot but the rest of his appearance was something impressed into the backs of my eyeballs. The ugly sutures that criss-crossed his head and body. His skin – where there was any – puce and yellow and glistening. His ribs looked like the broken hull of a ship-wreck, with ragged holes that exposed the dark and oily ridges of bone and sinew beneath. He looked worse than any corpse, if that is possible. A dead body will decay and turn to dust over time. Ned's grandfather seemed to have been in a state of constant putrefaction over the course of many, many years.

'This is an abomination,' one of the scholars was claiming, now. 'It has no place in the world.'

'It should be sedated.'

'Sedated? It should be destroyed!'

The others agreed.

'No!' said a new voice.

I had wondered if Ned had been responsible for the collapse of the sails, but I never thought that he had actually escaped from his prison at the top of the windmill. And yet here he was, throwing himself at his grandfather's feet. My heart swelled with pity for the boy. Pity, and fondness, too – there was compassion in him that was nowhere to be found in the cold, bare rooms of Wellrest Manor.

I wriggled to try and get a better view. Ned was on his knees, with his arms outspread.

'Please, sirs,' he said. 'You do not understand.'

'Who the devil is this?' said one of the scholars.

'Ignore him, gentlemen,' said Phineas, who seemed as surprised as I was to see the boy. 'He is a vagrant. Lives in the woods. He persists in disrupting my research.'

'You must not hurt him. He is my grandfather.'

'Your *grandfather*?'

'He is just ill,' said Ned. 'Terribly, *terribly* ill. Tell them, Pa.'

The old man sighed and said nothing.

'Please,' said Phineas, 'if we might return to the demonstration, I might explain *how* such a miracle might be achieved . . .'

'I can explain,' said Ned. 'You should start by looking in the attic.'

'Silence!' cried Phineas. 'You must understand, gentlemen, this boy is more animal than man. An imbecile. The village idiot. They do not suffer him to live among them.'

He swiped at Ned and the boy skipped out of the way. He ran around the back of the equipment and stood on a box to try and open the trapdoor.

'He keeps the results of his failed experiments up here,' Ned said. 'They are more shocking than anything you see in front of you.'

Phineas dived at him and knocked him from the box just as Ned unfastened the bolt. The trapdoor fell open. There was a strangely pregnant moment of silence when it seemed everyone assembled was awaiting the arrival of someone or something from the floor above.

'Mosca,' said Ned. 'If you would be so kind.'

There was a distant drone, which in an instant became violent as the swarm of flies exploded into the room. The lamplight seemed to darken. There were hundreds upon hundreds, bringing with them a warm stench from above. They seemed the presence of Death itself, a black and noxious vapour made of little wriggling bodies and agitated wings that found their way into one's ears and nose. Ecstatic to have been released into the world of the living.

There were more cries of dismay and disgust from the scholars, who began climbing over themselves to get down the stairs and out into the fresh air. Phineas and Ned rolled and fought amongst the apparatus, knocking over tripods and flasks and voltaic piles. In the chaos I tried calling out through my gag but nobody could hear me. I wriggled over to the end of the workbench and tried rubbing the ropes against the corner of the table leg, with no success. There was a spirit lamp above whose flame might have burnt through my bindings, but knocking it on to the floor would only have spilt burning alcohol over the wooden floorboards.

The last of the scholars fled, along with Mr and Mrs Gilly. Loyal to the last! I heard Ned groan as Phineas landed blow after blow upon him. And still more flies came in great, frantic waves from the attic room.

Ned's grandfather came and crouched beside me. I am ashamed to say I shut my eyes. I could not bear to look at him so closely.

He wordlessly slipped the gag over my head and untied the knots at my wrists and ankles. Only once I was free and standing and the man was standing a few paces back did I look at him, and only then from the corner of my eye.

'Thank you,' I said.

The flies congregated around his fingertips, around his mouth, around the ribs clearly visible through the gaps in his skin. He nodded curtly and gathered his clothes from the floor beside me. He put an arm into the sleeve of his old coat and, even in the midst of the chaos, I heard the clink of his keys.

By now much of the laboratory was a wreck. Phineas had watched his reputation vanish along with the last of the scholars, and it seemed he did not mind destroying every piece of apparatus if it meant he could throttle Ned personally. He had the boy pinned against the inside of the copper bath, his hands around his throat. I fought my way through the clouds of flies, arm raised to my eyes as if the place was ablaze. I seized Phineas by his shoulders and he whirled about and tried to strike me across the face.

'Devils! Villains! The pair of you!' he shrieked.

That was when I saw, through the fuzz of the swarm, his nose was gone. It had been dislodged during the course of their struggling and where it had been there was now a puckered and reddish hole. He put his fingers where his prosthesis had been. His eyes widened when he noticed what was missing and he clapped his whole palm over his face, as though his injury were a secret I had only just uncovered. He looked around frantically.

'Where is it?' he said. 'What have you done with it?'

Ned sat up in the bath rubbing his neck. Phineas turned back to him but Ned's grandfather planted himself between the two of them.

'Out of the way, old man,' said Phineas, spitting flies. 'Out of the way, or so help me God I will . . . I will . . .'

'Kill me again?' said Ned's grandfather. 'I would welcome it.'

'Give it to me, boy!' Phineas screamed.

Ned wriggled awkwardly out of the bathtub. Phineas lunged after him but the old sexton blocked the way and threw him off balance. He collided with the workbench where he had hidden me, knocked the spirit lamp from the tabletop, and sent a tide of flaming alcohol spilling over the floor.

The conflagration happened almost too quickly to be seen. The frame of the windmill was already mostly charcoal and the timbers were ready to burn. The flames leapt and caught the nosegays that hung from the ceiling. They found their way to the many flasks of volatile fluids; to the bundles of dried herbs; to the other spirit lamps. The entire laboratory soon resembled some garish, deafening carnival of coloured fireworks and exploding glassware.

Phineas picked himself up and looked from Ned, to me, to the old man, then spun around in the chaos. He stopped suddenly and gasped. His brass nose was in the wreckage, underneath a workbench. It glowed in the firelight, as if newly forged. He got on his hands and knees to fetch it and while he pawed through the flames a beam descended from the ceiling and barred the way between him and the rest of us. Ned seized my hand and pulled but I did not move. Even after everything it did not seem right to leave Phineas where he was. I called out but he could not hear. A second beam crashed beside him and he rolled further away into the burning ruins of the laboratory.

Ned tugged at my arm again. I looked up and through the smoke I saw the boards of the windmill's upper floor sag and crack. I did not wish to be inside when the contents of the attic fell upon our heads, and I was sure Ned did not either. I paced a few times around the fallen beam but could already feel my hair singeing and there was nothing to be done for Phineas. I turned away from him, turned back. Eventually Ned's grandfather took my other hand and led both of us through the flames and the flies, and we stumbled through the trapdoor and down the stairs and out into the cold, blue night.

It was strangely quiet outside the mill. The university men were still dim shapes hobbling among the trees, and there was no sign of Mr or Mrs Gilly. I wondered if they would have the gall to return to the manor, or even the village. I wondered if that would be a problem.

Victor and Clerval were still tethered at the trough, stamping and rolling their eyes. I untied Victor's halter and led them both to the edge of the woods. I could hear Ned saying something to the old man, over and over, and patting at his shoulders where his old coat was still alight. When we reached the trees we stopped and looked back at the windmill. It made for a hellish silhouette against the sky. The remaining sails showered debris upon the ground. The masonry began to fall from the topmost level. I thought I could hear Phineas howling.

'We must find you a physician, Pa,' said Ned. 'Or a surgeon. I do not know. How do you feel? Are you in pain? Pa?'

The old man did not reply. He just stood a little apart from us, still smouldering. His eyes were fixed on the blazing windmill. Ned tried again, and when he received no response he turned to me.

'Bede? Can you help him?'

I looked at him. Such a sad and kind face. It was badly bruised from Phineas' fists. I took his hand and squeezed.

'Perhaps,' I said. 'Though, I do not know what kind of help he needs.'

The sexton turned with his mouth slightly open, as if to make an answer, but at that moment the top level of the windmill finally caved in and sent a shower of glowing sparks up into the sky.

'Did you see him?' asked Ned.

'Who?' I said.

'Phineas.'

I shook my head. There was no sign or sound of him.

'Should we go back?' said Ned.

'I don't think there is anything to be done.'

As if to confirm this the walls of the mill collapsed further still, like one of Mrs Gilly's undercooked cakes. The horses reared and whinnied in distress.

'We should go before the rest of the villagers get here,' I said. 'The whole county will see this.'

'Go where?' asked Ned.

'You can stay at the house for the time being.' I had a sudden vision of us all sitting down to supper in the dining room. 'Yes,' I said, hauling on Victor's reins, 'I am sure Father will be simply *delighted* to see all three of us.'

Ned followed, with many a backward glance at the ruin of the mill. I knew what he was thinking, and I knew I had a great deal of explaining to do, if I wanted us to remain friends. And I did want that, very much. Given how my father was likely to react, Ned was probably the only person I had left in the entire world.

XXXVII

BEDE

The three of us stood at the door to Wellrest Manor and I raised the heavy brass knocker. There were two, in the shape of lion's heads, and they had not been polished in many years. The rain had left dried streams of greenish tears from the lions' eyes – a suitable reflection of the mood inside the house, I thought.

'Should we hide?' said Ned. 'Your father was not well disposed to us last time we met.'

'Absolutely not,' I said. 'No more hiding. My father shall know the truth.' I paused. 'At least, some of it.'

I knocked three times and waited. After a minute I knocked again. The sound echoed from the front of the house to the back, as if none of the rooms contained any people or any furniture and most of the dividing walls had been removed. I raised the knocker a third time but before I let it fall I heard muttering and shuffling feet.

The knob turned and the door opened. No Mr Gilly, of course. It was Father on the other side, his nightcap askew, holding a candle not much bigger than his thumb. The lord of the manor, attending to the door of his own house. The shame of it!

He squinted at me suspiciously, then at Ned and his grandfather. It must have been too dark for him to see. He brought the candle flame close enough for me to feel its heat upon my chin, and then his eyes widened and he put a hand to his mouth.

'Hello, Father,' I said. 'I am sorry for calling at such an unsociable hour.'

His face was already very pale, but it seemed to grow whiter still, and he took two steps back into the hallway. He shook his head.

'Oh, God in heaven! Obedience! No, no, it cannot be!'

I stayed upon the threshold.

'May I come in?' I said.

'Be gone, spirit!' He averted his face and stretched out one hand. 'I know you are here to punish me, but I will not admit you to the house! My own conscience is punishment enough!'

I looked at Ned and his grandfather. The three of us must have made a baleful sight to my father, old as he was and sleepless with guilt and sorrow. I stepped into the hall.

'There was a time, Father, when you would have dismissed talk of ghosts and spirits as the stuff of womanly fancy. Are you so changed, now?'

He was cowering behind a table. I went and knelt by him and took his hand in mine. He looked up, and his cheeks glistened in the light of his candle. He sniffed.

'You are not a vengeful ghost?'

'I am not, Father. I am Bede. Your Bede. In the flesh.'

'But,' he said, 'that cannot be.'

He raised a shaking hand and touched my cheek, lightly at first, and then more firmly, as if to check if there were any substance to me. Then he fell into my arms, and it seemed, while he wept, that I was the parent and he the child. Perhaps he had needed that ever since he had lost my mother.

We held each other on the hard wooden floor for a long time. Ned and his grandfather loitered awkwardly at the door. Eventually I stood up and helped my father to his feet, and I took his candle and lit the hallway lamps.

'It is a dream,' my father said.

'It is no such thing,' I said. 'I am here. I am alive.'

He still shook his head. I saw myself in the mirror, covered in soot, my hair scorched, the corners of my mouth raw and bloody from Phineas' gag.

'My word, Obedience,' said Father. 'What has happened to you?'

Then he finally recognized the figures behind me.

'You! Did you have a hand in this? What did you do to her?'

'Be calm, Father,' I said.

'They are devils!'

'They are friends, Father. Good friends. They are the reason I am still here at all.'

He frowned. His face softened and then hardened again.

'They stole from your mother!'

He thrust a hand down his nightshirt and produced the

locket on its chain. He had been wearing it around his neck, even while he slept. I nearly wept myself at the sight of it; at the thought of him clutching it to his heart while he tossed restlessly in his bed. It took me a moment to compose myself.

'They stole from no one, Father,' I said. 'They are entirely blameless. I took that from Mother. With her permission, I would like to think.'

Father gave up trying to make any kind of expression with his face, besides abject tiredness.

'I do not understand,' he said.

I took him by the elbow.

'Let us go to the sitting room, Father,' I said. 'I shall explain what I can.'

We reached the stairs and he glanced over his shoulder at Ned and the old man.

'What about your . . . acquaintances?'

I looked at them too. I caught Ned's eye and tried to smile, but he still seemed preoccupied.

'I wondered if we might make up a room for them,' I said. 'Since they have nowhere to stay.'

He studied the pair of them. His suspicions were not assuaged, exactly, but they seemed tempered with the beginnings of guilt. He sighed and then looked at his feet and was quiet for a while. In the end he said: 'Very well. I shall rouse Mrs Gilly.'

'Oh, do not trouble yourself, Father,' I said. 'Mrs Gilly is already very much awake. Though I doubt she is anywhere in the house.'

'She is not? I wondered that nobody else opened the door to you. Where is she?'

Where indeed? We had passed the university men not long after leaving the burning windmill, the wheels of their carriages sunk into a quagmire by the side of a farm track. They were so furious – and, as they still clamoured, so in need of their supper – they did not even notice us passing.

But we had not seen Mr or Mrs Gilly. A part of me worried that they might reveal our arrangement, and that I had been the 'gentleman' employing them. But, I reasoned, to do this would mean implicating themselves as the resurrection men, and then they might find themselves blamed with the thefts of bodies across the whole county of Oxfordshire. Besides, would the scholars not claim that Phineas had been the man in the mill? Their word surely counted for more than that of a pair of servants.

'I'm afraid Mr and Mrs Gilly have left our service,' I said.

'Left?' he said. 'Why on earth would they do that?'

'Because I dismissed them.'

'Dismissed them? Whatever for?'

I looked at him earnestly and, for the first time since Phineas had ambushed me, I felt the gears of my thinking machine whir back to life. Perhaps, I thought, the truth was not what Father needed after all.

While Ned and the old man raided the kitchen and prepared their sleeping arrangements, I made my explanations.

Father and I took tea on the single threadbare couch that remained in the sitting room and I told him how events had unfolded. I impressed even myself with my performance. I told him that I was as amazed as he was, to find myself alive. Perhaps it had been a mere fainting fit that had put me in such a deathlike sleep. Perhaps it had been something in the food. Whatever the symptoms my body had shown, my soul had rallied. Not only that, but in a quite incredible stroke of fortune, Mr and Mrs Gilly had dug me from my grave. At first Father looked delighted by this, but I quickly explained that they had not done so in the hope I was still alive. Quite the opposite.

His face fell and he waited for me to continue.

I told him that I had come to my senses in the back of a wagon. Mr and Mrs Gilly had taken my supposedly lifeless body to the windmill on the outskirts of the village. As soon as they had opened the sacking they had wrapped me in, I had come face to face with my fiancé. It was difficult to say who had been the more horrified. There followed an altercation and I was eventually and unexpectedly saved by the sexton and his grandson – yes, those two who had suffered such undeserved ill-treatment at the hands of the villagers! Good, honest men, the pair of them. They had known I would be too ripe a reward for any resurrection men to ignore, and Ned had gone to watch over my grave and perhaps catch the criminals once and for all. Unfortunately, in the confrontation that had followed, some of Phineas' equipment had caught fire, and the man himself had been unable to escape. Of course, I reminded Father, we had all seen how dangerous Phineas' experiments were, here in this very house. He had, in the end, been destroyed by his own research.

The story only became more satisfactory in the telling. It would not be long before the villagers investigated the ruin of the windmill. People would find the remains of the laboratory, the remains of the bodies, and, perhaps, the remains of Phineas. The scholars would testify to the horrors of the demonstration, and none of them had even known I was there, since Phineas had taken such pains to pretend the work was his own. It all made perfect sense.

If Father had any doubts about the explanation, they seemed outshone by his joy and relief that I was alive and well. After I had finished speaking he was quiet for a long time, before he leant in and patted my thigh and said: 'I cannot believe it, Bede. I simply cannot believe it.'

I wondered if he was referring to the fiction I had constructed, as much as my return from the grave. But he did not question anything out loud. Eventually he said: 'So, you think Mr and Mrs Gilly will not return?'

'Would you want them to?' I said.

'No, I suppose not,' he said. He sighed deeply. 'And I thought this household could not get any smaller.'

We sat with our thoughts and there was a creak on the floorboards outside the sitting room. I thought it was Ned or his grandfather – lost, perhaps, or still hungry after finishing off Mrs Gilly's dry, tasteless biscuits – but when I got up to open the door there was someone else skulking in the darkness. An ancient creature, to be sure, though not as ancient as the sexton.

'Who is it, Bede?' asked Father.

'It is Mr Mordaunt's footman.'

Perkins stooped before me as if he had bowed and forgotten to straighten again. He looked up at me and the candle flame shone in each of his wet eyes.

'Can we help you?' I asked him.

'Beg pardon,' he said, 'but I couldn't help overhearing.'

'Of course you couldn't. The door is still warm from where your ear was pressed against it.'

He gave a sheepish smile. 'So he's gone, has he?'

'Gone?'

'Mr Mordaunt. He's kicked the bucket.'

'I rather think so, yes. Though I would not put it in those terms. I am sorry.'

He looked down again and his body began to shudder. I could almost pity him — perhaps he had been as loyal as Phineas had said, had loved his master, even, though I could not imagine why. Then I realized: he was not crying but laughing. The sound grew and grew until he had to stifle his mouth with a bony fist.

'Are you quite well?' I asked.

'Never better,' he said, once he had composed himself a little. 'Lord have mercy, I'm free of the rascal. I knew it was coming. Knew he would come to some mischief, the things he was up to. The things he made me do for him, miss, they'd make your hair stand on end.'

I said nothing, knowing that I had probably done some of those things myself.

'I can only imagine,' I said. 'Then you are glad to be released from his service?'

'Right glad, miss, yes. Though, not so glad to leave the

family.' His face suddenly became very serious. 'Drove his father to drink, did you know that? And beyond, if you get my meaning. Poor Mr Mordaunt – the elder one, I mean – always having to cover up the things his son was doing. All the rumours. Well. You know what he was like. You saw it yourself, sounds like. Good riddance to him. I'll be delighted to not take his filthy coin any more.'

A thought came to me.

'Perhaps you would like to take ours?' I said.

'Miss?'

'As you no doubt heard, we will be rather short on servants after tonight. We will not be able to pay anything like the amounts Mr Mordaunt gave you. But I assure you, your duties will be a good deal less strenuous.'

He smiled again.

'I will certainly think on it. Perhaps I can give you an answer in the morning?' He paused. 'This is the first night in years I'll be able to get a good night's sleep, without him ordering me around.'

'By all means, Mr Perkins. Get some rest.'

'Thank you, miss. And a very good night to you.' He peered around me to see Father on the couch and made another crooked bow. 'A good night to both of you.'

He withdrew into the dark and I could have sworn he was whistling before he reached the end of the hall.

I closed the door quietly behind me and turned back to Father. He looked very small. I thought of what Perkins had said of the elder Mr Mordaunt, driven to drink and despair by his own son. I did not wish to be that kind of offspring.

'Well, there is some providence,' I said, returning to the couch. 'He would be a welcome addition to the house. Don't you think?'

'He is old and decrepit,' said Father. 'I think he will be a perfect fit.'

'Do you think he can cook?'

'No,' he said. 'But Mrs Gilly could not cook either.'

We both laughed, and the room seemed a good deal brighter than the handful of candles would allow.

We talked for a long time after that. At first our conversation was only of Phineas, and all that had happened since his arrival. But soon, almost without either of us realizing, we were speaking of Mother, and of the past, and of the future. I felt my heart growing. Father and I had not spoken of the future before – at least, never in terms outside of my marriage to Mr Mordaunt.

It was well past midnight when we finally decided to go to our beds. I bid my father goodnight and as I was leaving he swept a hand over the battered old couch and said: 'Do you remember how much your mother loved sitting here?'

'Sitting?' I said. 'I remember her draping herself over the whole couch, a novel in one hand and cake crumbs all down her dress.'

He laughed again, though his eyes were sad.

'I am glad there is so much of her in you,' he said, and he squeezed my hand. I sat down beside him again, and we held each other tightly until all but one of the candles had burnt out.

XXXVIII

NED

In that dark and shapeless time, when midnight is a distant memory but the dawn is still hours from arriving, I heard somebody creeping around my bedroom. My nerves were already agitated – I was plagued with visions of what had happened at the windmill and disorientated by the unfamiliar house. Pa had not spoken a word and I had not slept a wink. Now, it seemed, Phineas had returned to throttle me in my bed.

And then I caught that floral scent.

'Ned?' whispered Bede.

I sat up.

'What is it?'

'Come with me. Quickly.'

Even after everything I had witnessed, and despite my concerns for Pa, who was still creaking around the room next door, I could not help but obey. The spell she had cast over me remained quite unbroken. Perhaps she wished to talk, I thought. Perhaps she would offer me some explanation for the horrors in her laboratory that would allow me to love her as fully as I wanted; that restored her to perfection.

A ridiculous, childish thought, I now know.

I got up from the bed, still fully clothed, and followed her out of the door. She picked up an oil lamp from the floor and proceeded silently along the landing to the staircase. She had not changed her clothes either, nor had she washed her face, nor combed her hair. Mosca flitted about her, casting enormous shadows on the wooden panelling.

At the bottom of the stairs she went through the hall and opened the front door and we were halfway down the driveway before she spoke.

'You must think me a perfect monster,' she said.

I did not reply at first. We walked a little further.

'I do not know what to think,' I said. 'I saw everything, Bede. I saw poor Master Garrick. And the others.'

'I know. I would have told you, Ned. Of course I meant to tell you.'

I stopped a few paces from the gate, and she stopped too.

'So it was you, then,' I said. 'You took the bodies.'

'Yes,' she said. 'Well, Mr and Mrs Gilly took them. But I told them to do it. Worse than that, really. I tricked them into doing it.'

The last hope that it had all been a misunderstanding vanished into the cold night.

'But do you understand why, Ned? Tell me you understand why I did it.'

I wanted to, with all my heart. I looked at my feet, and thought again of Robert Garrick's toes, mindlessly clenching and unclenching. I heard her take a couple of steps towards me and she raised my chin with her fingers. She was wearing her gloves again, to conceal the many scars she had earned from her research.

'I think I do,' I said. 'I think you wanted to help people. I think you wish you could have helped your mother.'

'My mother, yes,' she said. 'And yours, and everybody like them. I have only ever wanted to help. We must all lose the people we love, but if we might have another hour, another day, another year with them . . . Well, I thought, if I could offer that to the world, I would feel my life had been of some use. I could even feel that Herbert Wellrest's life had been of some use. His motivations were closer to Phineas' than my own, but I thought that, if I could direct his work towards a more noble end, his ruin of our family would not have been for nothing.'

'And Mr Garrick?'

'An accident. An anomaly. I swear.'

We looked at each other. I was not sure if I believed her, or if she even believed herself. I loved her and hated her and for some time my soul wrestled with itself for the right words.

'You stole the residents, Bede,' I said. 'You did awful things to them. Without their permission.'

'Yes, and I know how wrong and wicked that must seem. But how else could I have done it? They will not allow me to study at the university on account of my sex.'

'And you were so sure of your success?'

Her face hardened a little.

'Yes, I was sure.'

'How?'

'Because I am brilliant, Ned. Quite brilliant.'

She stood framed by the gates and for a moment her pride seemed to have made her several inches taller. Then she became a little embarrassed and fell to examining her fingers.

'If that is true,' I said, 'could you tell me what is wrong with Pa?'

She took a while to find the words.

'I could. But whether I *should* is another matter.'

'What do you mean by that?'

'I mean, it is complicated. Perhaps he should be the one to tell you.'

'No!' I shouted, and Bede winced. My voice had surely carried all the way back to the house. 'I have been waiting for him to tell me all night, and he has not spoken one word! He has a hole in his chest where his heart should be, and he looks in a worse state than any of the bodies that you pilfered, and yet he stands and he walks as if nothing were amiss! I don't know what to make of it.' I paused. 'Tell me. How can it be that he is still alive?'

Again, a long time passed before she answered. In the silence Mosca landed upon my shoulder and did not move, as if he too were hanging upon her next words.

'I do not know,' Bede said. 'But I would like to, as much

as you. That is why I have asked you to accompany me. I wanted your permission.'

'My permission?'

'After everything I have done, you are right to be indignant. You are a kinder and more considerate soul than I, Ned.'

I was angry, and fearful, but I wanted to disagree with her on that point – I did not think her unkind, at all.

Before I could say as much, she spoke again: 'I think, perhaps, I have a great deal to learn from you. But tonight, would you permit me one last folly?'

'Folly?' I said.

She unwrapped her shawl from her shoulders and reached into her bodice. I heard the familiar sound of metal upon metal. She held out her hand and proffered me the keys to the graveyard.

'I would have asked your pa's permission, too, but I fear he is a little more stubborn than you.'

I looked at the keys and then at Bede and said nothing.

'Herbert Wellrest's greatest discoveries are buried with him. If what I suspect is true, there may very well be something there which can explain what has happened to your grandfather. And help him, perhaps, in his discomfort. So. I am asking you to return with me to the churchyard. And, with your blessing, I would like to open one final grave.'

I thought of Pa, wheezing away in his bed; I thought of Bede's mother, snatched from the world while her daughter was still a child; I thought of my own parents, taken even earlier than that, before I had known their faces. I understood, then, why Bede had done the things that she had done. And I found I could forgive her quite easily.

'Very well,' I said. 'Only, I do not have my shovel.'

XXXIX

NED

There was still a smell of damp smoke hanging over the graveyard. Once we were through the gate I went straight away to the remains of the cottage. It was still very dark and I could only see what the lantern showed me, and of that I was glad. The walls still seemed to be standing but the front door had been burnt away and the roof had collapsed. The furniture, the tea tin, the pots and pans – all black and blistered and glistening under the lamplight.

'I am sorry, Ned,' said Bede, and rested a hand on my shoulder.

'It wasn't your fault,' I said. 'The villagers have wanted us out for years. You weren't the one to start the fire.'

I searched around the debris, fragments of my old life crunching underfoot. I found my shovel where I had left it, leaning against the wall. It was not untouched by the fire, but the heat seemed to have hardened the wood of the shaft rather than split it. I hefted it and went back outside and started straight for the Nameless Grave.

'Are you quite all right?' said Bede. 'We can rest a moment if you would like.'

I shook my head and kept up a brisk pace.

'It will be dawn in a few hours,' I said. 'We should waste no time.'

When we arrived at the plot, Bede set down the lamp and we stood before the crumbling headstone for some time.

'Your grandfather,' said Bede. 'He never told you what was buried here?'

'No. I am starting to realize he kept a great deal from me.'

'My father is the same. I know it is done out of care for me, though. I suppose they think us children still.'

I looked at Bede's dirty face and at my own blistered hands and thought: no, I am definitely not a child any more.

'Shall we get started?' I said.

We cleared the ivy from the mortsafe as best we could and Mosca showed us to the keyhole on one side. I scooped out the dirt with a finger and Bede strained on the key until it snapped around quite suddenly. We both sat on our haunches and with a good deal of sweating and gritting of teeth we managed to heave the cage open and lower it to the ground on the other side of the grave.

I looked around the churchyard. If someone had been watching us over the wall, it was too dark to see them. I fancied I could see a very dim orange glow on the horizon, which I took to be the remains of the fire at the windmill. I certainly *hoped* it was that, rather than the rising sun.

I looked at Bede and lifted the shovel. Before the blade

bit the earth I was seized suddenly by a very irrational kind of terror. All the reverend's talk of sorcery and black magic came back to me, and the idea of some evil presence seemed more than plausible in the long and leering shadows of the oil lamp. I envisaged spirits and monsters and poisonous fumes escaping from the grave the moment I broke the surface.

'Ned?' said Bede. 'Is something the matter?'

I lowered the shovel.

'What exactly are we hoping to find here?'

'Besides Herbert's body? I do not know for sure. Books. Apparatus. Another diary, perhaps. The first contains many fascinating discoveries, but it ends rather abruptly. He seemed to be on the verge of something truly profound.'

'And what might be in the diary?'

'The final piece of his research. The secret to life itself. Perhaps, more specifically, the secret to your grandfather's life.'

She looked as if she might say more, but quickly and firmly shut her mouth.

Well, I thought, another book was hardly cause to worry. Mosca landed upon my knuckles and seemed quite as calm as I had ever known him. I took this as a good sign, raised the shovel once more, and started to dig.

The earth was very firm, and nothing like the other plots in the churchyard. More clay than soil, and full of stones, as though somebody had wished to make it as difficult as possible to dig there. I was exhausted as it was, and the work took twice as long as it should have. When I stood up to rest

I realized that Bede had joined me in the grave. She had found Pa's shovel and was working tirelessly, wordlessly through the unforgiving ground. I could not even say how long she had been there.

Down we went. The hole was over six feet deep and I felt sure the sky was starting to lighten and still I had found nothing. There was a part of me that wanted to leap out and fill the grave back in before daybreak, but I did not want to disappoint Bede – and I myself still wanted answers about Pa. We were in well over our heads when the end of my shovel split a black and spongey piece of wood. I bent and fished it out. I probed about for another minute or so and found a few more pieces, none larger than my hand, almost indistinguishable from the wet mud that they were resting in.

'Is that him?' said Bede.

'This is the remains of a coffin. A very cheap one, too.'

'What else?'

'There is nothing else.'

'What do you mean?'

'There is no body. The coffin is empty.'

She said nothing. I heard the lark in the yew tree over-head, a sure sign that the night was nearly over.

'Perhaps we just need to keep going,' said Bede.

I looked up at her.

'We must be seven or eight feet deep by now,' I said. 'And it is almost morning. We don't want to be found like this.'

I climbed with some difficulty out of the grave and stood on the edge. She followed a moment later and continued to squint into the hole as if it were her fault it was empty; as if she simply had to look harder, and something would appear.

'I don't understand,' she said. 'Where is the research? And more importantly, where is Herbert Wellrest?'

Somebody cleared their throat behind us – the thick, phlegmy cough of a man on his deathbed.

'He is here,' said a familiar voice.

The figure had a heavy, uneven tread and took several paces before emerging into the lamplight. Of course, I knew who it was before I set eyes upon him. But I waited until I could see every line on that old and ghoulish and beloved face before I said anything.

'Pa? What are you doing here? You should be resting.'

'I wish I could rest, Ned. More than anything!'

He turned to Bede.

'You are quite the talented pickpocket, my dear,' he said, not unkindly. 'But Ned should have told you – I do not sleep. I have not slept for a very long time.'

The lark continued to sing quite happily overhead. The sky behind the church steeple was beginning to pale, ribbed with clouds and coloured like the inside of an oyster shell. Pa came over and looked into the grave himself, and then sat down on the edge with a groan of effort. There was the feeling, as there had been on my birthday, that we were the only souls in the world that morning – only this time there were three of us.

'I think it is time,' he said, 'that I told you the truth. Believe me, Ned, when I say I never wanted to keep anything from you. Only, I could not find the words. Not last night. Not in the last two hundred years.'

A strange laugh arose in my chest but was strangled somewhere before it could leave my lips.

'Two hundred years? What do you mean?'

He sighed. Bede found my fingers with hers and squeezed. She looked at me steadily. The remark did not seem to trouble her in the slightest.

'Bede? Do you know something I don't?'

'Miss Wellrest knows half of the truth, but not all of it,' said Pa. 'In the windmill I said that I was the product of Herbert Wellrest's experiments. What I did not say was that I conducted those experiments, for the most part, on myself. I am Herbert Wellrest. Or rather, I was.'

I would not believe it. I tried to laugh again, but could not. I tried to swallow, but could not do that either.

'No, Pa,' I said. 'This is not funny at all.'

He turned and looked at me from where he sat. His eyes were shining.

'Sit,' he said.

I did.

'I do not feel like him,' said Pa. 'Not any more. When I think of Herbert Wellrest, it is as if I am recalling a man I read about once, in a book, a long time ago. But perhaps this is only an attempt to excuse all the wicked things that I did. In the name of science, of alchemy, certainly – but wicked, nonetheless.'

'What did you do?'

'I dug too deeply, Ned. And I discovered things that I

should not have discovered. The elixir of life, the philosopher's stone – it has had many names over many thousands of years – but while others were looking for substances and solutions or magical spells, I knew the answer lay in our bodies. I was the only one of my peers to throw off all shame, all decency, and to reduce a man's flesh to all its constituent parts. And in doing so I found it. That essence, that spirit that could keep a body alive for time beyond imagination.'

There was a long pause. I looked into the grave and thought I might leap to the bottom and begin heaping the earth upon myself.

'And what was it?' said Bede.

Pa looked at her.

'I cannot tell.'

'You mean you cannot remember?'

'I meant I cannot tell.'

'But was it a chemical? A salt? Some electrical charge?' She snapped her fingers. 'It is phlogiston, is it not? I know the theory has been discredited, but I always thought there might be something in it . . .'

Pa put his hand gently on her shoulder.

'My dear,' he said. 'Look at me. Look upon the very ruin of my being. The secret to eternal life could be as simple as a recipe for chicken soup, and I still would not tell you. Because it is not for us to know.'

'Then the answers are not here?' said Bede, hardly able to keep the disappointment from her voice. 'They are not in this grave?'

'No,' he said.

'Then why is the grave here at all?'

'Because I had very much the same idea that you had, Miss Wellrest!'

He laughed and was seized by a coughing fit more violent than I had ever seen. I put an arm around his shoulders and felt the knobbles of his spine through his several coats and thought there was no more pitiful thing on the earth.

'There came a time when I saw the terrible nature of my work, and I saw the destitution I had brought to my family – *your* family, Bede – and I decided it would be better if the world were free of Herbert Wellrest and his discoveries. I destroyed my diary. At least, I *thought* I did. I should have checked that the fire had done its job properly. And then I destroyed myself. I was on very good terms with the sexton back then, since he gave me access to the graveyard for my materials – it was no great inconvenience for me to fake my own death and have him dig me up. I arranged for the mort-safe to be placed over the grave, because I knew that my fellow alchemists might come sniffing about for my research.'

'But it was never buried here?' said Bede.

'I never said that it was. I believe I wrote that my greatest *secrets* would go with me to my grave. And in a way that was true – the biggest secret being that I was still alive, and my coffin was quite empty. That was really what all these bars and locks were for.'

Bede stared into the hole as if she still might find something of use in there. She said nothing. I could not find the words either. I could feel my blood heating at the deceit of it all – the years upon years of lies!

'I spent many years travelling,' Pa went on. 'I have seen more of the world than one might see in several lifetimes. I wandered and I wandered and as the years passed I found myself aimless and wretched. I thought myself no help to the world whatsoever. So I returned to my home, here, and I took on work as the sexton. I suppose I hoped I could at least be useful. And I wanted to make up for my mistreatment of the dead, when I had been Herbert Wellrest.'

At this he took off his gloves. The sight of his ragged fingers was still a shock to me, though I had seen worse by now.

'What I did not realize during the course of my experiments was this: that the human body will continue to degrade even if its lifespan is unnaturally long. This was the curse I should have foreseen, but did not. I concocted a solution that helped to numb the pain. But cups of tea will only achieve so much. My spirit lingered, despite the failings of my body. Why, you saw yourself! Even a bullet to the heart will not extinguish my meagre flame. To own the truth of it, for many, many years, I wished to die.'

This was too much for me to bear. I leapt up and stormed away from the grave, with no intention except to get as far from both of them as possible. I heard Bede calling after me but I ignored her and kept going until I reached the husk of our old home. I went inside and found the charred remains of a stool and slumped upon it and surveyed what was left of the cottage. A good thing, I thought, that it had been burnt to ashes! My old life had been nothing but falsehood!

I sat there and let Mosca run over my hands. He, like Bede, did not seem disturbed by the news either. Was I the only one whose world had come crashing down around them? I put my head in my hands and I wept.

I heard Pa's boots crunching over the floor behind me.

'Ned,' he said. 'Forgive me.'

'Go away,' I said. 'I don't even know who you are.'

'I meant what I said, Ned. I was Herbert Wellrest in a different life. But Herbert is gone. Now I am your pa. I have been for as long as I have known you.'

'How?' I said, and I stood up and knocked over the stool. 'How can you be my grandfather, if you are over two hundred years old? How could my mother have been *your* daughter?'

'Again, I must beg your forgiveness,' he said. 'It is true, I did not know your parents. Your mother, as I understand, was very young and very poor. She had already lost her husband to cholera. She had not the means to keep you, so she entrusted you to God. It is not uncommon, I am told. She brought you to the church and she left you on the altar.' He smiled for the first time that morning. 'I still remember that day, being woken by your mournful cries. I still remember your face, red and round as a plum; how you pummelled me with your little fists when I tried to swaddle you. To look at you now, you would not think you had such violence in you!'

I swayed on my feet, I felt fainter with each new revelation.

'She abandoned me?'

'Not abandoned at all, Ned. You were a gift. One that I was overjoyed to receive. I told you that for a long time I wished to die. The day I found you was the day I stopped wishing.'

I blinked a few times. He looked back at me, his bad eye quite steady, the smile still upon his wrinkled face, and pulled me tightly to his chest.

We held each other in the blackened ruins of the cottage while the sky turned pink and gold under a cool sun. The thought that we might be discovered, by the reverend, by the villagers, seemed entirely insignificant in light of all that had been said.

Through tears – of sadness, of relief, of pure tiredness – I saw Bede loitering by the cottage door.

'I think,' she said, 'we should be going.'

'What of the grave?' I said. 'It's too late to start filling it back in!'

'I am not sure we need to,' she said. 'I wonder if Phineas might take the blame for that as well. It will not be hard to convince the villagers, when they discover what he was up to at the windmill.'

We made our way over the broken wall and through the woods, each of us in thoughtful silence. Pa was very slow, but there seemed no rush and Bede and I matched our pace with his. The sun rose higher still and set a glowing halo around every new leaf.

We were perhaps halfway back to the manor when I noticed Pa was speaking very quietly behind me. Bede had noticed, too. We looked at each other and seemed to exchange an unspoken worry that the events of the night and the morning had been the last straw for his two-hundred-year-old brain.

I slowed a little more until I was very close to him.

'Look after him,' he was saying. 'Do not let him from your sight.'

'What is that, Pa?' I said. 'Look after who?'

He jerked upright, as though he had been interrupted quite unexpectedly.

'Oh! I am sorry, Ned. I was speaking to Mosca.'

I stopped and he nearly walked into me. He had never spoken to Mosca in my whole life, or so I thought.

'Mosca?' I said. 'You can understand him?'

'I do not know about that, but I like to think he can understand me. He has been a most faithful companion. My *only* companion, both as Herbert Wellrest and as your grandfather.'

Not for the first time that morning, I could not find the words I needed.

'Surely,' said Pa, 'you do not think I would conduct experiments upon myself without a few carefully controlled trials? That would have been very foolish of me. No, my first experiments with extending our mortal lives involved only very simple animals. Mosca here was the first successful result of the procedure.'

He held out a finger and Mosca circled a few times and then landed upon it. Pa grinned.

'Your fly,' he said, 'is nearly as old as I am.'

XL

NED

We emerged from the woods opposite the gates to Wellrest Manor, crossed the road and slipped into the estate. The day was warm and the earth was exhaling all of the rain that had recently fallen in a thick mist. Bede and I were a few yards down the driveway when we realized that Pa had not kept up.

We went back and found him waiting outside the rusted iron bars. With every wheezing breath his body swelled like a bullfrog.

'Pa?' I called.

I wondered, for a moment, if I should refer to him as Herbert, or Mr Wellrest, but quickly dismissed this as absurd. He was, in all his manners and appearance, still Pa.

'A moment, if you please,' he said.

'What's the matter?' I said. 'Are you tired? We can rest once we are inside. Quickly — there will be people on the road before long.'

He stood and scratched his head through his hat. His

shoulders slumped a little. Then he nodded, as if coming to some conclusion with himself, and he looked up at me and said: 'I think I should go.'

'Go? Where?'

'Somewhere else.'

Bede and I looked at each other. We crept back through the gap in the broken gates.

'You do not need to worry about my father,' said Bede, 'if that's what you are thinking. You are my guests. You may stay here as long as you wish. Both of you.'

Pa made a tiny bow.

'I do not doubt your hospitality, miss,' he said. 'But it is not your toes, or your father's, I worry about treading upon.'

'Whatever do you mean?'

He turned to me.

'Ned, I am ashamed.'

'Of what, Pa?'

'In so many ways, I have kept you in the dark. I did not just withhold my life from you. I withheld *yours* from you, too. Since you were a baby, I have kept the entire world at bay, so you might know a peaceful, untroubled existence. But a toad under a stone may be said to have that. What about a full life? A *lived* life?'

'You have kept me safe, Pa! Can I ask for more than that?'

'Yes, Ned. I think you can. You have been safe, certainly. But the church wall does not just keep things out. It has also kept you *in*. You know nothing of the society of men – or women, for that matter.' He paused, long enough for me to understand his meaning. 'When I look at you now, I wonder if I have done you more harm than good.'

I clasped at his sleeve.

'Nonsense! Our life was quite marvellous, before we met Bede!'

She snorted behind me.

'Well, that is very kind of you,' she said.

'No,' I spluttered, 'that is not what I meant.'

'And what did you mean?' said Bede, raising a singed eyebrow.

'I should have said, our life was marvellous, *even* before we met Bede.' Her eyebrow dropped, and a faint smile appeared upon her lips. 'But in truth it was a different life. And perhaps I was a different Ned. This new life, well – it is all the *more* marvellous for having met you.'

She looked at me and an expression rippled across her face that I could not decipher.

'Tut,' she said. 'You are a sentimental creature, Nedric.'

I did not know what to say to that. I did not know if she was happy or sad or disappointed or tired or hungry.

'This is precisely what I mean,' said Pa. 'Your life *has* changed, Ned. And I am sorry it has happened so quickly and so uncomfortably.'

'I would not call it wholly uncomfortable,' I said, and deliberately made sure I did not meet Bede's eye.

There was another long pause and eventually Pa nodded and said simply:

'Time.'

'What of it, Pa?'

'That is what you need, I think. Time. And space. To grow a little.'

It took me a moment to realize what he meant.

'But you cannot return to the graveyard. Where will you go?'

'Oh, not far,' he said. 'And not for long.'

I could not say why, but I felt quite sure he was not being completely honest.

Before I could press him further there was the sound of a cart further down the road. Bede and I looked at each other in alarm and ran and hid behind one of the stone gateposts. Pa did not move. He just stood in a shaft of sunlight and closed his eyes. I hissed to him but he did not seem to be at all concerned. I put my back to the damp, green stone and waited for the mutterings of disgust.

The creak of the cartwheels slowed and I heard a woman's voice.

'Well, who'd have thought. The old man's up and about!' There was a pause. 'You look dreadful. More dreadful than usual, I mean.'

The Meat Maid! Here was a piece of luck. I came out from my hiding place and there she was, pulled up in front of Pa, her wagon loaded with the bony carcass of a cow and a brace of rabbits.

'And you,' said Pa, opening his eyes, 'look all the more beautiful.'

'Hush yourself,' the Meat Maid said. 'I don't accept compliments as payment. Besides, did your boy not tell you?

I've got a new customer who pays twice as much as you do.'

She heard my feet in a puddle and turned to see me.

'Good morning,' I said.

'Ah, here he is! And his fly, to boot! The whole household!' she cried. 'Lordy. You don't look much better than your grandfather. And who's this?'

Bede had joined us in the road. The Meat Maid leant forward on the seat of her cart. She narrowed her eyes and licked her pale lips.

'Say, there's talk all through the village of a fire up at the old windmill. You wouldn't know anything about that, would you?' She scanned the three of us. 'I'd say you all look a trifle *scorched*.'

The three of us waited for someone else to reply. Nobody did. My mouth hung half-open like a fish's. The old woman laughed and tossed her silver hair.

'Don't you worry,' she said. 'I'm not in the habit of spreading rumours about my customers. Speaking of which, I'm meant to be meeting one of them here. So you'll all need to give us some privacy.'

'I do not think your customer will be here today,' said Bede.

'Why do you say that? You don't even know who he is!'

'It is Phineas Mordaunt, is it not?'

The Meat Maid sat back and let the reins fall in her lap.

'And how would you know that?' she said.

'This is my house. There is nothing that goes on here without my consent.'

'Your house! So. You're the lucky lady he's marrying.'

She paused and spoke the next words from behind her hand, while she vigorously wiped her nose. 'Sure you'll be very happy together.'

Even knowing that Phineas was gone, my blood still boiled at the thought. Bede just shook her head.

'I am afraid the wedding has been cancelled. And that is one rumour I am happy for you to spread.'

'Oh,' said the Meat Maid. 'Had second thoughts, has he?'

'You might say that.'

'So he's not at home, then?'

'He is not.'

'Where is he?'

'I do not know. But there are rumours that he has been visiting the windmill, night after night. Performing all sorts of strange rituals. Of course I do not give credence to such things, but . . . If there has been a fire, I hope he was not involved.'

The Meat Maid's mouth twitched.

'I see. Well. There's a shame. He was due to pay me a pretty penny for this heifer. Wanted to take the whole thing off my hands! I don't suppose you want to buy anything, do you?' She turned to Pa. 'You're awful pale. Couple of fresh rabbits to keep you going? I *say* fresh. Couple of days since I found them.'

'It is a tempting offer, miss,' said Pa. 'But I was rather hoping you might do me another favour.'

'A favour!' the Meat Maid screeched. 'And me trying to run a business!'

'I am not asking for your wares,' said Pa. 'But I was

wondering if I might ride with you a while.'

There was silence on the road, broken only by the slurp of mud as I shifted in my boots. I knew what he was suggesting, and it did not bring me any comfort.

'Ride?' said the Meat Maid. 'In this here wagon? Where to?'

'Where are you going?' he asked.

'All over,' she said. 'But I should think I'll be in Northampton by tomorrow morning.'

Pa smiled.

'Do you know, in all Herbert Wellrest's years of wandering, I believe he never saw Northampton! How funny. And it is only in the next county!'

'Herbert who?' said the Meat Maid.

'An old acquaintance,' said Pa.

The old woman looked confused. When Pa did not elaborate she leant over the side of her wagon and spat.

'Well, come on then, if you're coming,' she said. 'You'd better ride up front with me, or people will think you're for sale. They'll think I've thrown my hand in with the resurrection men!'

Pa smiled and took a long, deep breath as if a great burden had been lifted from him. Perhaps he had simply passed it from his shoulders on to mine, because I found I could barely move from where I stood. I understood what he wanted for me – time, space, and all that those things can offer – but I was still not entirely sure I wanted it for myself. I suppose the truth is that we cannot choose when or how or whether to grow up.

'Thank you,' Pa said to the Meat Maid.

He hobbled around the wagon and gave me the embrace of a man travelling a good deal further than Northampton. He stood back and looked at me, and at Bede, and his face was as bright as I had ever seen it.

'I wonder,' he said, 'if this is the reason why I have lived so long.'

'What do you mean?' I asked.

'To see you delivered to one another.'

I did not look at Bede and did not need to. I had no doubt she was rolling her eyes.

'Look after him, Miss Wellrest. I have no doubt you will. I have asked Mosca, too, but he is not the most reliable of servants.'

Mosca was not even listening. He had lighted upon the cow's eyeball and was feasting with great enthusiasm.

Pa ruffled my hair with a gloved hand and then put his arms around me again.

'Goodbye, Ned,' he said. 'Go well.'

'Goodbye, Pa,' I said. 'We will be here whenever you are ready to come back. Perhaps you can let us know when you're coming. If you're coming.' I paused. 'We can make sure to put the tea on.'

He grinned his toothless grin, then turned and tipped his cap towards Bede.

'Miss Wellrest. I wish you every success with your research. And if, in the course of your work—'

The Meat Maid clicked her tongue.

'How long are you going to be, old man? I've got other

customers waiting for me!'

'Forgive me, miss,' said Pa.

He went around the front of the cart and heaved himself up and sat beside the old woman. Mosca flew about his head a couple of times and landed on the back of his hand. Pa whispered a few words to him and gave a gentle laugh, as if in response to something Mosca had said. Then my fly came spiralling back to me and took up his customary spot on the tip of my ear.

'Right then,' said the Meat Maid. 'Off we go.'

She plied the reins and the cart wobbled and its wheels churned in the sludge. It had gone not more than a dozen yards before the mist thickened between us and obscured Pa where he sat, more upright than I had ever seen him, one hand raised in farewell. I watched until he and his strange carriage had disappeared completely, and the only sign that he was still up ahead was the wet clop of the horse's hooves in the road. Soon this was gone, too, and there was only birdsong and the quiet sounds of the world growing under the spring sun.

Bede held my hand and leant in as if to whisper something in my ear. I caught the smell of her burnt hair, and then, without warning, she gave me a quick, warm kiss on my cheek.

'He will come back,' she said.

I raised a disbelieving hand to my face and was so flushed with love and with loss that I found myself unable to speak.

'And I am sure,' Bede continued, 'we will be able to read a great many more books before he does. Perhaps by the time he returns, we will have found a remedy for him.'

'A remedy?'

'A cure. For his long life.'

I could not help smiling at that.

'A cure for life,' I said. 'Goodness, Bede. If only such a thing were possible!'

I listened again for Pa but the road was quiet and deserted, now. Bede turned away and gently tugged at my elbow and led me back through the decomposing gates of the estate. The mist closed around us, and hand in hand we wandered up the driveway and into the brightening gloom.

ACKNOWLEDGEMENTS

For bringing this book to life and sending it forth into the world, my undying thanks: to Kesia Lupo, the faithful and tireless Igor in my laboratory; to Barry, Rachel L, Rachel H, Esther, Elinor, Jazz and all of the Chickens; to Claire McKenna, copy-editor and champion of oppressed flies; to Micaela Alcaino for the outrageously beautiful cover; to my agent Jane Willis for support and guidance from day one; to Mary, Dave and Duncan (again) for putting me up, and putting up with me; to Jac, Jas and Hugo for all the barn-based loveliness, and the good company, and the inspiration of Church Hanborough; to Laura, my light in the gloom, always.

This book relied on the research of many people far more rigorous and learned than the author, but particular thanks must go to Kathryn Harkup, whose book *Making the Monster: The Science Behind Mary Shelley's Frankenstein* was a dark, diverting, stomach-churning delight.

SONG OF THE FAR ISLES

Oran's home is on the far isle of Little Drum where everyone lives and breathes music.

When their way of life is stopped by an order of silence from the ruling Red Duchess, it is Oran who must go in search of the island's last hope – a mythical instrument made of whalebone with the power to change hearts and minds.

Thank you for introducing us to such an unforgettable world. Gets you right from the first page.
CERYS MATTHEWS, BBC RADIO 6 MUSIC

Paperback, ISBN 978-1-912626-67-0, £7.99 • ebook, ISBN 978-1-913696-03-0, £7.99